THE I
TRUMPET

Other books by Stephen Mark Rainey

Dark Shadows – Dreams of the Dark (with Elizabeth Massie)
HarperEntertainment, 1999
Fugue Devil & Other Weird Horrors
Macabre, Inc.; 1993

THE LAST TRUMPET

STEPHEN MARK RAINEY

WILDSIDE PRESS
Berkeley Heights, New Jersey

Threnody, copyright © 1986; original version appeared in DEATHREALM #2, 1987; and in THE NEW LOVECRAFT CIRCLE (as *The Spheres Beyond Sound*), 1996.

The Spheres Beyond Sound, copyright © 1987; original version appeared in TALES OF LOVECRAFTIAN HORROR #2, 1988.

Fugue Devil, copyright © 1991; original version appeared in FUGUE DEVIL & OTHER WEIRD HORRORS, 1993.

The Devil's Eye, copyright © 1996; original version appeared in TALES OF LOVECRAFTIAN HORROR #4, 1996.

Spiritual Radio, copyright © 1989; original version appeared in CHILLS #6, 1992.

Sabbath of the Black Goat, copyright © 1993; original version appeared in THE SHUB NIGGURATH CYCLE, 1994.

To Be As They, copyright © 1995; original version appeared in MISKATONIC UNIVERSITY, 1996.

The Fire Dogs of Balustrade, copyright © 1996; original version appeared in NEW MYTHOS LEGENDS, 1999.

The Horrible Legacy of Dr. Jacob Asberry, copyright © 1993; original version appeared in MIDNIGHT SHAMBLER #10 (as *The Horrible Legacy of Dr. Jacob Rigney*), 1998.

The Grey House, copyright © 1985; original version appeared in CRYPT OF CTHULHU #81, 1992.

S, copyright © 1994; original version appeared in THE AZATHOTH CYCLE (as *The Pit of Shoggoths*), 1996.

The Herald at Midnight, copyright © 1991; original version appeared in NOT ONE OF US, June, 1992.

MISFITS, or, A New Arrival at Paradise Lost, copyright © 1989; originally appeared in MIDNIGHT ZOO, Spring, 1991; and in QUICK CHILLS II, 1992.

The Last Trumpet
A publication of
Wildside Press
P.O. Box 45
Gillette, NJ 07933-0045

www.wildsidepress.com

SECOND EDITION

This book is dedicated to . . .

Douglas McArthur Craft, for steering me
to just the right books at just the right time. . . .

Jacques Tourneur, for his everlasting influence. . . .

Maurice Zam, for irrevocably snaring
a certain young fellow, somewhere around 1963,
with his recording of A Child's Introduction to Music. . . .

And to my old hometown of Martinsville, Virginia,
which pretty much did me right over the years.

Table of Contents

Introduction
by Stephen Mark Rainey

The stories in this collection represent the work of many years, having been composed for many different purposes and published in a wide variety of books and magazines. A number of you who are familiar with my work have occasionally wondered if certain of my tales with particular common, underlying threads might ever be published together, thus presenting the definitive beginning and ending (if such is possible) of what Robert M. Price has sometimes termed "The Fugue Devil Cycle." Well, here they are, packaged as something resembling a chronology—a chronology based not on the dates the stories were written but on a rough sequence of events that unfolds within their contexts.

All of these tales have appeared previously, but all have been revised for this collection—some only minimally, others quite extensively. When I originally wrote them, especially the earliest ones, I had no real intent to link one to another beyond tangentially correlating some of them to H. P. Lovecraft's *The Music of Erich Zann.* But the first of these, titled *Threnody,* somewhat inadvertently became the cornerstone for an ever-increasing number of works designed to explore some of the myriad possible tenets of the original theme. It was in *Threnody* that certain characters and settings crystallized and became pivotal elements of tales that were to follow. Aiken Mill, Beckham, and Barren Creek—communities in the fictional Sylvan county, located in the mountains of southwestern Virginia—first came into being in *Threnody,* as did the Asberry family that plays a pivotal role in this first tale as well as in subsequent storylines. (Actually, the town of Aiken Mill originated in an earlier, otherwise unrelated story titled *The Arms of Doom,* which I did not feel warranted inclusion in this book.) These settings are patterned after the locality where I was raised in Virginia, a place that has—thankfully—largely retained its unique rural, southern flavor, in contrast to so many other communities I've known and cared about, which have been transformed into the miasma of generic strip malls, congested commercial areas, and characterless suburban sprawl that are the trademarks of what our materialistic, overpopulated generation so adroitly terms "progress."

Some of you will have heard this little aside before, but I think it bears repeating here. While there is a distinct parallel to HPL's Arkham in "Beckham" and its resident school of higher learning, the actual inspiration for this community is the town and college of Ferrum, Virginia. The college's founder was named Samuel Beckham, and the occasional moments "on location" in my stories are based directly on my experiences at this off-the-beaten-track and subtly alluring locale. In Franklin and Henry Counties, Virginia, there are numerous places of commerce bearing the name "Beckham." The similarity to Arkham, while undeniable, was (at least initially) a happy coincidence.

Fugue Devil, the original version of which appeared in my first collection, *Fugue Devil & Other Weird Horrors* (Macabre Inc.; 1993), remains one of my personal favorite tales, as its premise was drawn from a particularly traumatic dream I had as an adolescent. It was a true night-horror, one that woke me in a cold sweat three separate times. Each time I managed to get back to sleep, the dream took up right where it left off. Except for one other instance that might possibly compare, I have never had such an experience since that time; a fact I very nearly lament. At that young, impressionable period of life, this dream left an indelible mark in my brain, and in 1991, after 20 years of (at least occasionally) struggling to find a way to transfer relevant portions of the dream into a viable work of fiction, at long last *Fugue Devil* found its way onto paper. Perhaps not altogether strangely, its sequel, *The Devil's Eye*, also came from a dream–one that occurred more than 25 years after the original. This second dream did not represent a sequel to the story *Fugue Devil* per se; it actually followed the events of the actual dream that I first had in 1971, there or abouts.

I have always been drawn to music, and over the years music has frequently served as a powerful creative catalyst to my writing. It was only natural that, when I read HPL's *The Music of Erich Zann* back in college, I found myself swept away by the concept of music–and sound–as a *force*, something that possesses inherent power, be it spiritual or purely physical. Over the years, as I have found myself being called back to Aiken Mill and Barren Creek, I often still hear the strange, dreamlike music that haunts those places. The stories that developed after *Threnody* simply demanded to be written, like lyrics to a subliminal, rambling piece of music that refuses to find any sort of resolution without the words to accompany it.

I hope that as you read you will hear those ghostly strains yourself, perhaps so dim and distant that it plays just beyond your grasp. Sometimes I think it is best not to try to understand just what it is or why it is there. It is both comforting and disturbing, for it represents the familiarity of people, places, and things I have known intimately in the past, yet always hints that something else entirely might lie behind it—or perhaps waits at the conclusion of the fugue.

Enjoy.

*

You may visit the author's web page at http://members.aol.com/mark-rainey or contact him by email at markrainey@aol.com.

Threnody

I never knew my father's father. My parents had been city dwellers since long before I was born, though before them, all our generations since the early eighteenth century were native to the Appalachian mountains of Virginia. Grandfather lived in the old house atop Copper Peak, which my father's family had inhabited since its inception in this land. I had never been to the place before, though over the course of my life, the stories birthed there, the pictures, and my dad's related memories had combined to create a mental image that I came to find was not far off the mark in reality.

Grandfather was dead and buried now. His house and property were destined to be sold, a fact that somehow did not settle to my liking. My father's attitude that the place had outlasted any practical value seemed almost peculiar, as he had lived there through his adolescence and generally reflected on those days with some degree of affection. Still, his reluctance to talk much about his family hinted at what I sometimes took to be shame. My father's two brothers–my uncles Frederick and William, whom I had only met in passing, many years ago–had both recently left the area and taken no personal interest in the property or its potential financial value. The reasons for this I never questioned; but I now found myself fantasizing about what life in the mountains must have been like in those simpler but more rigorous days, and what family secrets might lurk within the shadows of the ancient dwelling. Over two centuries of history had been viewed from its windows.

Few people, even those who live among them, consider the Appalachian mountains mysterious or oppressive. Unlike the Rockies, or the wilds of Canada, the Appalachians do not harbor many grave threats to man. There are few dangerous animals, the weather is usually moderate, and pockets of population are generally not too few or far between. However, as with all wild terrain, there are corners left that men seldom travel. Copper Peak lies in the western arm of Virginia, amid a range of treacherously steep, densely wooded ridges. The nearest town to our family place is twelve miles away; a little hamlet called Barren Creek that nestles in the valley between Copper Peak, Thunder Knob, and Mount Signal. There is only one road on Copper Peak, which leads from the house to the highway into town; in the last ten years, it has fallen into disuse as my grandfather's health precluded him traveling even those miles into Barren Creek. I have never quite understood how he existed. My two uncles had apparently delivered food and other necessities to him, and brought his mail from the Barren Creek post office, but I can scarcely imagine a man of his years and failing health subsisting in such an isolated environment. Nonetheless, he seemed to thrive there, and my father was never compelled to suggest his relocating.

After Grandfather's death, I took it to heart to visit the old house, knowing that if my dad sold it, my chance would probably be gone forever. I was due for a week's vacation from my business, so after minimal consideration, I decided that Copper Peak was where I would spend it. My father at first seemed displeased with my decision, but eventually changed his mind, telling me that doing so might shed some light on an incident that had "profoundly affected him" when I was a young boy. I had no recollection of what he might be referring to, but his cryptic references certainly served to heighten my curiosity.

I drove alone from my Washington, DC residence, with a set of maps and written directions provided by my father. The mountainous countryside along Interstate 81 filled my view for the better part of the trip; southwest of Roanoke, the road rose and the green mountains turned to steeper, rock-walled towers. When I turned off the Interstate onto the single-lane highway into Barren Creek, I found myself entering a picturesque, quaint world of pastures and woods, occasional farmhouses, and rare drivers passing in the opposite direction. Barren Creek lay a few miles west of a small community called Aiken Mill, which I judged to be very wealthy by the size and style of most of the houses I passed. Beyond the town, the road narrowed, and I found myself alone in a thickly wooded, rapidly rising countryside through which the road snaked and curled. Between Aiken Mill and Barren Creek, I did not encounter another motorist going in either direction.

Barren Creek has a population of about 200 people. The "town" consists of several small buildings on either side of the road, including a bank, a post office (a mobile home painted red, white, and blue), a tiny grocery store, and a greasy-spoon diner. A few of the townsfolk were about, most of them old timers with missing teeth, wearing T-shirts and faded overalls. Several of them waved as I passed, to which I responded in kind. Then, a mile or so beyond this strip of urbanization, a gravel road turned to the right and disappeared into the woods high above me. Checking my directions to be sure, I slowed and turned in, realizing I had arrived at my destination.

The road was little more than an eroded rut down the mountainside that had been poured over with gravel. At places, the hill grew so steep that my tires spun and spat rock, and I began to think that I might not be able to take the car all the way to the top. But my Japanese coupe proved to be a sturdy little animal and successfully negotiated the treacherous path. Ahead of me, a patch of daylight marked a break in the foliage. I passed over a rickety wooden bridge, beneath which ran a spidery, shallow stream, identified by my father's directions as "the" Barren Creek, the source of which lay on this very mountain. And then, just beyond, I caught my first sight of the Asberry House, the birthplace and home of my father's father's fathers.

At first I was surprised by how small it seemed. The few photographs I'd seen made it appear larger, or perhaps seeing it amid the rearing trees created a different sense of scale than did the tiny proportions of a picture. But the atmosphere of the place was much as I had imagined. Shadows fell darkly upon the house from the thick, sheltering branches, and an undefined but unmistakable smell of age saturated the cool, early spring breeze. The weedy, unkempt grass that passed for a lawn disappeared into thick, wiry brambles a few feet from the house in every direction, as if being consumed by creeping, predatory vegetation. The house's wooden siding was stained and speckled with gray and green lichen.

Still, the building appeared sound and seemed like a natural part of the tranquil environment. I could imagine my dad as a boy, playing in what would have been a well-trimmed yard, while smoke curled from the chimney and the aroma of some splendid meal being cooked drifted across the clearing. Again, I felt a pang of dismay that such a fundamental relic of my family's past would soon be either in the hands of strangers, or, more likely, demolished and replaced by some sterile piece of architecture that passed as someone's idea of a summer home. For a vain moment, I entertained the idea that I might buy the place; my profession as a graphic designer supported me comfortably, but I could barely afford my single apartment in DC, much less an additional piece of property I could visit only infrequently. I would never be able to live here, for nowhere nearby could I secure employment suitable to my talents.

My dad had given me the keys, as he had been here shortly after Grandfather's death to remove a few valuables and generally straighten the place up. But after placing my few belongings just inside the front door, I immediately set out walking, hoping to make the most of the remaining sunlight and familiarize myself with the surrounding land. I soon discovered several overgrown trails that must have been struck by my forefathers over the past two centuries. Following one of them, I came to find the small spring whence came Barren Creek a short distance away from the house. The stream wound down the mountainside, mostly parallel to the gravel road; I followed it for a time until I came to a sheer drop-off of at least a hundred feet, where the water leaped into space and plummeted to the valley below. In the summer, this stream all but dried up–hence its name, which had been coined by some family member in the late 1700s. The scene was so quietly impressive, so stimulating to my city-numbed nerves, that I knew I *somehow* had to persuade my parents to retain the rights to this wonderful tract of land.

Upon returning to the house, I decided to begin a brief exploration of the interior before I started thinking about dinner. I had no idea what Dad might have already removed, but, happily, I found a wealth of fascinating paraphernalia remaining: beautifully preserved antique furniture, photo albums of countless, as-yet-unidentified family members, and–most interestingly–a number of stringed musical instruments that appeared to have been hand-made. Hanging in the little back room was a mandolin, a classical guitar, two violins, and a dulcimer, all exquisitely finished and in fine condition. I took this room to be a workshop, where my grandfather must have made these instruments himself. In the tiny den, I found some exceptionally old books, an antique radio, and a reel-to-reel audiotape machine that looked to be of early 1960s vintage–apparently the most modern piece of electronics in the house. Fortunately, there was electricity, running water (both hot and cold), and an indoor toilet, so I anticipated a comfortable, if utilitarian life over the coming week.

Darkness fell early, and soon the woods came alive with the sounds of insects and nightbirds–something to which I was entirely unaccustomed. I sat down about seven o'clock to a dinner of chicken sandwiches and iced tea that I had packed. The kitchen had been more or less cleaned out, and I figured that tomorrow I would visit the little store in Barren Creek to pick up a few necessary items. While I ate, I paged through some of the books I'd found that looked interesting, including a couple of volumes on local history (courtesy of the Aiken Mill Public Library; someone in my family had not been above stealing), an original 19th-century copy of *Uncle Tom's Cabin* by Harriett Beecher Stowe, and a book of music by one Maurice Zann entitled *The Spheres Beyond Sound.* I was not well-versed in musical theory, but this volume contained some odd and fabulous illustrations that immediately caught my interest.

I ate and read to a chorus of chirping and yowling from outside that was distracting at first, but that after a time faded to the background of my awareness. The pictures in the Zann book completely captivated me, for they consisted of prints and drawings of imaginatively stylized subjects: lizards, birds, fish, skeletons (animal and human), and strange, monstrous-looking things one might expect to find in a science-fiction movie. When I began skimming the text, I discovered that this book was truly no "normal" guide to music theory. Upon finding lines that read

". . . vibrations of this exact frequency and volume are required to complete the summoning process . . ." and "by assimilating the perfect tones and pitches, the very essence of primal power may be acquired . . ." I decided to start reading the book from the beginning.

I soon found that the strange illustrations were perfectly complementary to the written contents. The author's basic premise was that music could open gateways to other realms of existence—not just in the mind, but in the physical world. Now for me, music is indeed a spiritual experience. It may be hypnotic or violently stimulating. I listen to and appreciate all kinds of music, from folk, to jazz, to classical, to rock, to New Age. When I was younger, nothing delighted me more than to sit for hours wearing my headphones, carried away by the power of music. Zann contended that certain combinations of tones could actually alter space—that the correction modulation of frequency could even reach beyond the barrier of death. Needless to say, my initial reaction was that *Spheres* was a work of pure, intentional fantasy, but, as I read further, the details became increasingly technical and beyond my grasp, leading me to assume that the work was meant be regarded as factual. This book occupied me well into the late hours. Even though there was much that I simply could not comprehend, the writer's sober, clinical writing captivated my imagination. I found myself almost shaking with excitement as I read this passage:

> . . . I have seen the power that the following strains will summon. The rhythm and cadence are extremely vital. The switch from the 3/4 to the 7/8 time signature followed by the 5/3 line illustrated below must be instantaneous, without hesitation or pause. The standard tuning E, A, D, G, B, E in perfect A must be altered to D-flat, A-sharp, E, B-sharp, C, E-flat to facilitate the playing of the proper notes. The volume produced by each instrument on each beat must range between 77 and 89 decibels for the summons to be effected. Depending upon atmospheric conditions, results may be seen, if the process is completed flawlessly, from within three minutes to one hour.

Farther into the text, there were passages relating to other types of musical power, from hypnotizing human subjects to communicating with the dead. But, to me, the most astounding aspect of all was the theory that certain musical arrangements could transcend the limits of time and space to be heard by *things* existing in other universes. The concepts of parallel or alternate dimensions have been explored by both scientists and fantasists for years, I suppose, but never had I seen such a lucid and calculated thesis on the subject as this. After a time, I began to wonder why my grandfather would have owned such a book and if he had given its contents any credence. I supposed the subject might have merely intrigued him, as it did me, especially given his apparent interest in music. Upon checking the front of the book, I learned it had been published by an independent firm in Providence, Rhode Island, in 1929, as a limited edition. Putting the book aside, I found that my imagination had been thrust into high gear, and being alone in this old house suddenly seemed a chilling prospect.

When I at last began to prepare myself for bed, I found my hearing to be unnaturally sensitive, my state of mind strangely apprehensive. My chair legs scraped the bare wooden floor at a shocking volume, sending a harsh shiver up my spine. I stopped and held my breath for a moment, half-expecting to hear . . . something . . . other than the cacophony of the night creatures in the woods. When I heard nothing further, I went to the bedroom, made the huge, oak-framed bed with fresh linens from the closet, slipped out of my clothes, and buried myself deep within the covers, leaving the living room light burning and the door cracked so I wouldn't be engulfed by the total darkness of the mountain night.

I awoke early, to an absolutely brilliant morning, unable to remember when I had drifted off to sleep. I had slept heavily and peacefully, so it seemed, and I now felt refreshed, free of the odd anxiety that had gripped me during the evening. Morning birds chirped outside my window in happy contrast to the eerie wails of the night creatures. In daylight, the house took on a fresh, new quality, and some of my previous enthusiasm for the locale returned. I was hungry, and, realizing I had next to nothing in the house to eat, I immediately left for the general store in Barren Creek. The town was practically deserted at this hour, but the store was open. The proprietor, a Mr. Avery, greeted me cheerfully enough, asking me from whereabouts I came. When I told him I was the grandson of the late Thomas Asberry, he merely shrugged and offered his condolences. Apparently, Grandfather wasn't part of any close-knit group of locals. My family, like many of the back-country dwellers, had valued its privacy and seldom gathered with neighbors.

When I returned to the house, I prepared a large breakfast of bacon, eggs, and toast; after eating, I let my attention return to the weird volume of Maurice Zann. In the golden daylight, it no longer seemed as much a warped, dreadful recording of factual data as a fanciful product of some writer's bizarre imagination. I decided that, for the morning, I would forget it, explore some more of the mountain, and conduct a more thorough search of the house itself. There would still be a host of relics from my grandfather's day, and before, that would help me put together a more complete picture of my heritage.

About ten o'clock, I set out walking, heading north, in the opposite direction of yesterday's expedition. I discovered another worn trail that led along the crest of Copper Peak and followed it, taking in the exhilarating view of the surrounding valleys and slopes. Off to the east, far below me, I could see a few tiny buildings, which I took to be Barren Creek. Farther beyond lay Aiken Mill, a larger community, but still separated from "civilization" by a tall, knobby ridge. Many miles to the west, I could see another little hamlet, which, if I recalled rightly, would be a little college town called Beckham.

About a half mile from the house, I came upon a flattened area beneath a canopy of limbs, and, to my surprise, found it to be a small graveyard. There were maybe two dozen markers of varying shapes and sizes, all weathered with age, most nearly obscured by creeping flora. I strolled into their midst, noting the engraved names that were still legible: Nicholas Asberry, 1761–1834; Stuart Asberry, 1820–1914; Suzette Asberry Washington, 1823–1902; James Druid Asberry, 1895–1938; Sarah Asberry Collins, 1811–1899. I found myself excited, for here lay my direct ancestors, those whose names I might have heard only in passing over the years. Here, the past surrounded me; the very earth contained the blood of my progenitors.

My parents had not told me specifically where my grandfather was buried. "In our family plot, in the mountains," Dad had merely said. I let my eyes rove among the stones, seeking. Then, in a far corner, standing alone . . . yes, a fresh marker above a patch of newly turned earth. I approached it, positive of what I would find.

I was correct. Thomas Cadden Asberry, my father's father, born in 1910. The remains of some flowers drooped next to the obelisk-like stone, probably those my father had placed here upon Grandfather's burial. Thin shoots of grass were just beginning to burst from the mound of earth, and brown spots of mold had broken out on the granite. I stood there for a time, not quite sure if I should grieve, or offer a prayer. Finally, I murmured a low "Rest in peace," finding nothing within myself worth conveying to the dead. Then I turned and left the graveyard, feeling vaguely disconcerted. I didn't know why.

For a time, I wandered aimlessly, at last finding myself back at the waterfall I'd discovered the previous day. The air was quiet and still, and gazing at the tiny houses and green slopes in the distance, I came to realize that some odd strain of music seemed to be running through my head. It was low, harmonious, and pleasant, but altogether unfamiliar. I am not a competent songwriter, and it seemed strange that something I'd never heard before could somehow wend its way out from my subconscious.

For a while longer, I stood musing, then started back for the house. I decided I would make a light snack and then sift through a couple of the closets I had seen. I had to admit that suddenly I had become fascinated by the past; until recently, I had always been ambivalent about life before my time. Occasionally, when Dad would speak about his life, my curiosity would be momentarily aroused, but immediately forgotten when I returned to my ordinary affairs. Here, I supposed, with little else to occupy my mind, the past simply loomed larger and more tantalizing.

By the time I reached the house, my enthusiasm for delving into its closets and cupboards had peaked. I built a substantial ham and cheese sandwich for lunch, chased it with a cold beer, and then went to the bedroom to begin my foraging.

My dad had packed away most of the clothes and incidental personal items. But I soon came upon many neat little articles, such as an ancient shaving kit complete with boar's-bristle brush and straight razor, a slightly battered pocket watch, and a few bottles of age-old cologne, mostly still full. There were some more books stacked in a corner, including a Bible, a dictionary (vintage 1939), and an exceptionally brittle-looking, moldy volume called *The Encyclopedia For Boys.* And then I spied some cartons that immediately caught my interest: a number of six-inch reel tapes for the machine I had seen in the other room. I pulled these from their corner, finding four in all, each labeled with faded black ink in crabbed script that I assumed to be Grandfather's. Two of them were sermons recorded at a local church that Grandfather must have attended; one was a radio show from 1964; and the last was labeled "Zann," recorded in 1966.

I immediately took the latter one into the living room, found the tape machine in the corner, and proceeded to set it up for listening. I prayed the machine would work after so many years of probable disuse. Upon plugging it in, I found that everything seemed to function well enough. The reel began turning, and I stood anxiously waiting as the small speaker hissed and crackled. Then a voice that I knew immediately was Grandfather's began to speak: a slow, deep drawl with a pronounced southern Virginia accent, not unlike my dad's. The voice sounded tentative and somewhat nervous, perhaps due to his inexperience talking to a machine. What he said was this:

> "I am making this recording to test a few of the passages from the Zann text, on pages 121 through 128 of *The Spheres Beyond Sound.* I am Thomas Asberry, I live on Copper Peak outside of Barren Creek, Virginia. I am making this recording with the help of my neighbors, John Eubanks, Fred Wharton, Ray Martin, and Bill Miller. I am in the backyard of my house now, facing the crest of the mountain. Uh, we have practiced select verses, or, uh, lines out of the book, but this will be the first complete performance of what Zann calls 'the summons.' My neighbors and myself have all read the text, and we believe that if we follow the directions, as set down by the writer, we will actually experience the, uh, revelations he has foreseen.
>
> "I have decided to record this activity on my recorder. We don't honestly know what to expect, but if we should be successful, then it is possible there may be some danger. Zann's text indi-

cates that the, uh, existences, uh, on the other side are not necessarily malevolent, but they are destructive in nature, like a shark in the ocean. The means to send back the results of the summoning are printed on pages 135 through 137 of the text, and this part we played in full at several practice sessions.

"As I have said, I believe the writer of this book is sincere, for the simple reason that I have had proof. Two months ago, I took my fiddle up to the graveyard and played the piece on pages 39 and 40—the prelude to opening the barrier of death. As I played, as surely as I am standing here now, I saw the corrupted bodies of my relatives appear to stand before me, as solid as the earth under my feet. As I was so frightened, I quit playing and they vanished, but on two occasions, I have gone back to the graveyard and heard weird music, though there was no one there to be playing it. I believe it was an answer of some kind to the invitation I played. But I haven't responded. And I don't go back to the graveyard anymore."

Now I felt a tremendous surge of excitement, of complete disbelief in what I was hearing. But I continued to listen, hypnotized by the fear in the low voice on the tape, not sure now if my grandfather were wholly of sound mind. I could sense that he was terrified of proceeding with this plan of his . . . yet the longing to test the mysteries of Maurice Zann's book so outweighed his fear that he was willing to risk unknowable consequences. There came a series of tonal pluckings and whinings as the group tuned their instruments–probably the very same ones that hung in the small workshop next to the living room. A couple of unfamiliar voices said something incomprehensible; then my grandfather spoke again:

"It's getting dark now, and we're about to start. I will admit that all of us are pretty afraid, but we believe that the things we might learn are so incredible and so important that they warrant whatever risk. I think from what we have learned so far, we will be safe."

There was a pause, and a few more background voices. Then my grandfather's voice said, "So, you ready?" and, after a moment, a sudden discordant jangle rattled from the speaker. Harsh plucking and flat strumming echoed through what must have been a still mountain night more than thirty years ago. The noise seemed to have no rhythm or melody. Insect-like chirps arpeggioed up and down unknown scales, bass thumps jumped from one time signature to another without any pattern or structure . . . so it seemed. What I was hearing sounded more like a random banging of instruments by inexperienced hands than a complex latticework of music holding some deep-hidden power. But as I listened, I caught strains of some unearthly harmony occasionally breaking through the aural chaos. I began to hear tones that were not of stringed instruments, but of deep woodwinds or brassy pipes. The harmonic overtones of the mandolin, guitar, violin, and dulcimer were producing sounds unlike any I had ever heard, even in the most radical of electronic fusion. And yet . . . something about the music struck a familiar chord deep inside me. As if I must have heard such a recording before—perhaps when I was too young to remember it.

Beyond this cacophony, a definite melody seemed to coalesce, but from somewhere distant, mostly drowned by the brash orchestration. I turned the volume up on the machine, straining to catch the sequence of the evasive notes. I began to get distortion over the speaker, but I shut my ears to the pain, concentrating only on what lurked beneath. Yes . . . a melody was forming, combining in arias of thin, reed-like whistles and lower, rich tones that could only be blown from a French horn.

And then, beyond that, another distinctive tune, but so faint as to be lost in the crashing of insane strings. I sat there for a time, separated from my surroundings by a spell of mesmerizing power. My thoughts seemed to dissolve, and I allowed myself to be absorbed by this raw energy that explored every realm of ecstasy, tranquility, horror, and agony.

Suddenly, it was over. I sat facing the rear window of my grandfather's house, peering toward the depths of the forest. There was a clatter from the speaker as the musicians lowered their instruments and simultaneously breathed exhausted sighs. For a full two minutes, no sound came except for a soft sigh of breeze and few crickets beginning their chorus for the evening. At last one of the background voices said, "What's that? Anything?"

My grandfather mumbled something low. Then: "No. It's nothing." I waited again as silence returned, picturing the group of men looking around expectantly, probably with fear-widened eyes and sweaty, trembling hands. Then, Grandfather said, "Wind's picking up."

Sure enough, the drone of the breeze was growing stronger. It rose and fell several times, whistling by the microphone that probably sat unprotected somewhere near the players. But still, nothing more could be heard except for the increasing chatter from the forest. Almost five minutes went by without a word from any of the men.

Then, Grandfather said:

"Well, it looks like nothing is happening . . . so far. Guess we'll have to wait and see. The book said it could take a little while. I guess the weather has to be right, too, for the message to get through. But these are good conditions. Sky's clear, it's pretty

> cold . . . sound really carries. Wind's holding, I'd say between five and ten miles an hour. I suppose we could've done something incorrectly . . . damned piece of music ain't meant to be played by human hands . . . but it sure seemed like we did it right.

Outside, here in my own time, the afternoon sun was well on its way into the west. It would be dark within the hour. I felt a shiver run up my spine. A gust of chilly wind had swirled through the house.

> To save tape, I'll shut off for the moment and come back at the first sign of anything happening. Still damned peculiar . . . absolutely nothing. Nothing at all.

There was a click as the tape was shut off all those years ago. Another click followed as it was turned back on some indeterminate time later.

> It's been thirty minutes now. No sign of anything unusual. The crickets are going nuts, as you can hear, but apart from that, everything seems normal. Pretty disappointing, but also kind of a relief. Maybe it's better if nothing happens. I guess it ain't right for Christian men to fool around with powers that only the Lord should know about. 'Course, I suppose there's a lot this family has done that ain't considered right and true. It's common knowledge that the Asberrys make the best whiskey outside Franklin County . . . but I reckon in the eyes of God that's a small sin compared to messing around with the powers that be.

I frowned. I wondered if the Asberrys' "shady" side–moonshining–had been the source of my dad's discomfort in sharing his family's past with me. My father was a decent and proud man, and, having broken from his rural mold and established himself in an well-to-do urban environment, it would be like him to feel a sense of guilt about having a less-than-upright background.

Now, though, I wondered if there might be other secrets my family had kept hidden . . . darker things . . . occult things. Perhaps the music of Maurice Zann was only one such example. Might this old family have been delving into unknown, forbidden lore since before they settled here from the Old World?

I have always considered myself rational, well educated, and reasonably wise in the ways of the world. Still, the purely intuitive side of my nature felt the stirrings of some primal dread; instinct had overridden reason, leaving me confused and uncomfortable. The woods and wilderness that I had found so charming and restful now seemed fraught with perilous mystery.

Another couple of clicks came from the player. Then my grandfather's voice said:

> "Forty-five minutes now. Still nothing. The boys and me are starting to breathe a little easier. John's gone inside to make coffee. We can sure use it after this. I guess it's better this way. Maybe we messed up, or maybe the Lord just said it ain't to be so. Anyway, if nothing happens in the next few minutes, I think we'll all sleep much better tonight. After this, I reckon I'll be forgetting all about what happened before, up at the graveyard. I'll put that book away and never bother with it again. I should never have taken it from Daddy in the first place."

So, the book had been in the family even before my grandfather. Interesting.

> "Well, unless something happens tonight, I might as well give up on this recording. I'm pretty tired . . . all of us are right worn out, matter of fact. It's been hard work. So, for now, I'll be ending all this up . . . uh, unless the need arises later. So . . . signing off."

Grandfather ended on that uncertain note. There was nothing else on the tape, which disappointed me, as I had hoped for at least some explanation or commentary on the night's activities. Their attempt had surely failed, and I found nothing in the house to suggest they had repeated the experiment at any other time. And nothing mysterious seemed to have befallen my grandfather in the intervening years.

And what of this whole premise, I wondered to myself. Could I place any stock in the concepts my grandfather had sought–and failed–to prove? Surely not, I thought. There had indeed been some unusual, elusive depth to the music on the tape, but, surely, nothing that could convince me of any mystical power.

My grandfather sounded like an intelligent man, with a modicum of formal education. I wondered just what his experience in the graveyard had been that encouraged him to seek the greater power hinted at in Zann's text. Had he merely suffered some frightening manifestation of his own imagination? Frustration began to eat at me, for it seemed that this mystery was destined to die with no promise of resolve. Deciphering the technical data in *The Spheres Beyond Sound* was completely beyond my ability.

There had to be some other way of gathering information. Perhaps the neighbors who had aided my grandfather's performance could be of assistance, if any were still alive and of sound memory.

Then I remembered the strange tune that had entered my head while I was walking in the graveyard. Had not Grandfather spoken of hearing supernatural music when he had gone there? Could I have shared such an experience, here, more than thirty years later? Suddenly, I realized that I had to return to the woods to see if the same thing might happen again.

Late afternoon was creeping over the mountains, but I calculated that I could easily get to the cemetery and back before dark; and maybe tomorrow, I could search for the men who had accompanied my grandfather on the tape. There might yet be hope for this venture.

I disconnected the tape machine and returned the reel to its carton. Then I set out walking, carrying a flashlight in case darkness fell upon me sooner than I expected. The worst hazard would be the steep drop-off near the trail. Since I was a child, I have seldom felt the thrill of fear, the sense of foreboding cast by the unknown. That feeling was upon me now, and though I was skeptical of it, I also held for it a certain amount of respect.

It didn't take me long to reach my destination. The graveyard was immersed in a pool of shadow as the sun dropped beyond the wall of trees; but I sensed something different, an atmosphere I had never felt before. Small whirlpools of wind were flitting among the gravestones, lifting earth and dead foliage into writhing dances in midair. Strange dark patches grew here and there that were not shadows. A low rumble seemed to issue from the ground, as if something huge and distant were stirring from sleep. And, in the air, the faintest of high-toned wails blended with the whistle of the breeze in a wistful, eerie dirge.

None of these elements was spectacular or even blatant. But they combined to create a sense of atmosphere gone awry, a subtle *wrongness.* But my conscious mind now confirmed that these phenomena could not possibly be ordinary acts of nature. I knew now that the music of Maurice Zann was, in fact, the reason for them.

But the original attempt to utilize that music had failed. What conditions could have changed that allowed my thoughtless playing of the tape to summon some thing—or *things*—like that which now seemed to struggling into existence? I had been so curious about the music itself that I had never considered the possibility of it actually working the effect that my grandfather had hoped—or feared—to witness.

I left the graveyard and ran down the path that led to the waterfall. All I could think of now was getting away from this place.

Behind me, a weird, wild shriek suddenly tore through the forest; something animalistic, subhuman. It was joined by another, and then another, like a choir of ghastly, agonized voices. Something beneath my feet boomed deeply; then the ground shook so violently I was sure the surface must have been rent and that the denizens of the underworld would be crawling out of their blazing pits. More chilling cries from the graveyard sent me running even faster, down toward the house that I considered my only retreat.

Suddenly, before I realized it, I had reached the precipice where the stream pitched into space. I caught the trunk of a small tree just in time to save me from hurtling over the edge, nearly dislocating my shoulder in the process. A stab of pain halted me in my tracks.

Then, my eyes caught something moving in the valley below. The sun had just reached the horizon, and on this side of the mountain, facing east, only a shadow filled the depths below. But in that darkness, something even darker, something gigantic, seemed to be crawling across the floor of the valley. My eyes fixed on that mass of blackness, mesmerized by its immensity. My lungs stopped working, and for a moment, I felt I was falling. Somehow, I was able to keep holding onto that tree; it was the only thing that saved me.

From the woods behind me, there now came a multitude of shufflings and scrapings, as of many bodies moving through the foliage. Guttural groans and hoarse cries drifted through the dark woods toward me. A surge of panic sent me flying back from the edge and down the trail again. But the woods had grown nearly pitch black, and I could no longer see where I was going. I suddenly slammed into a hidden tree, somehow avoiding being impaled on broken branches. Reeling from the force of the impact, I reached out to find support . . . and gripped a moist, muddy limb that seemed to hang too limply from something unseen. Then, to my horror, that limb moved of its own accord, and I felt something hard and firm take hold of my wrist. I jerked my arm back purely from reflex, and as I did, a shrill wail exploded from the shadowy figure before me. I launched myself past it and began my flight anew down the treacherous path, blindly hoping to reach the house without killing myself.

Many times in nightmares I have found myself fleeing from some terrible threat. As often as not, my car is my refuge, for in mobility there is hope of safety. I was now living one of my nightmares, and my one goal was to get to my car and escape from this terrible mountain. And, like in so many dreams, the darkness engulfed me, slowed me down, obscured my path. I cannot count how many times I lost my footing or was snagged by grasping branches. Somehow, I at last reached the house, and I could see the kitchen light glowing invitingly. With profound but temporary relief, I pushed my way through the back door, slamming it behind me and leaning heavily against it.

I didn't care about the few belongings I had brought with me. My only concern now was to find my keys and get away from here with all possible haste. From outside, I could hear the restless chatter of the night creatures, more urgent than usual, and their chirps and buzzings spurred me on. I ran into the bedroom, searching desperately for my keys, which I found on the bedside table; grabbing them up, I turned and headed for the front door, not bothering to turn off the lights or lock the door.

The moment I shakily inserted the key into the car door, I heard a grating rumble from the woods just above the house. Looking up, I could see the tops of the dark trees shaking and pitching back and forth violently. The wailing sounds returned, drifting down from the darkness, drawing steadily nearer. A lump of terror rose in my throat, for it now seemed that there was no way I could get down the mountain in time to escape whatever was coming.

I jerked the car door open with a burst of frenzied strength, slid into the seat, and willed my hand to carefully insert the key into the ignition. I somehow accomplished this on the first attempt, fired up the engine, and flipped on the headlights.

The car faced the side of the house, and caught in the beams of the headlights stood a figure whose appearance nearly stopped my heart. It was a parody of a man, or had once been a man. It stood facing me on two spindly legs, its body a mass of dark, moss-covered earth. Two black sockets gaped from its mud-encrusted skull, empty, but seemingly possessed of sight. For a long moment, it did not move, only stood there apparently regarding me. Then, at either corner of the house, two similar figures appeared, both facing me but making no move in my direction.

Then, out of the empty air, I heard the mad strains of that mystical music, and to my shock, those corrupted bodies began to whirl and leap, spinning and pirouetting in a grotesque, fiery dance. And at that moment, above the roof of the house, a great mass of blackness rose into the night sky, blocking the glittering stars that had begun to appear. The night fell utterly silent; no wind cut across the mountaintop, no insect chirped. Only the notes of the supernatural music floated into the sky. The whirling figures ceased their dancing and dropped to their bony knees, prostrating themselves before the black shape that hovered above the house. I began to perceive at the far reaches of my senses the wistful notes of my grandfather's stringed cacophony.

As I sat there, the features of the huge thing before me gradually came into focus. I could see what appeared to be thick, arthropodic legs, dozens of yards long, and in the midst of the solid central mass, a myriad of tiny, flickering lights grouped in dense bunches. It was a gigantic spider-thing with a thousand eyes that glared down at me as if ready to pounce. The worshipping corpses began a new wailing chorus.

As the glare of those thousand eyes bore down upon me, I realized why grandfather's original performance had failed to summon this entity, whereas the playing of the tape had succeeded: I had turned the volume on the machine up to catch the subtle undertones of the music. The lower, most subtle elements of the "live" performance on acoustic instruments had failed to reach the volume prescribed in the Zann text. Yet the very same music, played at a higher decibel level, had been in the exact range to complete the summoning process.

Then another cold fear seized me: due to the failure of his attempt, Grandfather had never recorded the passage that returned the extradimensional horror to its rightful place. There was no way to send the thing back!

Now, strange whispers, voices from somewhere beyond this plane of time and space, began to swirl through the air around me like buzzing bees. Panic motivated my hand, and I slammed the gear lever into reverse and spun the steering wheel, turning my car down the road away from the house. In mad fury, the car screamed and bucked over the potholed road, several times nearly skidding into the woods on either side. I did not slow down, though, for fear of smashing myself into a tree was not nearly so real as the otherworldly threat I was leaving behind.

At last, I reached the bottom of the mountain and sent my car hurtling down the winding highway toward Barren Creek, never looking into the rearview mirror to see what might be following.

The music and whispering faced from my hearing, though my terror did not subside. Once, while speeding down a long, curving decline that allowed me a brief view of Copper Peak, I swore I saw a portion of the sky blocked out by a gigantic, spiderlike shape resting on top of the mountain. But the road curved again, and Copper Peak slipped once and for all beyond my line of sight.

In Aiken Mill, I stopped to fill my gas tank, which had fallen dangerously close to empty. As I nervously pumped the gasoline into my car, my eyes darted repeatedly down the road whence I came, half-expecting to see some crawling, pitch-black silhouette advancing from the distance. But nothing appeared, and I paid the nervous-looking attendant who must have though I had escaped from the nearby Catawba Sanitarium. By the time I reached Interstate 81 to head back home, I had seen nothing more, and the terror that consumed me slowly began to abate.

And yet for me, the real fear lies ahead. Whatever the music of Maurice Zann summoned, it must still lurk on the fringes of this world, somewhere in the mountains around Barren Creek. The only way to send it back is by playing the proper musical arrangements from *The Spheres Beyond Sound,* and the only copy of that book in existence seems to be at my old family house. Even if I could find the right passage, someone who could read music would have to play the piece. As it is, I have been unable to find another copy of that book, or any record indicating such a book ever existed. And I will never, never return to that place in the mountains, at any time, for any reason. I have urged my father to sell the house, but to avoid going there at all costs. Of course, I discussed nothing about the events that had transpired there with my father; yet as irrational as I must have sounded, he seemed to accept my words without question—and with a curious attitude of understanding.

As I said, however, the real terror for me has yet to come. For surely, those animated corpses were those of my own relatives, their eternal souls somehow drawn back to their wasted bodies. Even now, they must dance and worship the black overlord of death that Zann's music called from beyond. My father had said that I might come to some understanding of an "incident" from my own childhood; and while I do not specifically remember it, I know that I *have* heard my grandfather's music before. It somehow marked me as an Asberry to the things from outside, and thus my fate has been sealed. At times, I can hear those demonic notes pounding in my ears, as if the long-dead Asberrys are beckoning me to join them. Whatever paradise might await others in the life after this one, I know it is never meant for me; as long as that black spider remains free in this world, the gate to the other side is blocked and guarded. Eventually, my time will come, and when it does, I will become one of those damned, dancing parodies that bewail their fate and bow to the demon master from dimension beyond death.

The Spheres Beyond Sound

From the day Kenneth Asberry was born, his grandfather hated him. Certainly not for any deed the young one might have committed–for what ill could a mere infant inflict upon a man with such physical strength, keenness of mind, and what some might call the wisdom of ages tallied in his favor? No, sadly, the hatred Thomas Asberry felt for his grandson was directed thus simply for want of a more appropriate and deserving object. For quite some time, the Asberry patriarch's righteous wrath had been leveled at the wife of his son, but this spirited and meticulously refined hatred had been derailed by her untimely demise. Therefore, Thomas naturally enough turned every ounce of his smoldering ire toward the offspring of the one he considered to be the engineer of his favorite son's downfall.

Throughout his youth, Thomas's son James had been close to his father in temperament, taste, and, most notably, physical attributes. James's prodigious, hawk-like nose, for example, served to make his profile virtually identical to his father's—not to mention any number of his paternal ancestors'—and, similarly, generations of Asberry men, including James, possessed exceedingly long and narrow, almost fragile-looking fingers that would prove deceptively powerful to one inclined to shake an Asberry by the hand. As an adolescent of unexcelled intellect (a common and renowned trait among the family), James remained quick-witted, unfailingly trustworthy, and even spiritually enlightened, much as his father had been at a similar young age. Thomas raised his son with love and devotion, and just after James's 11th birthday, was forced to do so alone, for James's mother was taken by a brain tumor. Up to then, she had schooled James and his brothers at home; but now, unwilling to send his youngest to any public school, Thomas assumed that burden as well. James learned quickly, and, to Thomas's mind, was far better schooled than he ever could have been down in Aiken Mill. While Thomas hardly neglected his two elder sons, neither of them came close to receiving the attention he reserved for James, whom he considered his "best and last gift from Heaven."

Thomas loved the traditions and romance of the past, and he perpetuated the ways of his progenitors with the kind of care that only one thoroughly steeped in the lore of a great many ages could appreciate. The Appalachian mountains of southwestern Virginia stood as timeless monuments to the world of his forefathers and provided him with a rich environment where he could live and work in reasonable comfort, with almost complete security. The earliest Asberrys had settled the region in the late 18th century, populating its valleys and hills with enough members to ensure their longevity, but rarely mingling with neighboring families, privacy being one of their primary and ongoing concerns. Spreading beyond Sylvan County had never been a priority for those early branches of the family tree, nor was it for Thomas, who, even in his younger days, found little allure in the idea of venturing forth from the old family homestead. Despite the inevitable influx of population and development of the world around Copper Peak, little about the Asberry house and property had changed in 200 years, nor about the town of Barren Creek, which the Asberrys themselves had named, in the valley below.

Thomas never denied the wisdom of progress (to a certain extent), and had seen to having the house wired for electricity and outfitted with hot and cold running water back in the days when such things were rarities. But stock products of "civilization," such as telephones and televisions, could only be unhealthy distractions to the mind in search of spiritual purity, so he refused to allow them a place under his roof. His one concession to the modern age of communication was an old radio set by which he could learn about current events elsewhere whenever the mood took him. However, these news stories usually disgusted him in short order, so the radio spent most of its time in a dark corner, unspeaking. His wife, before her passing, had frequently pestered him to install a telephone, arguing with almost convincing fervor that such a device would simplify life rather than complicate it; but not wishing to subject himself to unwanted intrusions by outside parties, he staunchly refused, stating flatly that anyone desiring to communicate with the family could always do so by mail.

The Asberrys' reclusive nature, like so many of the families whose lineage went back to the early mountain settlers, was at least partly due to the demands of its primary business, and that was the manufacture and distribution of homemade, untaxed corn liquor. A mainstay of the Blue Ridge Mountains' culture, this enterprise could be found in prolific quantity if one knew where to look; in fact, Franklin County, just next door, was often referred to as "The Moonshine Capital of the World," even by its most respectable public citizens, a fact plainly evidenced by the brazen welcome signs along the highway leading into Boones Mill. Sylvan County's supervisory body tended to avoid such blatant promotion, but the product in question hardly suffered any shortage of demand because of it. The Asberrys regularly peddled their wares in Barren Creek, Beckham, and Aiken Mill, usually without interference by any local, state, or Federal revenue men, and townsfolk respected the family name sufficiently to never go calling at Copper Peak without invitation. Whenever the community grew thirsty for the best whiskey in the state, one could be sure that a member of the Asberry family would soon be down with an ample supply of the goods for a reasonable price.

For Thomas, however, the family business had grown to be scarcely more than a profitable sideline. His true passion was music. Be it studying the compositions of the masters or composing his own work on his handmade instruments, he poured his heart and soul into that form of the arts he believed to be closest to the divine. A woodworker of no little skill, he loved to build his own stringed instruments and had set up a small workshop in the house where he could practice his favorite craft at his leisure. Throughout the house, the products of his proud efforts hung in prominent places: exquisitely rendered violins, guitars, mandolins, dulcimers, and even banjos, several examples in every room, and, though decorative, all had seen considerable practical use. Thomas–and his sons after him–had been thoroughly trained from an early age in the finer aspects of making music. He was adept at playing traditional styles, from classical baroque, to blues, to American, English, and Celtic folk music; but he had also studied numerous other, more challenging forms, from primitive African, to modern jazz, to even more experimental types, all of which he attempted to interpret on his strings.Complementing his interest in all things musical, Thomas took great pleasure in the written word, and among his extensive collection of music-oriented books could be found any number of rare and obscure volumes; but one, in particular, gripped his interest like nothing else he had ever discovered. In this one, which had been passed down from unknown generations of Asberrys, the author sought to extend the boundaries of musical theory into areas that most laymen might label supernatural. The text was an arcane, complex study of music and its influence on mankind through the ages, going back even into pre-Biblical times. But beyond its historical and philosophical treatises, the author had, with convincing scientific aplomb, proposed that the very vibrations of music reached into realms beyond the physical, hence the profound significance of music in the ceremonies of virtually every religious order, Christian or otherwise, throughout the history of the world. The author contended that, when refined to degrees unimagined by most "conventional" minds, certain musical compositions could actually build bridges between the ordinarily perceivable, three-dimensional world and other, unseen realms—even those that might exist beyond the barrier of death. This book was Thomas Asberry's most prized possession: *The Spheres Beyond Sound*, by one Maurice Zann.

Thomas kept any secrets he might have learned from the Zann book to himself, but he freely shared his musical knowledge and skill with James, who—to Thomas's delight—appreciated many of the same musical values as he. When James was a teenager, he and his father would often sit on the back porch facing the woods atop the mountain's crest and play together, on violin, guitar, mandolin, or dulcimer. Sometimes the two older sons, Frederick and William, would join in, and the melodic, delicate sounds of the stringed instruments would echo through the forest like the calls of jubilant birds, swirling and dancing on the breezes to be heard by others at the base of the mountain, far, far below. Thomas had even gone against tradition and purchased an audiotape machine so he could record these wonderful performances for future listening.

One day, while delivering a shipment of his family's most popular goods to his usual customers at the Barren Creek general store, several of Thomas's neighbors, having heard the ghostly strains of music from the mountain, accosted him and told him how deeply moved they had been by the sound. The neighbors, with no slight effort, eventually convinced him to break from his shell of isolation and occasionally join them in their own gatherings, where homemade liquor and homemade music went happily hand-in-hand. In time, Thomas and these men could be seen playing at various public events all around Sylvan County; sometimes providing the hearty kick at the local bluegrass festivals, other times the happy, hopeful music for a wedding, and, at others, the somber, sometimes grim background for a wake or funeral. Appearances of this nature for Thomas were admittedly rare; however, such activities did serve to stimulate young James's interest in both his father's and his own creative abilities. This made Thomas proud and seemed to indicate that, one day, James would be ready to learn some of the mystical secrets of Maurice Zann's *The Spheres Beyond Sound.* Throughout James's teenage years, this was his father's strongest hope, his purest ambition.

But when James turned 20, something happened to estrange father and son. On a number of occasions when James went into Beckham to make his routine deliveries, he had remained gone for hours on end, a few times failing to return until very late in the evening. Thomas had warned the lad many times that associating with townsfolk could be dangerous–especially in the little college town, where large numbers of outsiders naturally gathered.

Finally, one evening, James did not come home at all. When he reappeared at midmorning on the following day, his explanation sent the worried and sleep-deprived elder Asberry into an almost fatally violent fit of fury: James had, during his sojourns to Beckham, become acquainted with a young lady who attended college there. At first, she had been nothing more than a loyal customer for the Asberry corn product, but, over time, she became an object of fascination for James, who began making trips to the college specifically to see her. Something of a romance had developed between them, and now facing a frighteningly irate Thomas Asberry, young James was even proposing to bring the creature home to meet his father and two brothers.

James's voice had always been of deep timbre, steady and confident in tone. Now, however, it was thin, reedy, and plaintive. "Dad, she's very special to me. I've never met anyone like her."

"Of course you've never met anyone like her," Thomas growled. "There is no one like that on Copper Peak."

James was a young man of considerable stature, and, though his father had preserved himself well for his 60-some years, the elder Asberry could hardly have posed a physical threat to his son. Still, James cringed and flinched nervously with every fierce exhalation from his father's lungs. In a voice barely more than a whisper, he said, "Dad, she's going to be here this evening."

A silent explosion rocked the foundations of the old house, and James threw up his hands and backed away in terror as his father took a single step forward. "That," Thomas said, voice soft and menacing–which, to James, was far worse than the severest bluster–"is unacceptable."

"But, Dad, it's too late. I can't get in touch with her to tell her not to come. Not without . . . a phone."

"You can get your hind end down to the college and put a halt to this arrangement. Right now."

James shook his head in exasperation. "She's got classes in the daytime, and I don't know where to find her. There's no way. Dad, please. Just meet her. You will like her. I'm sure of it."

And so, for the first time, Thomas Asberry found himself at loggerheads with his son. Unable to prevent the inevitable, he spent the rest of the day anticipating—and dreading—the moment when he would confront the only individual ever to turn his son's head from the path Thomas had set for him. The boy kept to himself all afternoon, mostly hiding in his bedroom behind closed doors, ostensibly reading and writing in the journal he had begun keeping. There he remained until dinnertime, and it was shortly after the tense, silent meal that James's special girl arrived on Copper Peak. She drove up in a small, gleaming black foreign car and parked in the gravel drive right in front of the house. Thomas had sent his two older sons on a delivery to spare them this ordeal. Now, as he waited for the inevitable knock at the door, he sat in his favorite rocking chair glowering at the anxious-looking James, allowing his anger to simmer under pressure, so that when he released it the results might be spectacular indeed.

The knock came, and when James hastily opened it to admit his guest, Thomas nearly died of a seizure.

She was a monster: a tall, slim thing with large, dark-painted eyes, orange-dyed hair cropped close around a lumpy skull, and ghastly, chalky-looking makeup that turned her face into a leering, corpse-like mask. She wore a glistening coat of black leather and obscenely tight black pants that ended in high, spiked heels. Thomas had never seen such a thing, and had his joints allowed him to rise from his chair with any expediency, he would have ejected her bodily from his home. As it was, he could only meet James's pale, pleading face with an icy, stabbing stare.

"Dad. . . ." the young Asberry stammered. "This is my . . . friend. Dauphine."

Thomas's eyes did not leave his son. His glare grew sharper, colder.

The girl looked nervously to James. Weakly, she addressed Thomas. "I . . . I was born in New Orleans . . . on Dauphine Street. That's how I got my name."

Thomas's pale gray eyes continued to stare icily at them. The girl turned to James and shrugged. He offered her something that resembled a comforting, reassuring look, and then said to his father, "I don't know how else to tell you, Dad, so I might as well say it up front. Dauphine and I . . . we're going to get married."

Even his old joints could not prevent Thomas exploding from his chair, adrenaline and horror blazing through his veins like magma. His tongue had frozen with shock, and he nearly collapsed back into his seat as a jolting stab of pain burned in his chest. How could this happen? How could all those years of tenderness, love, and mutual respect have culminated in this, the ultimate disaster? How could James's cultivated mind have been so utterly perverted?

What could this debased creature from the world beyond want with his boy?

At last Thomas's tongue loosened. He hissed, "What is the meaning of this? Where did you get the idea you could betray your father? Undo everything we've worked together for? Where?" He gestured ferociously at the girl. "From this?"

Dauphine looked indignant but said nothing. James meekly shook his head. "Dad . . . I have to. I just have to."

"This is what happens at those schools. People from all over the world come here. To our backyard. And this is what they do. Look at her, son. *Look at her!*"

"Dad. . . ."

"James, you see here the decadence of the cities, all rolled into this little painted package here. You see the sickness that I have always tried to protect you from. *Look at her!*"

Dauphine put on an arrogant sneer–which her makeup grotesquely accentuated–and placed her hands cockily on her hips. "He's not going to let up, is he?" she said in a soft voice, thick with forced patience.

The young Asberry was speechless. He slowly shook his head, his eyes begging his father to listen to reason. The icy wall between them only grew more frigid.

At last, James mumbled, "Dad . . . Dauphine is carrying my baby. She's pregnant."

Now, everything within him spent, Thomas simply lowered himself into his chair, letting his weight rock it slowly back and forth. His fingers had gone numb and he could hear nothing but a thunderous roaring in his ears. This could not be *his* failure. He did not deserve such cruel treatment. This was pure, unadulterated evil: the very thing he had sought to keep from his doorstep ever since he was a lad himself . . . that his entire family had kept out for two centuries. Of all of them, only he had failed.

No. It was the sickness from outside. It had insidiously infected his son. But he should have known better! James had grown too curious and ventured too far from his home, from his upbringing. It was all too often the way of youth. Yet Thomas, in his day, had resisted such temptation. All of the Asberrys had resisted such temptation! He knew what was right, and he stood by it. His strength of character had been sufficient to curb that which tempted him before it could subvert his will, his principles. He had always been certain that the same would be true of James.

But now . . . this diseased creature stood in his own living room, exerting its influence over James with even a faint glimmer of pride in its dark, opaque eyes.

He glanced at his son, his heart momentarily melting with a pang of regret and sympathy. The boy just didn't know better. It was not too late. Surely, it was not too late!

But James said, "A grandchild, Dad. Doesn't that mean anything to you?"

"Nothing of my own blood would ever come from *that,"* he whispered, pointing at Dauphine. He drew a deep, fury-tinged breath. "I suggest you destroy the child, send this creature away, and come back to me, James. It's not too late."

Dauphine's undead face flushed with disbelief and horror. She stared wide-eyed, first at Thomas, then at James. Her voice cracking, she said, "Do you hear that? Is that how your family is? You said he was strict, but . . . but James, this guy is a complete asshole. Are you sure he's your old man?"

James turned sorrowfully to her, unable to face his father's withering glare. He took her hand tenderly and shook his head. "I'm sorry. I didn't think it would be like this."

"Come on," she said. "Let's get out of here. You can come with me. I've got room at my place. You don't have to stay here . . . not in this goddamned looney bin."

For several long moments, James stood there, torn and hurt. His eyes finally turned to Thomas's, desperate for even a gleam of sympathy, but they found none. Dauphine's eyes bored into James's with a kind of raw power that turned Thomas's stomach. His son stood no chance against such manipulation. All those wonderful years together . . . they were being crushed under the spiked heel of this she-beast from the degenerate outside world he hated.

Fight her, son.

But then, the final, terrible words came from James's mouth, and Thomas simply closed his eyes and prayed his heart would stop beating so he wouldn't have to listen to its terrible clanging.

"I'll go with you."

And James left. He got into the car with the creature and disappeared into the night. The house had fallen silent but for the soft tick-tocking of the clock on the fireplace mantle. Outside, even the insects and nightbirds had ceased their whistling and jabbering. With a pained groan, Thomas rose from his chair and testing his legs, wondering if they would support his weight after the shock he'd suffered. For the moment, at least, they held, and he shuffled to the mantle, staring at the hands of the clock that so slowly but inevitably crept into the future.

In just a few short minutes, a lifetime of labor, of caring, of love, of nurturing, had been undone by a monster.

Those eyes of hers. Black and empty. Their soulfulness was nothing but a reflection of the poor boy's who gazed into them.

Thomas picked up the old clock—an heirloom from his grandfather's day–and hurled it into the fireplace, watching ambivalently as it smashed into useless pieces against the brick.

It was over. Everything was over. He had lost his favorite son, and nothing and no one could ever repair the damage.

He slowly walked to his bedroom, closed the door, and took his oldest violin and bow from their place on the wall. He worked his fingers back and forth for a few moments to limber them up . . . and, then, for the next several hours, the house was filled with the most piteous and doleful music that any instrument in the history of the world had ever produced.

Outside, a hot, angry wind began to sweep over the house, whispering Thomas's name.

For months, Thomas did not know where James had gone. His two other sons, who had always cared deeply for their brother, offered their father as much support and care as they could, but he refused to acknowledge that James had ever existed. As far as Thomas was concerned, his youngest son had died. Frederick and William took on James's former responsibilities in the business without complaint, and they continued to play with their father on those now-infrequent occasions that he felt compelled to share his more conventional music with anyone.

Then, the letters began to arrive. They were composed in James's familiar, elegant script, and upon seeing that handwriting for the first time in so long, Thomas's heart momentarily leaped. But when he read what the boy had to say, any chance of reconciliation melted away like icicles beneath a blazing sun. In his explanation for his unconscionable behavior, James wrote that he truly cared for Dauphine, and he wished his father would at least try to understand his feelings. In the beginning, he and Dauphine had been attracted to each other because of the vastly different worlds whence they came; but these subtle feelings soon blossomed into true passion, and then . . . the rest was self-evident. He and Dauphine had been married by a justice of the peace. The baby was due in a month, and, for the time being, he and his wife were living with Dauphine's parents in Georgetown.

When the baby came, James named him Kenneth George, after Thomas's own father. But there could be no softening of the elder Asberry's all-consuming, righteous indignation. He would never accept the child of his wayward son as any relation of his, for the blood of its mother was corrupt and vile. As long as that child existed, the Asberry family line was diseased; tainted. Even if James were to leave the woman and return home in true penitence, Thomas would never be able to take him back. Not after what he had done . . . not after fathering a child such as he had.

Years went by, and Thomas grew older and only more bitter. His two remaining sons moved into homes of their own—still on Copper Peak, but away from the main house, where their father brooded endlessly. Frederick and William faithfully continued to maintain the family business; in fact, profits from the Asberry product had skyrocketed in recent days, affording the entire family as comfortable an existence as they desired. But Thomas stayed in his own spartan house, content to while away the hours with his music, his memory too long for the damage to his spirit to mend itself.

The Spheres Beyond Sound had become Thomas's Bible, his constant companion, and many were the days that the sound of unearthly music emanated from the house, disconcerting even to Frederick and William, who worried that their father's mental state might be failing. Surely, sounds such as those that screeched from Thomas's room could not be the product of a rational mind. When Thomas began to play, his sons avoided the house and grounds, for the tones that rang out sounded more like tortured screams than music, and sometimes they thought they heard more than a single instrument playing—even though this was patently impossible. Strange echoes and weird harmonics often accompanied the chaotic melodies: oddly delayed notes; half-intelligible syllables and whisperings; long, sustained tones that seemed to come from monstrous vocal cords rather than catgut strings.

But what his sons didn't realize, Thomas thought, was that he was saner, more in tune with his own soul than he had ever been in his life. As he played the simplest compositions from Zann's book, he began to find a kind of peace; not an assuagement for his pain and anger, but a means to focus his negative energy, to transform it into a source of strength and determination. In the book, he found simple truths and grand revelations. He found fugues and toccatas, symphonies and sonatas; compositions of every variety, some for entire orchestras, others for a soloist. Some could not be given a name or classified; they were mere combinations of sound intended to set in motion a desired series of vibrations, the effects of which might be tangible or intangible. That which would seem mere fantasy to untrained, uneducated eyes had become the foundation of Thomas's world. His faith was complete and justified; for though it was not until the rift with his son that his devotion to Zann became total and complete, he had, in his younger days, seen proof positive that *The Spheres Beyond Sound* was anything *but* a book of fantasy.

Even before James's birth, Thomas had studied the Zann text, devoured its words to find the arcane truths that might be revealed within. That worlds existed beyond this one, Thomas had no doubt, and to use Zann's music to discover and explore them had always been his most ardent desire. But the bridges between worlds were tenuous and fragile, and could lead to terrible dangers as well as enlightenment. For, according to Zann, certain of these distant realms might be places of pure chaos, populated by things that, if not overtly hostile to the hopeful seeker, might in their very ambivalence be quite deadly. Zann gave no names to the places and inhabitants his music might reveal, but he bestowed upon them epithets such as "The Madness Out of Time," and "The Shadows Beyond Space." There were stern admonitions by the author to be fearful of approaching things unknown, and to respect every tenet of his text as the unmitigated truth.

While in his early thirties, Thomas Asberry had decided to test the veracity of this fabulous volume, and to do so chose a spring night when his wife and two infant sons had gone to Barren Creek to visit one of her cousins. He had altered the tuning of his viola exactly as Zann prescribed to facilitate the playing of unusual progressions. Then he had gone to the edge of the forest, sat down, and simply absorbed the atmosphere of the night for a considerable time, listening to the harsh trills and soothing songs of the plentiful night creatures. A soft breeze whispered through the branches, providing a low, rustling percussion as a background. His mind was calm and serene, and not ripple of fear disturbed the tranquility of his soul. He knew that he was ready.

Lifting his bow to the viola, he began to play. The discordantly tuned strings screeched and buzzed in mimicry of a melody, but to Thomas's ears, the notes were pitch-perfect. Now and again, his fingers would pluck an individual string, and the harmonics would ring eerily through the forest, sustaining themselves for seemingly impossible lengths of time. As his wrist deftly guided the bow over the strings in smooth, circular motions, increasing the tempo of the fugue, he began to hear tones that sounded like the rich, mellow voice of a French horn. With a thrill that jolted his heart, he realized that these new sounds were not being produced by his instrument, but were coming from *elsewhere.* His eyes desperately searched the black forest for a sign of the source, but he dared not lose his rhythm, his momentum. It wasn't until he had nearly reached the end of the piece that something moving at the corner of his eye finally captured his full attention.

A few yards to his right, behind a number of pillar-like trees, a pale, ghostly mist seemed to be coalescing out of thin air, swirling and oozing in an oddly sentient manner–as if it were aware of him and seeking to reach him. In ecstatic shock, he watched as the mist assumed a hazy but definite shape, its contours suddenly taking on a distinctly disturbing aspect. The hair on the back of his neck and hands had risen as if the air were electrically charged, and he found he could no longer hear his music over the pounding of his heart.

The luminous mist solidified, and what Thomas's bulging eyes now apprehended was a grayish, aqueous-textured thing hovering several feet above the ground, emitting a kind of deep, warbling hum. It had a long, conical trunk and a huge, domed "head," not unlike a jellyfish, with dozens of long, snakelike tendrils sprouting from beneath the bulbous cap, several of which ended in wicked-looking, clawed talons. A vast array of gold-colored, globular eyes gazed at him with cold disregard, much as he might take note of a spider crossing the floor at his feet. The warbling sound became an angry buzzing, and the golden eyes flashed with a light that seemed to come from deep within the thing's pulsating body.

The entity suddenly scooted toward him on its cushion of air, conveying an attitude that did not bode well for Thomas's continued good health. Deciding that *now* was the proper time, his trembling fingers began to pluck the opening notes of the musical passage that would reverse what he had done, thus closing the door on this unhappy intruder. He unleashed a series of rapid, nightmarish arpeggios, and, suddenly, the advancing thing halted as if it had struck an invisible wall. Its angry voice chastised him with a sound like hornets swarming, and several tendrils slashed at the air alarmingly close to his head. Quickly, the thing's body seemed to lose its definition, and, within moments, it had reverted to the insubstantial mist that he had first seen. As he continued to play, the mist began to dissipate, like a column of smoke coming apart on a breeze.

Then, it was gone. No trace remained of Thomas's visitor, not even an echo of that low, warbling drone. The only reminder of the whole bizarre event was the total silence of the forest; all of the woodland creatures within hearing distance had ceased their calls, as if they, too, held their breath in anticipation of something terrible yet to come.

But nothing did more did come. After a time, the nightsongs began again, and the stars above glittered over a forest that appeared as normal and prosaic as it might on any other night. Only when Thomas had stared, slack-jawed, into the depths of the wood for two or three eternities did he realize that he was completely alone in his own backyard, and that his clenching fingers had shattered the neck of his favorite stringed instrument.

Without actually meaning to, he opened his mouth and screamed loud and long to the denizens of the night; not in horror, nor in mortal dread, but in complete, utter, and rapturous joy. Later, people in Barren Creek would claim to have heard his whooping and hollering, most of the opinion that one of the Asberrys had availed himself to one jug too many of their famous corn product. Truly, Thomas was intoxicated, absolutely giddy with his sense of achievement. But this youthful display of exuberance was soon tempered by his rigid self-discipline, and he solemnly returned indoors to contemplate the evening's episode in a somewhat more objective light. And, characteristic of his family, and of himself,

Thomas Asberry's sense of achievement soon gave way to a new sense of purpose.

His favorite viola had been repaired by dawn the next morning.

Thomas had never reproduced that experiment again, but only because he felt it unnecessary. The truth of Zann's book had been proven, and within its pages lay more knowledge than one man could ever possibly absorb. Over the years, he continued to delve into the text and construct other, different types of musical bridges, some of which produced similarly miraculous, if less traumatizing results. And all along he had been grooming James to continue where he would eventually leave off, since, as with all men, the time would come when Thomas would have to pass from the realm of the living. But this dream had been violently dashed, and while most men would simply accept the inevitable and move on with their lives, Thomas—even after so many years—could release neither his son nor the beast to which he had mated from culpability.

James continued to write regularly, keeping his father apprised of events in his life, despite the fact that he never received a single reply. He had become something of a success in his life away from Copper Peak, having secured a slightly better-than-menial position with some human resources outfit in Washington, DC. Thomas's grandson was growing into a well-adjusted, intelligent youth; wouldn't it be wonderful, James wrote, for Thomas to finally meet him? Wasn't it time to set things right between them?

Thomas continued to ignore his son's entreaties. James Asberry had no place in the family or in Thomas's heart; and as for the little bastard that the beast had spawned, well, the devil—or that which commonplace minds accepted as the devil—could simply have him.

Then it happened. James's wife, Dauphine, who had become "less exotic in her appearance and attitude" in recent years, had taken an overdose of some recreational pharmaceutical and shuffled off to her own sphere beyond sound. Apparently her recent "conservatism" had not been as complete as James liked to believe. Thomas, once past his resentment toward the creature for denying him his spite, eventually became jubilant. Not since his experience with the thing from outside, so long ago, had he known such exhilaration. It was beautiful. Beautiful! For a short time, he entertained thoughts of bringing James back home, thinking that, somehow, his son's good name and family status might be salvageable. But Thomas had cultivated his hatred too long and too diligently to be swayed by sympathy or pity. His heart quickly hardened again, and while Frederick and William sent their brother letters of condolence, Thomas turned a blind eye to the worthless alien he had once sired.

Then, Thomas fell very ill. He was getting old, and his two remaining sons were obliged to move back into the house to help take care of him. He knew that he could not be much longer for this earth, and, though Frederick and William were good sons and respected his talents and devotion to music, they had never been of a mind to learn what he had learned, to carry on where he must necessarily leave off. To pass beyond, leaving not the legacy he had intended for so many years, but an abandoned, valueless child . . . this calamity burned in his soul, and he knew that he must do *something* to resolve it before he was no longer capable.

A letter arrived from James, who would surely be ignorant of his father's condition, but who must have sensed that, with the passing of years, Thomas's health and mind might be failing. With positively embarrassing humility, he begged for forgiveness for himself and acceptance for his son. Kenneth was 12 years old now and knew of his grandfather only from the stories James told him of life in the old days up on Copper Peak. With his heart stuttering more often than it was steady, Thomas finally decided that, yes, now was the time to do what must be done. He simply could not go to his grave leaving his affairs so hopelessly unsettled.

One bright and warm September afternoon—the first day of autumn—Thomas Asberry ordered his two sons to deliver a large shipment of liquor to Aiken Mill, which would keep them occupied for a considerable time. He set up his audiotape device and retrieved his old viola, and after consulting a few crucial passages in the Zann book, he began to play. For a good quarter hour, anyone who might have happened upon the house on Copper Peak would have been treated to an insane viola concerto that rose to the heights of sonic chaos—only to be followed by another, similar but distinctly different variation on a theme. Then, for several long hours, not a sound came from the mountaintop. As night fell, not a single cricket chirped. Not a bird called tentatively for a mate in the darkness. No breeze rustled the leaves that had begun to fall from the oaks, maples, and poplars that towered regally over the house.

Locked in his room, Thomas composed a letter with trembling hands, barely able to hold pen to paper. Once he had completed it to his satisfaction, he read over it, hoping its intended reader could make out the crabbed, awkward script.

The letter read:

My Dear James,

It is truly a tragedy that we have allowed ourselves to live without each other's company for all of these many years. You must know the bitter heartache I have suffered since the unfortunate incidents that led to the complete separation between us. That the years we did spend together were so wonderful and rewarding to the both of us has only made living without you all the more difficult. I will admit to you that my anger has been so severe for so long that I simply have not been able to bring myself to approach you in any other manner.

But I now write to you in the hopes that, at the end of my life, I may be able to wipe away the stain that has blackened our memories and cast a shadow on our good family name. It is my sincerest hope that you accept this gesture as coming from my heart.

Enclosed is a tape recording of some music that has been dear to me for a very long time. You will find it unusual, I do not deny, but I encourage you to listen to the entire recording. You cannot guess how important this music is to me, and how much I had always hoped to share it with you under very different circumstances. The tape is intended for both you and your son Kenneth, and I am certain that you will come to understand exactly why I consider this my last and most important gift to you.

I fear we shall never see each other again in this life. I am failing, and may in fact be gone by the time this package reaches you. Hopefully, when I have passed into that which lies beyond, the world will be a better place for what I am leaving behind.

In all sincerity,
Thomas Asberry

Thomas packed the letter and tape in a mailing carton and addressed it to his son in Washington, DC. He then wrote a note to his other sons, in case he did not last until they returned, instructing them to mail the package immediately. He wanted it put into the mail on this very evening.

Satisfied his arrangements were complete, Thomas settled himself in his rocking chair, realizing that life was, in fact, ebbing from his ancient body. The room was dark and growing steadily darker with each painful breath that he took. He was positive now that he would be gone by the time Frederick and William returned. He would love to have seen them again, but he was leaving them well provided for, and he knew it was better that they be spared the ordeal of witnessing him breathe his last.

And so, there he sat, finally content, secure in the belief that he had redeemed himself and set things to right. Perhaps he should have done it long ago, but it was too late to indulge in any regrets. The fact that the tape recording contained no barricade, no means of sending back that which was called forth, would likely mean a problem for someone at a future time, but Thomas could not bring himself to be concerned about that. The music on the tape would fulfill its purpose, and whatever happened beyond that, he simply did not care.

There was so little time left. Voices from the other side were calling to him, singing in sweet, beckoning voices. He thought that, from somewhere, far, far away, he could hear the sound of a viola. Here, in his house, he was alone; but he knew that something waited for him just beyond the periphery of his senses. He could feel it. Hear it. His dimming eyes grew dimmer.

And the darkness fell complete.

Frederick and William returned from their errand to find their father's body comfortably reclining in his favorite rocking chair, his skin still warm to the touch. Next to him lay the package addressed to James and the note he had left for the two brothers. Saddened by their father's death, but still bound to follow his wishes, they promptly carried out the instructions he had so painstakingly written and saw to mailing the carton before concerning themselves with any post-mortem arrangements.

When Thomas was buried in the small family cemetery, just a short distance from the house he loved, his face, which had been so pinched and hardened from years of bitterness, wore a radiant, blissful smile.

Fugue Devil

I was fifteen years old when my family moved to Beckham, Virginia to live. My dad had been hired as an English professor at the local junior college, after years of applying at countless other, larger colleges and universities. We came from Atlanta, where he'd been a newspaper copywriter, in the fall of 1974, just in time for me to enroll as a freshman at Beckham High. Being city-bred, I wasn't sure how I would take to relocating to a mountain community of barely a thousand people–not counting the six hundred or so college students who took up residence during the academic year. I was a afraid I'd be thrown into a classroom of backwoods rednecks and KKK shitkickers; exiled to some quaint country home miles from the nearest neighbors, with my parents and older sister the only company I would ever see outside of school.

I was half-right. Beck-Hi, as it was commonly known, did contain its share of long-haired dopeheads, junior bigots, and teachers whose eyes betrayed their hatred of the few black children in their classrooms; but, on the whole, the school–and the town–seemed to follow the more progressive sociological path paved by the college. Our house was indeed off the beaten track, but a few kids lived within walking distance, and the miles of unbroken woodland offered me an opportunity for exploration and adventure unlike any I could have imagined in Atlanta.

That was the year I learned about the Fugue Devil.

Ronnie Neely told me about it one day while riding home on the schoolbus. He lived about a mile past my place on Route 2, and being kind of lonely out there, he took to me immediately upon learning how close my house was. He became my first and best friend in my new hometown.

I remember that afternoon well: we'd been talking about the kinds of music we listened to; I was partial to good old rock and roll, *Radar Love* by Golden Earring being my favorite at the time. Ronnie was a country boy and loved bluegrass. His father had been an accomplished fiddler, so he told me.

"You know, my dad used to know an old man up on Copper Peak, out toward Aiken Mill," he said. "He was a musician who worshipped the devil. Dad said you could hear horrible sounds coming from up there on Halloween and on the Witches' Sabbath. He played the fiddle to call up demons and stuff. They say there's this one called the Fugue Devil, and since the old man woke it up, it comes out every seventeen years looking for souls."

"Really? Who was the old man?"

"People don't speak his name. And nobody goes up on Copper Peak anymore. I guess he's probably dead now, and in Hell."

"Cool."

"Sherry Wilson's dad saw it one time. That's what made him blind."

My heart leaped at the mention of her name. "Sherry's dad is blind?"

"Shoot yeah. She'll tell you about it, if you ask her."

Sherry Wilson. She was a slim, golden-haired beauty with wide brown eyes and perfect legs, a ninth grader who'd captured my notice from day one in school. I'd never spoken to her, but how I wanted to meet her. She lived up on Mt. Signal, a humpbacked ridge a mile or so north of my house. From my backyard, the mountain looked like a big tortoise shell, and at night I could even see the lights from Sherry's house. I'd often gaze up there and imagine she was looking down at my house, dreaming about me the way I did about her, sharing our unspoken love across the distance.

Now maybe I came into manhood late or something, I don't know. All my friends in Atlanta had been going out with girls for quite a while, and some of them had even gotten laid. But I'd always been more interested in model airplanes and playing baseball, and I guess there were even whispers that I must have been queer. But when we arrived in Beckham, my hormones suddenly caught up with me and literally drowned me with an insatiable desire for this winsome lass. Now, to hear that her dad had seen a demon, and it had *blinded* him. . . .

I *had* to meet her.

"You know her pretty well?" I asked.

"Kinda," Ronnie said. "I can introduce you, if you want."

"You like her?"

"Well, yeah, I like her, but not like . . . you know. It's Stephanie Asberry for me, man."

"Ah. Okay."

Ronnie was tall and bony, with longish red hair. He lit up a Winchester little cigar—the driver never cared if people smoked as long as they sat in the back of the bus—and offered one to me. I ended up nearly coughing my lungs out because he didn't tell me it was best not to inhale them.

"Don't light up in front of Sherry," he said. "She doesn't like men who smoke."

I nodded. That was important information to remember.

My stop was next. I stood up and gave Ronnie a wave. "See you tomorrow, huh?"

"Yeah. Be cool."

The bus groaned to a halt, and the rear doors hissed open. I jumped out into the chilly mountain air, noticing that the sun had already dipped beyond the ridge to the west. For to the northwest, I could see the tip of Copper Peak towering above the forest. Straight ahead of me, Mt. Signal rose like a huge castle for the queen who lived at its summit. Her bus would probably be dropping her off about now.

I hurried up the long gravel driveway to my house. Smoke was pouring from the chimney. My mom had probably built a fire, even though it hadn't gotten that cold yet.

How I would have loved to sit next to a fire with my arms wrapped around Sherry, maybe under a fur blanket, seeing her eyes filled with longing for me. We'd kiss, and she'd whisper, "I love you, Mike."

Yeah. That's how it would be.

My sister Tammy was seventeen. She'd starting smoking pot before we left Atlanta, and was always trying to turn me onto it. I wouldn't do it. Most days after school, instead of taking the bus home with me, she'd catch a ride with some other seniors and go over to the college. I guessed she was looking for connections now that she was in a new town. She'd even meet up with Dad and ride home with him some evenings, stoned out of her mind. My parents knew—they *had* to have—but they never said anything. They wanted to pretend that it wasn't happening.

Dinner at our house had become a tense thing, a gathering of family around an utterly silent table, except for the sound of flatware clanking. Tammy seemed to enjoy knowing that she could have such a profound effect on everyone. That night, her eyes were glassy and red while we ate. You could smell the reefer on her.

When I was younger, my dad had been a stern man. With Tammy, he seemed to have turned into a pansy. I couldn't understand what it meant.

My mom had made coffee, and when dinner was over, she asked, "Tammy, would you pour us a cup, please?"

Tammy nodded and rose to get the coffee pot. She poured Dad's first. It went straight into his empty salad bowl.

"Oh, shit," she whispered. Then she burst into silly laughter. "Sorry about that!"

I started to laugh in spite of myself.

Then, to my surprise, my father reached over the table and smacked me across the face.

"That wasn't funny, *son,* so I suggest you can the laughtrack." He gave Tammy a scowl, but then his attention turned to me. "You'd better go to your room."

"Dad, I didn't do anything."

"Go."

I gave Mom a pleading look, but she just shook her head and sighed, averting her eyes from mine.

Adults have their quirks, and I knew my parents had their share. I could understand their reluctance to confront Tammy about her extracurricular activities. But I could not understand them taking their frustrations out on me. It just wasn't like them.

I did as I was told without a word. As I left, I heard a chair scrape the floor, and I looked back to see Mom getting up to leave the room.

My Dad gave Tammy a harsh glare. Her face grew about five miles long, and she poured his coffee for him. I stopped in the hallway just out of their sight, peering around the corner to watch them. Tammy sat down next to him.

"You haven't told her, have you?" Dad whispered.

"No, of course not. She's probably figured it out by now, though."

"Look, Tammy, I swore it would never happen again. You know I'm sorry for it. What do I have to do to convince you?"

"You didn't have to do that to Mike."

"He'll get over it. It's no big deal."

"Yeah, sure. I trust you're not going to touch him . . . the wrong way?"

"Now you look here," he said, raising his voice dangerously. "I know what you think about me after what I did. But Tammy, we have to work it out and come back together. How long are you going to put us all through this?"

She glared defiantly back at him. "As long as I feel like it, Dad. Because I don't think you're really very sorry about it."

"You're wrong about that."

"I don't think so."

"God, Tammy, if your mother ever finds out . . . if *anybody* ever finds out. . . ."

"I know. It's the end of your life as you know it." She slid her chair back and rose from the table. I ducked out of sight and headed for the stairs to my room. I stomped my feet as hard as I could, not caring if I shook the house or broke the floorboards.

I finally understood it all. Yes, naïve little me, I saw exactly what had happened. Dad had molested Tammy, and she'd agreed to keep it quiet–for a price. Somehow, I didn't exactly feel sorry for her. Mom must have suspected *something,* though she probably thought it was just about drugs. The only thing I didn't know was how long this had been going on. In the city, I'd heard about this kind of thing; it had happened to some of my classmates. But it couldn't happen in my family. *Not mine.*

I shut my bedroom door, turned on the radio, and lay back on the bed, not knowing whom to hate, whom to feel sorry for, whom to turn to for help. Blue Swede began chanting, "Ooka, ooka, ooka-chaka, ooka, ooka, ooka-chaka. . . .

"I can't stop this feeling deep inside of me. . . ."

It was dark as sin in the backyard. In Atlanta, streetlights had burned outside my windows all night long. I reached over and switched off my lamp, gazing out toward the black forest, the mountain looming over my house, and the tiny lights up there where my precious queen lived. What was she doing now? Having dinner? Doing her homework? And her parents–did she and her dad ever–

Christ!

Sherry's dad couldn't even see what she looked like.

An early autumn wind sighed through the trees, rustling the leaves that had begun to gather in the yard. It was a lonely sound, melancholy and bitter. Why did it sound like the music my heart made–a dirge that drowned out the song on the radio? How could my family, my normal, decent, Christian family, ever sink into the kind of depravity that you only heard about in the ugliest of stories?

I lay in the dark for hours, hoping Dad would come and tell me I was wrong, that I was *stupid* for even thinking such things. I tried to convince myself that I'd jumped to conclusions, that somehow I'd just misread everything I'd seen and heard. But I knew I hadn't.

As I finally began drifting off to sleep, my door opened softly. The light from the hall burned into my eyes, so that I couldn't tell who was standing just outside. I expected it to be my father.

It was Tammy. She came in and laid something on my nightstand, then turned and disappeared without a word, closing the door noiselessly. I gaped after her for a moment, not quite sure I was really awake.

Turning on my lamp, I looked to see what she had left me.

It was a hand-rolled cigarette—a joint. And a butane lighter.

I started to crush the joint in my hand, but then I stopped. Instead, I opened my nightstand drawer, placed the items inside, and covered them with some notebook paper.

Maybe it was time to see just what it was all about.

"Mike . . . this is Sherry Wilson."

She stood next to Ronnie, giving me a tentative smile. Her hair was full and wavy, not flat and lifeless like so many of the girls'. She wore a medium length gray jumper over a red, long-sleeved sweater, her long legs crossed demurely as she leaned against the wall. She held a stack of books in one hand.

"So," I said, careful not to trip over my tongue, "you wanna sit with Ronnie and me at lunch?"

She shrugged. "Sure, I guess so." Her soft voice held only the barest hint of a southern drawl, even though she'd lived in Beckham all her life. She turned to accompany us to the cafeteria, her tight-fitting top revealing a figure that was just beginning to turn glorious.

"Where are you from, Mike?"

"Atlanta."

"Mike wants to know about the Fugue Devil," Ronnie interjected. I felt my face go red.

"You've already heard about it?"

"Ronnie told me."

"Bad news. It's dangerous to know about the Fugue Devil."

"Dangerous? How come?"

"Because if you know about it, it knows about you."

"Get out of here."

She gave me a stern glare. "I'm quite serious."

Needless to say, I didn't believe there could be such a thing, but I was intrigued by the story—and by what she might have to say about her father.

We entered the lunchroom and got in line. Sherry waved to several of her friends gathered in a corner. They looked in our direction and giggled.

"This is the year it's supposed to come," she said. "Every seventeen years it flies up from Hell in search of souls. If you know about it, it knows about you. And if you see it, it will come for you."

"Every seventeen years," Ronnie said. "Kind of like locusts."

"At midnight of the autumn equinox it appears. Everybody from

Beckham to Aiken Mill stays inside and closes up their houses on that night. Sometimes it just goes away. Sometimes it doesn't."

"Sounds like an old folk tale," I said. "Kinda like the St. Simons Island lights, in Georgia, or the headless ghost that wanders down the Gainesville Midland tracks at certain times of the year."

"Yeah," Sherry said. "But the Fugue Devil is real."

"Tell him about your dad."

"Well," she said, drawing out the word dramatically. "We don't much like to talk about that."

"If it bothers you, don't," I said, not wanting to appear the least bit inconsiderate to her.

"So what, nobody else is listening," Ronnie said. "Go on, tell him."

"Daddy only told the story once, when I was very small. But I remember it because it scared him to tell it. He didn't used to believe in the demon. So on that night, seventeen years ago, he looked out the window at midnight. And there it was, coming through the trees toward our house. It was so terrifying, Daddy's eyes just couldn't take it. He went blind, and he's been that way ever since. He won't talk about it with anybody, so if you meet him, don't ever ask him. He doesn't like me talking about it, either."

"But you do because it makes you special," Ronnie said with a mock sneer. Sherry punched him in the arm. Hard.

"But that doesn't sound like it took his soul or anything," I said.

"He thinks it did, in some way," she said mysteriously. "It has its own methods that we don't necessarily understand."

"So, how does this thing know how to find you . . . if you know about it?"

"It has a giant bloodhound. It sniffs you out."

"A giant bloodhound. Right."

"It's true."

She looked like she meant it. Her father must have really told her a whopper to explain his blindness, I thought. It seemed like carrying an old story a little too far.

We got our lunch and went to sit down. We ended up next to a bunch of Sherry's friends, so apart from a little small talk, we hardly got to say anything else to each other. But I watched her as inconspicuously as possible—not very successfully. I simply couldn't take my eyes off her. She moved so delicately but with such self-assurance. Even the way she lifted the forkfuls of mystery meat to her mouth was graceful. Once in a while, our eyes met, and my heart would flutter. I couldn't read her expressions, but I'd never been able to read girls anyway—as if anyone ever has.

As if to emphasize that point, when the bell rang, my sister came into the cafeteria for the next lunch period. She saw me as I was dumping the leftovers from my tray into the garbage can, and she walked by to say "hi." I didn't even want to look at her, much less speak. I guess she'd figured out that I knew what I had happened with Dad and her.

"Mike, you don't understand anything. Don't be mad at me."

I didn't answer. I slid my tray through the slot in the wall, where an anonymous pair of hands grabbed it and pulled it out of sight.

"This doesn't concern you, Mike, see? Nothing between us has changed. How about you just let Dad and me work it out, all right?"

I shook my head and started to leave. She grabbed me by the arm.

"Don't go away mad, Mike. You don't understand."

I finally turned around and looked her in the eye. She wasn't stoned, but she looked tired.

"What I understand," I said, just loudly enough for people nearby to hear, "is that Dad molested you, and you're trying to pay him back. But all you're doing is digging yourself in deeper. You could have gotten help. You could have even come to me. But you've decided to blackmail him, so you can do whatever you want. What about Mom, Tammy? You don't give a shit about her, or me, or anybody but yourself. You make me as sick as he does."

Her look of contempt only confirmed what I already knew. I turned and left, feeling that the devil was indeed real, and it was living in my house.

"This weekend is the equinox," Ronnie said, blowing the smoke from his Winchester. "The night of the Fugue Devil."

The bus bumped down Route 2 with Ronnie and me the last passengers left. Somehow, the story of the Fugue Devil had lost some of its charm.

"Nice," I said. "You going to board up your house?"

"No, but Mom and Dad will be in bed early with all the curtains closed."

"What about you?"

"I reckon I'll just be asleep."

"You know . . . I was kind of thinking about going out to watch for it."

"Huh?"

"I mean, it only comes around every seventeen years. We weren't even born the last time it came, and we'll be old by the next time. I want to get a look at it."

Ronnie stared at me with big, surprised eyes. "You serious?"

I leaned over to him and asked, "You ever get high before?"

"Not really. But I've drunk moonshine. You're in the moonshine capital of the world, you know."

"I got some grass. You want to smoke it with me?"

"When?"

"Tomorrow night. At midnight."

He whistled. "You don't believe in the Fugue Devil, do you?"

"Hell, I don't know. But I guess I'll find out tomorrow night."

He shook his head dubiously. "Have you ever got high?"

"Nope. This'll be the first time."

"Damn, man. I don't know." Ronnie's face was pale. Was it fear of trying drugs for the first time, or was it something else?

"C'mon, let's do it. You in?"

The bus slowed down and shuddered to a stop in front of my house. I stood up and grabbed my books. Ronnie stared at me thoughtfully for a long moment. "If you see it," he said at last, "it will come."

"Hell, I want to see its dog."

He laughed sharply, then gave me a resigned shake of his head. "Okay. I'm in."

An explosion of satisfaction spread through my chest. I could barely believe what I was scheming.

"So, come to my house before midnight. Knock on my window if I'm not already outside, and we'll go out to Mr. Miller's field. It's just up the ridge a little ways."

The doors opened, and I hopped out. As the bus rumbled away, I waved to Ronnie. He leaned out the window peering after me, shaking his head again.

"Don't chicken out on me, man!"

"I'll be there!" he called back.

I looked toward my house. Mom's car was parked in the driveway. I didn't want to talk to her, though I knew I would have to. She'd barely spoken this morning before I'd left for school. I knew she must feel angry and ashamed, her feelings too private to divulge to anyone else. What if I told her what I knew? Would it make it easier for her or hurt her all the more?

She was sitting in the living room when I came in, listening to an Al Martino record. *Daddy's Little Girl.* She didn't look up.

"Hi, Mom."

"Hey."

I couldn't do it. She obviously had guessed everything, and there was nothing I could say to her, not now. She still had on her housecoat, and her eyes had a dim, faraway look. I couldn't bring myself to intrude. She would have to make the first move.

The night of the equinox, I went to my room right after dinner—another grim, silent affair—and did my homework. My father had apologized for hitting me and punishing me, but he'd said and done nothing to explain himself. He'd looked uncomfortable, as if he'd had something to tell me but that wouldn't come out. I didn't know how to feel about him anymore. I kind of hated him, but, in a way, I pitied him. I knew that as long as this wall of failed deception divided our family, there would be no chance for reconciliation.

Tammy had gone out to the college. About nine o'clock, I heard my parents' voices drifting down the hall from the living room. They were raised in anger, and I gathered that the dam had finally burst. I couldn't make out what was being said, but I wasn't about to creep from my room to try and listen. I focused on my math paper, forcing myself to keep my mind on the value of *x*.

"I didn't mean for it to happen!"

"But it did. How many times?"

Their voices were growing clearer. I heard a door slam. They'd gone outside.

"So what's it going to be, Emily?"

"I'm going to Martha's."

The car started, and tires spat gravel. So. Mom was leaving. She hadn't even come to tell me goodbye, or that she would be back soon, or that everything would work out in the end. That was what Mom and Dad had always stood for. Things working out.

And she was leaving. I would be alone in the house with my dad. *Did she not even care about that?*

I crossed the room and looked out my window that faced the driveway. I saw the headlights of Mom's car turn up the road toward Beckham. In a moment, she was gone. The back door slammed again, and I heard heavy footsteps approaching my room. I quickly sat down at my desk, hunched over my paper. The door opened.

"Mike, your mom's gone to visit her sister in Roanoke. I don't know when she'll be back."

"Okay."

"I'm going to grade some papers. Please don't disturb me for the rest of the evening, all right?"

"Sure, Dad."

"Good night."

"Night."

He closed my door, and his footsteps retreated down the hall. I heard his bedroom door close. Something fell to the floor with a crash. Mom's jewelry box.

After that, I didn't hear anything from the other end of the house until I went to the bathroom around ten o'clock. A low noise came from behind Dad's door. I detoured from the bathroom and softly made my way down the hall. Before reaching the end, I could tell that the sound was muffled sobbing. My dad was crying.

Back in my room, I opened my drawer and took out the joint and the lighter that Tammy had given me. Just looking at it scared me, yet it fascinated me. Was this how my sister fought back? Was she so ashamed that she couldn't talk to anyone, only drag herself down with drugs and wild behavior? I was still hurt and mad as hell at her, but I wanted to understand. Maybe this was the means.

In a couple of hours, I'd be going out with Ronnie to look for a devil. I didn't even believe in it, I didn't think, but all the same, I was nervous. Combined with the anticipation of getting high for the first time in my life, the anxiety set my stomach fluttering. My hands and feet were cold, going on numb. All my overpowered senses cried out for release.

I lay down on my bed, wondering about my mother, hating my father, and not knowing what to think about my sister. And I dreaded what I was about to do.

Oh, Sherry, I need you so.

I turned to peer out the window toward her house. I could see the lights up on the mountain, twinkling like little stars.

At eleven o'clock, they went out.

Ronnie showed up at twenty minutes till midnight. I'd already put on my coat and gone outside to wait for him. My father had cried himself to sleep, I guessed. There hadn't been a sound in the house for over an hour.

"This is it, man," he said. "I think we're crazy."

"You scared?"

"Naw, man. Well . . . actually . . . how about you?"

"Kinda."

"Yeah." He lit a Winchester and gave me one.

We headed out of my yard, into the woods leading up and around Mt. Signal, toward Mr. Miller's field, about half a mile distant. Fortunately, we'd both had brought flashlights, for beneath the trees the darkness was impenetrable. Our footsteps crunched loudly in the dry leaves. Far in the distance, the cries of whippoorwills and ground owls echoed like mournful choirs.

"You got the stuff?"

"I got it."

"You don't suppose we'll have a bad trip or anything, do you?"

"I don't think so. Not if we keep our shit together," I said, nearly biting my tongue at the thought of Tammy. In reality, I had no idea how the pot would affect me. But I did know one thing: I was going to prove myself stronger than any pot, stronger than my dad and my sister . . . and even my mom.

We made our way through the limbs that slapped at our faces and clothes. Every now and again, I'd peer up toward the mountain's summit, trying to catch a glimpse of Sherry's place, but here there were too many trees in the way.

"Talk to Sherry any more?"

"Not really," I said. "I sure wish she was here now, though. Except that she probably wouldn't go for the pot, huh?"

"I doubt it. But I wish Stephanie was here, too. We could double-date."

"Be great, wouldn't it?"

"God, yes. I'd let Stephanie shit on my face just to see where it comes from."

"Man, you're sick!"

"But it's a good kind of sick."

I laughed. The cool night air felt wonderful, revitalizing. Out here with Ronnie, it was like I could almost forget everything that had happened. Even Mom's leaving didn't seem quite so bad. Tomorrow, things would work out. Tonight, I had me a demon to watch.

Ahead, I could see a break in the trees and a wide, misty gray space beyond. To our right, the small white shape of Mr. Miller's farmhouse nestled in a shallow valley, pale smoke rolling from its chimney. All the lights were off.

We walked out into the tall grass and waded up the hill to a circular mound about twenty feet in diameter. A few dark shrubs grew around its sloping sides. We cleared a space at the top and sat down, facing northwest. Copper Peak rose above the ridge before us. To the left, out in the distance, a scant few lights burned in Beckham. The college lay farther south, beyond our line of sight.

I reached into my pocket and withdrew the joint. I held it up for Ronnie to see.

"Ready to burn it?"

"Yeah," he said. "What time is it?"

"A couple of minutes till midnight."

"Do it."

I placed the joint between my lips, flicked the lighter, and touched it to the tip. I sucked in a deep lungful of sweet-tasting smoke. I'd heard you were supposed to hold it in; but it was like the smoke expanded inside my chest, and, a second later, I coughed it out in a big gray cloudburst.

Ronnie took the joint from me and puffed tentatively. Then he drew in a long breath. He also coughed it up immediately.

I tried again and this time was able to hold the smoke in longer. My throat burned, but the sensation was not unpleasant. When I blew the smoke out, a sudden dizziness made my head reel.

We passed the joint back and forth several times, each drag of the smoke making me feel more lightheaded. I began to notice an almost subliminal humming sound around me. When I looked at my feet, they seemed to be a mile away. My whole body appeared anchored on the ground, while the rest of me–my spirit–floated freely, looking down.

"Jesus," Ronnie whispered. "I feel weird."

"Yeah. It's kind of neat."

"Look at the stars."

I peered at the sky. A few thin clouds drifted past a brilliant starfield, and a three-quarter moon hovered above the ridge. The chilly breeze that swirled down the slopes was just shy of uncomfortable.

Out toward Copper Peak, I glimpsed a flicker of light. My eyes turned toward it but were slow to focus. Making my body obey my commands seemed a supreme act of will. The joint, almost gone now, came back for a final drag. I sucked the smoke in and tossed the roach into the tall grass.

"What the hell's that?" Ronnie asked, pointing to the northwest.

The light I had seen on Copper Peak was now rising into the sky, a tiny golden globe moving up into the heavens. As it ascended, it began to zoom back and forth in a zigzag pattern, traversing the sky from horizon to horizon. It moved quickly, soundlessly; within a matter of seconds, it reached a zenith directly over our heads.

"My God . . . that's it!" Ronnie whispered.

"You're full of shit."

"Look at it!"

I had to struggle to keep my eyes on the ball of light. But now I could see that it was trailing sparks, and, in its heart, something dark was taking form. I saw a pattern of limbs emerge, like a distorted fetus within a fiery amniotic sac. A distinct figure was beginning to take shape: something with arms and legs, and there was something else up there with it.

"I don't believe it," I said.

"Is it the grass, man? Is it making us see things?"

"You don't hallucinate from grass. And we're both seeing the same thing."

"Christ. Do you know what this means?"

"It means it's real. Man, it's real!"

"It means we're dead, Higgins. We're fucking dead!"

The brilliant shape disappeared over the ridge behind us. I could see a wispy trail of black smoke, like the remnants of some nonsensical sky-writing. Within moments, the smoke had dissipated in the breeze. We had only our memories as evidence we'd seen anything at all.

"If you know about it, it knows about you," Ronny said. "And if you see it, it will come for you."

Without a word, we simultaneously turned and galloped down the hill toward the woods. My feet kicked the earth, seemingly hundreds of feet below, my head swimming in a murky sense of unreality. As I ran, I forgot where I was; I knew only that I had to run, to hide, to escape. When we reached the woods, we tore through the tree limbs as if they were mere shadows, ignoring the cuts and lashes we received. I may have tripped and fallen, perhaps more than once, but I remembered nothing more until I reached the relative safety of my backyard.

We hurtled into the yard, gasping and panting. Our eyes scanned the sky, peered into the woods; our ears strained to catch the slightest hint of movement anywhere around us.

"It's out there, Mike. What are we going to do?"

"How can we make it leave us alone?"

"There is no way."

I swore under my breath. I'd gotten us into this, led Ronnie to what must be certain death. But *he'd* told me about the thing. *He* was the one who started it all in the first place.

As if he knew what I was thinking, he began to whine, "Why the hell did Sherry have to tell me about it? Damn bitch! Why'd she have to tell me?"

That was too much. I could accept the responsibility for what we had done, but I would not allow him to cast blame toward Sherry. I leaped at him, shoving him roughly to the ground. "You leave her out of this. It wasn't her fault."

"If she hadn't told us about it, we'd never have gone out there."

"We could have decided not to go. We could have kept on believing it was just a story."

"Bullshit. If you know about it . . . you look for it."

I realized he was right. The temptation of such a tale was simply too great.

"How many other people might have seen it?"

"I don't know," Ronnie groaned, dragging himself from the ground. "People just don't talk about it. They try to forget, so people like us *won't* look for it."

"Too fucking late," I said. "What are we going to do?"

"I gotta get home."

"We better stay together. You can't take off alone."

"You'll let me stay here tonight?"

"Yeah, I guess so. *I* don't want to be alone."

"Let's get the hell inside, then."

We turned and trotted up to the back door. I was about to open it when I heard a rumble and saw lights coming up the driveway. It took a moment for me to realize it was a car.

It was Tammy coming home in Dad's LTD. She parked beneath the balcony over the turnaround, switched off the engine, and opened the door to climb out.

Suddenly, I heard a heavy crunching sound in the woods on the other side of the driveway. A slow, deliberate tread approached the house, accompanied by a low snuffling sound. My heart slammed into overdrive.

Tammy shut off the headlights, and the driveway was submerged in almost total darkness. The crunching sounds drew nearer.

"Tammy, turn the lights back on!" I cried. "No, get up here! Hurry up, just get the hell up here!"

"What are you yelling about?"

Ronnie joined in, "Just hurry! Come on!"

She began climbing the steps. I looked past her into the woods, toward the source of the heavy footsteps.

High above the ground, a pair of glowing, golden eyes stared at me from the cover of the trees. They moved back and forth slowly, as if sizing me up.

I screamed. A moment later, Ronnie saw them. He screamed too.

"Jesus Christ, what's wrong with you?" Tammy asked as she reached the top of the stairs. "Are you nuts?"

"It's out there!" Ronnie cried. "It's seen us!"

"What are you talking about?"

My tongue was frozen. I gaped stupidly at Tammy, unable to explain. The footsteps began to recede into the woods. She must have heard them and turned around. But she saw nothing. It was gone.

The back door opened, and there stood my father, still dressed but disheveled. He flipped on the porchlight, which illuminated the driveway to the edge of the trees. I stared into their depths, searching for any movement. There was none.

"What's going on out here?"

"I just got home," Tammy said. "They were out here yelling."

"I thought you were in bed," Dad said to me.

"I . . . I couldn't sleep."

"Ronnie, what are you doing here? You've got to go home, son."

"Mike said I could spend the night."

"Mike didn't ask. I don't know what you young men think you're doing, but you won't be doing it here tonight. Mike, inside. Ronnie, you get on home."

His face turned ashen. "I don't . . . I can't. . . ."

"Do your folks know you're out this late?"

"No, sir."

"Then I suggest you get moving."

"What if . . . could you take me home?"

"No, I could not. You apparently got here on your own. You may leave the same way." Dad gripped me by the shoulder and gave me a tug. "Let's go."

I raised a hand toward Ronnie, but Dad slapped it away and pulled me by the arm into the kitchen. I struggled free and nearly sent my fist right into his face; somehow, I restrained myself.

Tammy came inside after me, and Dad closed the door. I saw Ronnie peering in through the window with pleading eyes. He looked back into the darkness, then at me.

"Dad, there's something. . . ."

"Get to bed, Mike. It's too late for this crap. We'll talk tomorrow."

"But. . . ."

"Go."

The command was final. He locked and deadbolted the door, then turned and stalked out of the kitchen and down the hall toward his room. Tammy gave me a long, icy stare, her hands on her hips. I leaped for the back door and fumbled with the lock, but I could already see that Ronnie was gone.

I hurried to the kitchen window and looked out toward the front yard.

I could see him in the moonlight, racing down the hill toward the road. He looked back once, but I don't think he could see me. He rounded the corner at the bottom of our driveway and turned left without breaking stride. I'd never seen anyone move so fast.

I felt Tammy's eyes boring into the back of my head. I watched the retreating figure disappear beyond the trees at the end of the yard. He had nearly a mile to run. I stared out the window long after he was gone.

My sister did not hear me when I whispered, "I loved you, Ronnie."

Brilliant daylight was streaming into my eyes when I next opened them. I didn't remember falling asleep.

I was lying on my bed, still dressed. It all came flooding back: going out to Mr. Miller's field with Ronnie, smoking the joint, seeing the light in the sky, and then . . . those golden eyes peering at me from the woods.

Ronnie . . . he had run home by himself.

It had to have been the pot. I'd had some kind of bad trip. *Tammy!* She knew how pot affected you. She'd been smoking for a year or more now.

I slid off the bed and hurried to the kitchen. The clock over the table read eight-forty-two. The house was quiet. Too quiet.

"Tammy?" I called. My voice echoed emptily through the house. Glancing out the back door, I saw Dad's car was gone. He must have already gone out on his errands, like he always did. Like he did when we all loved each other, and everything was simple and sweet, and Saturday mornings meant cartoons and playtime, with no worries, and. . . .

Mom. She was at my aunt Martha's. I had to call her.

I went to the living room phone and dialed the number. It rang once . . . twice . . . three times. No answer. I slammed the phone down. Where the hell could they be? I was home alone. *Completely* alone. Vulnerable.

"Oh, shit."

I was just about to go back to the kitchen when the phone rang. I spun around and grabbed it up. "Hello?"

"Mike? This is Julia Neely, Ron's mother. He wouldn't happen to be over there, would he?"

A cold iron fist grabbed me, stealing my breath. It took a moment to stammer, "No . . . no, ma'am. He isn't here."

"He was gone when we got up this morning. We saw him when he went to bed last night. But he doesn't usually get up early on weekends. Did he say anything to you about what he might be doing today?"

"No, Mrs. Neely," I said, not knowing what else to tell her. "He isn't here."

"I'm worried about him. His bike is still here with a flat tire, so he didn't go off riding."

My voice was about to fail me. All I could do was breathe into the receiver.

"If you see him, please tell him to hurry home."

"Okay."

"Thank you, Mike."

"Yes, ma'am."

I dropped the receiver into its cradle, feeling like I'd just told the most horrible lie of my entire life. My hands were shaking.

Jesus Christ. It had gotten Ronnie.

There was no other possibility. He had raced for home with the devil literally at his heels. I tried to think rationally. Maybe he'd fallen and hurt himself along the way. What if he were lying in a ditch somewhere with a broken leg or something? He could need help. Wasn't that the most logical explanation?

But I'd seen the thing in the sky.

Even under the influence of the marijuana, I knew I hadn't imagined or hallucinated the monster. Ronnie had seen it too. We'd heard it in the woods near the house. Where was it now? Did it lurk somewhere nearby, waiting to catch me alone?

Like now?

Sherry. She would know.

I opened the drawer where we kept the phone book and looked up the listing for Wilson. I didn't know her dad's first name, and there were five Wilsons in town. I knew she lived on route 7. There . . . Wilson, Kirby C. I quickly dialed the number.

It was her voice that answered, "Hello?"

"Sherry? It's me, Mike Higgins."

"Hi, Mike." Her voice sounded cautious.

"Sherry, last night . . . Ronnie and me went out to Mr. Miller's field. We saw the Fugue Devil. I think it got him."

"You saw it?"

"Yeah."

"And Ronnie?"

"He ran home, not long after midnight. The thing was near my house. I *saw* it. And Ronnie's mom called this morning and said he was gone."

"God."

"What am I going to do? What can I do?"

"What do you mean? You know about it, it knows about you. And you saw it, so. . . ."

"There's got to be some way to stop it."

"No. There isn't."

Well, when does it come? How long does it stay?"

"I don't know. As long as it takes."

"Who else knows about it? Somebody must know something about it."

"Nobody that does will admit it."

"You did!"

There was a long silence. "Mike, don't you understand? I didn't believe it, either. I always thought it was just some story my dad told me."

"It isn't. I saw it. I swear I did."

"I know."

"You do?"

"My mom just talked to a friend of hers. Some kids from the college have disappeared. I guess they heard about the Fugue Devil and drove up to Copper Peak last night. The cops found their car this morning, empty."

"Maybe they're okay, somewhere. . . ."

"No, Mike. There was blood. Lots of it."

Not knowing anything else to do, I locked myself in my room. I had thought of taking my bike out and riding toward Ronnie's house, to see if I could find him. But I was too afraid to go out on my own. I sweated and fidgeted, actually praying that my dad would get home so I wouldn't have to be alone in the big, silent house. Every creak of floorboards settling, every rustle in the yard sent cold chills up and down my spine. I'd never been so terrified in my entire life.

Just after eleven, I heard Dad's car in the driveway. I ran out to meet him, overcome with relief. He got out and began unloading several bags of groceries from the trunk.

"Hey, Mike, come give me a hand with these."

I went down and took a couple of the sacks. Dad looked weak and beaten. Standing close to him, I found myself feeling dirty, as if the ugliness inside him also tainted the air around him. But, for the moment, it was a discomfort I was willing to suffer.

"Where's your sister?"

"I don't know. She was gone when I got up."

"She must have gone to the college with those damned friends of hers." He didn't hide the disgust in his voice. And I could scarcely conceal my disdain for his own double standard.

I turned to go up the steps. A row of dense evergreen trees separated me from the backyard. On the other side, I heard something moving in the woods. A low grunt, like a dog snuffling, came from the hillside beyond the yard. My heart skipped a beat and I froze.

Animals often came out of the woods. It was just an animal. I paused on the steps, catching a glimpse of movement through the evergreens.

Dad came up behind me. "Get a move on, son, these bags are heavy."

Reluctantly, I proceeded up the stairs. At the top, I stepped aside and let him pass. I turned and peered into the backyard, up the hill into the woods.

I didn't see it until it moved. A pair of huge, black eyes were staring at me. Cavernous nostrils flared as if to catch my scent. Bluish splotches covered its dull gray back and sides. A stiletto-like tail pointed rigidly from its hind end.

It was a monstrous hound the size of a horse, standing between two thick pines on tall, muscular legs. Worst of all, something moving behind it was causing the trees to sway and tremble. Limbs clattered above the dog and leaves cascaded over its head. The heavy footsteps in the dry leaves seemed to shake the ground. A huge silhouette on two legs materialized beside the dog.

The thing that had taken Ronnie.

I barely caught a glimpse of two deep-set golden eyes staring at me before I spun around, dropping my sacks of groceries. Glass shattered. I shoved my way past Dad, knocking one of the bags from his arms. But as I pushed the door to the kitchen open, something tugged at my collar. I frantically turned around, fists flailing blindly.

The blow caught my dad squarely in the jaw. His remaining bag pitched over the railing to smash on the driveway below. His look of shock lasted only a second. Then he charged at me with an angry snarl.

"You little shit! What the hell's wrong with you?"

I was pummeled by fists that, if stronger, would have knocked me cold. I raised an arm in a vain attempt to defend myself, but a blow to my solar plexus drove the wind out of my longs. I went down, gasping for breath.

"You want another one? Huh?"

I saw his foot draw back for a kick. I managed to croak, "Something . . . out back. Out back!"

He hesitated. I pulled myself toward the door, out of his immediate reach. He looked at me in bewilderment. "What are you talking about?"

"There's something in the backyard. It's after me."

He took a couple of uncertain steps back. He peered around the corner of the house. "There's nothing there."

I should have known it. Dad didn't know about the Fugue Devil. It certainly would not show itself to him. I whispered, "It was . . . an animal. Some kind of animal."

He stared at me with puzzled contempt. "God damn, son."

"I'm sorry . . . I didn't mean to hit you."

His expression softened, and he peered down at the ruined groceries. He looked as if he were about to break down. "That took all my money," he whispered.

I began to cry. He seemed to draw up something inside, and he came to me, extending a hand to help me up. I suddenly wanted to tell him everything, to admit what I'd done, to be his little boy again. I fell into his arms, and there was a strength in his embrace that I hadn't felt in a long time.

"I'm sorry too, son."

There was no ugliness radiating from him now. For the moment, I could almost believe he was the same dad I'd known as a child: a strong, protective, loving man untouched by whatever disease or evil had worked its way into his heart. I felt safe, even when I heard heavy, crunching footsteps retreating into the depths of the woods.

A minute later, a car pulled into the driveway, followed by a chorus of female voices bidding their farewells. Tammy was coming home.

And Dad left me standing there to cry alone.

After that, I expected Dad to come to me, to repent, to bring Mom home, to make us a family again. I just wanted things to be put right, to feel safe. As a family, we could overcome the evil I had brought upon myself.

But late that afternoon, my mom called and talked to Dad. I heard him say something from time to time, but mostly he listened. At last, when he hung up, he came to my room and said, "Your mom is getting a lawyer and says she wants to have me brought up on charges. She's going to be coming to take you and Tammy away."

My heart sank. Everything familiar, everything I had ever known and loved was being stripped away. And, outside, there lurked a devil. It was waiting for me.

"What's going to happen?" I asked.

"I don't know. We probably won't be seeing much of each other."

"Where will we go?"

"All that will have to be worked out."

"Dad," I said, feeling tears coming on again, "I don't want this to happen."

He stared at me for a long time. I couldn't tell what was going on behind those clouded eyes. At last, he said, "Maybe it's for the better."

Then he turned and went out. His footsteps shuffled down the hall to his room. I heard his door close gently.

I went to my desk and picked up my radio. It shattered into a dozen pieces as it struck the wall with a resounding crash.

Somehow, I'd survived the previous night. I remembered Sherry's words: "Sometimes it goes away . . . sometimes it doesn't. . . ."

As long as it takes, she'd said.

I knew it wasn't going away. It was going to stay until it did to me whatever it had done to poor Ronnie.

Ronnie. He acted tough, but he was just a funny kid, sensitive and mild. Gone. God, how horrible it must have been. He'd known the thing was after him. I remembered the pleading look he'd given me through the window just before he'd taken off running.

He'd tried to blame Sherry for revealing a secret that was potentially lethal to all who shared it; he'd *needed* to blame somebody. But Sherry hadn't even believed in it herself. *Was* she to blame? If she'd never told us, Ronnie would still be alive, and I might have a chance to see a reconciliation of my family. Damn, why didn't she know what would happen?

Deep down, I knew better. I had to cast aside all blame. *I* had taken Ronnie to his death. *I* had condemned myself to an unknown but surely awful fate.

Me, myself, and I.

I stared out the window into the pure blackness. It took several moments for my eyes to pick out the tiny lights at the top of the mountain. I was seized by the deepest, most bitter melancholy I had ever known. My heart wept like a sweet violin. There was so much love in me with no channel, no release. Such unresolved love could only turn to misery. I became racked with convulsive sobs.

Through my tears, I saw the lights at Sherry's house go out. But a moment later they came on again. And then . . . off.

Something was intermittently blocking my view of her house.

Something was coming down the mountain.

Oh, God . . . this was it.

I left my room and went down the hall to my parents' room. My father sat on the bed with a stack of papers at his side. He held a red pen in one hand.

"What is it, Mike?"

"Dad . . . there is this thing, it's called the Fugue Devil. It was called up from Hell many years ago, and now, every seventeen years, it comes out to take souls. If you know about it, it knows about you. And if you see it, it will come for you."

"What in God's name are you babbling about?"

"It killed Ronnie last night. When you sent him away, it got him. It got some other people, too, from the college. Maybe they were students of yours."

Dad stood up. "What the hell kind of story is this? What's the point?"

"The point is, Dad, that now you know about it. And I wouldn't be at all surprised if you see it tonight."

I had willingly accepted the slap across the face and the sentence of bedroom imprisonment until my mother came to pick up Tammy and me the next day. I locked my door, turned out the lights, and knelt on the floor next to my bed to pray. I knew I had only minutes of life left, if that.

But for hours, nothing happened. Dad went to bed around midnight, I guess. I heard him brush his teeth and go to the bathroom. Tammy had gone out somewhere, as usual. I actually wished to hear the thing coming for me, to get it over with. My heart could not withstand such furious pounding, drawn out for so long. Surely, I was being toyed with.

Then, just after one o'clock in the morning:

A thump came from the basement. I heard a heavy creak. Then another. At last, it was in the house. By now, I felt I would welcome death. It would be the release I ached for. But when I heard the heavy *thud* on the steps, I realized I was wrong. Terror flooded my veins, and a new desire to stay alive seized me with unexpected vehemence. But there was no chance, no hope. The Fugue Devil collected souls.

Something was scraping the paneled walls, something hard and sharp. The floor groaned beneath an immense weight. And from outside my window came the snuffling sound I'd heard before in the woods. The contents of my stomach rose to my throat. Blood rushed through my ears like the banshee scream of jet engines.

It was in the hall now. Boards popped and screeched as the heavy steps approached my door. I heard a strange buzzing sound, like a swarm of bees, rising and falling rhythmically. Its *breath!*

The door handle turned. I could barely see the rectangle of blackness expanding as the door slowly opened, revealing a huge, vague shape: something tall, broad, hunched in the hallway. A pair of golden eyes blazed at me from near the ceiling. And as it crossed the threshold, the true shape of the thing began to crystallize.

The Fugue Devil had the head of wolf, with five bony horns protruding like a crown atop its skull. The massive body looked to be covered with reflective scales or plates, like armor. Its arms were long and muscular, manlike, but ending in talons resembling an eagle's. On its back, a pair of gold wings arched over its shoulders, half-folded like a bat's. From its bristly throat, it emitted a low, grating buzz, which rose to a thunderous rumble.

No . . . I did *not* want to be taken by this thing! It was so tall it had to lean forward so its head would clear the ceiling. It bent even lower to regard me with undisguised malevolence, tilting its head oddly, as if in vague *recognition* of me.

No wonder Sherry's dad had gone blind.

"Please," I whispered. "Go away."

Its canine jaws spread in a wicked parody of a smile. I felt the temperature in the room rising. The smell of scorched flesh assailed my nostrils.

"Don't take me, please," I sobbed. "Please."

I heard the sound of huge paws thumping across the yard outside, moving toward the other end of the house. The sniffing came from near my dad's window.

"Take him. Take my dad. Leave me alone. Please. Please!" The word came out as a screech.

The Fugue Devil stared at me with those brilliant eyes. I could see that they had depth—as if they were merely lenses that revealed some new and infinitely remote and dark dimension. There was in that gaze something more than intelligence. I began to realize that this beast-like horror was merely a physical manifestation of something else entirely; a horrifying shell to clothe a deeper, spiritual force that came from somewhere far, far beyond the little mortal world that I knew.

I was not so much terrified now as *humbled.* I was looking at a mere symptom of a consummate evil.

A talon rose toward my face. The scream I longed to release hung in my throat. All that came out was a whimper: "Not me. Please . . . not me."

A searing heat swept over my body. I closed my eyes. This had to be death. Yet, after a moment, the feeling passed. The air cooled quickly.

When I opened my eyes, the room was empty. But I could hear the thumping of the devil's footsteps out in the hall, heading away from my room. A door creaked. The footsteps stopped.

And the screaming began. The buzzing rose in a wavering harmony. A sharp, agonized wail was cut short by a quick ripping sound, like wet newspaper being shredded. A few moist gasps followed, then another shrill scream. It died slowly this time, ending with a muted rattled, as if something were stuck in my father's throat.

I remained perched on the edge of my bed, unable to move. I heard a rough scraping sound, then the splintering of wood. The rhythmic thumping began outside the house, and leaves rustled in accompaniment as the thing returned to the woods. The sniffing and snorting of the hound faded, as did the footsteps moments later.

After a minute or two more, I realized I could hear a faint hissing sound, wavering unsteadily, from the far end of the house. It was an agonized, weak sound: my father's tortured breathing. Life somehow remained in his body. I went to my door to listen. The sound was desperate, futile, blended with intermittent sobs.

Within a minute, the breathing stopped.

And then, I heard the downstairs door slam and footsteps coming up from the garage. Tammy. I kept silent, waiting to see what she was going to do. Her footsteps went down the hall, toward her room, then on to the bathroom. Then they stopped. I heard her voice call softly, "Dad?"

A moment later, her horrified shrieks filled the house, and I collapsed on the floor. I gathered a lungful of air, and my misery erupted in a howl that went on and on, until my vocal cords simply failed.

That was seventeen years ago.

At first, my sister and my mother thought I had murdered him. But when the police came, they absolved me immediately, for he had been killed by something incredibly large and powerful; in fact, the coroner went so far as to say that it would have taken a crazed bear to inflict the kind of damage my father's body suffered. The killing remains unsolved, as do the disappearances of Ronnie Neely and the college students whose car was found on Copper Peak. The official report theorizes that all were victims of some wild animal, never minding the fact that no physical evidence was ever found—no hair, no saliva, not *anything*—to implicate a bear or rabid dog. And I, of course, could offer no explanation.

My sister and mother eventually recovered from the shock; Tammy, in particular, seemed to take the death remarkably well. While they never had any inkling of what had killed my father, they always seemed to have an intuitive understanding that his death had been a part of something much bigger than a random act of violence. Mom grieved for a long time, I know; as much for having lost my dad to his worst side during his last months as for his actual death. But she never talked to me about her feelings. Her suffering remained hers alone, which forced me to be forever an observer to what became a crippling, withering battle for her sanity.

She won out in the end.

I, however, have carried the burden of my guilt for these years with no relief, keeping it locked inside myself, much as my mother did with her grief. While the thing that tore my father limb from limb was not of my making, the bargain I made with it makes me as guilty as if I had killed him myself. And I have never learned to forgive.

Sherry Wilson told me the Fugue Devil was a collector of souls, and I believe she was right in more ways than she knew. While it may have destroyed my father, it placed a lien on my own soul as everlasting as the death it brought its other victims. I have wondered for seventeen years if Sherry's father also made some bargain with the demon, to exchange his sight for his life. It is a subject I would like to have broached with him, had he not taken his family to another state shortly after the night my father was killed. I never saw Sherry again.

So, in the ensuing years, my struggle for my heart and soul has taken me through doctors and clergymen, an institution, and countless prescription drugs, all of which have been as effective as sugar water against cancer. For since that night, I have been completely mute; after that final scream, my tongue was frozen for all time. I cannot talk of the world, of love, of hate, of people and their affairs; I read it as a cruel joke, for my ability to use a pen is unhampered. Yet it is a story I have refused—until now—to commit to paper.

Last night was the equinox.

It was with great deliberation that I made the decision to leave the meager existence I have managed to eke out in Atlanta over the past few years and return to Beckham. I resolved to own up to my sin and pay in full the lien on my soul with my life. I intended to go back to Mr. Miller's field, the place where the Fugue Devil made its first appearance to me, and to make sure that I was there at midnight to witness its next arrival.

So that is precisely what I did. I arrived there well before time, remembering in fullest detail every step I'd taken with Ronnie on that night long ago. I made a place for myself on the small knoll in the middle of the field and sat down to watch the sky. Old Mr. Miller still lives in his house in that shallow valley. The stars were clear.

At midnight, I was struck blind. Just as my tongue prohibited me from speaking of that horror, now my sight was taken from me, denying me the glimpse I needed to draw the beast back to me. At a minute past, my eyesight was restored—just in time to see the last vestiges of black smoke in the sky like demonic skywriting.

The Fugue Devil proved itself the master engineer. I don't understand the strange laws that govern the black spirit worlds whence it comes, or the conditions that allow its interaction with us at the specified time every seventeen years. I know only that I am condemned yet again, and that for the beast itself, my father's death must take on a whole new sweetness, trapped as it is within my memory.

So, my story is here, like a roadmap to this world for the thing on the other side, for now the reader has dangerous knowledge.

The Fugue Devil will appear again at its prescribed time, in the prescribed place.

If you know about the Fugue Devil, it knows about you.
And if you see it. . . .

The Devil's Eye

"If you know about it, it knows about you. And if you see it, it will come for you."

He'd heard those words seventeen years ago, spoken by his younger brother Ronnie: now dead and gone, taken away, probably ripped apart, if there was anything to the stories told. Didn't used to think there could be any truth to them; just rural legends that had a way of cropping up in communities tucked away from the rest of developed civilization, the way Beckham was. Well, Ronnie had believed the line, and he'd died for his belief. Just a kid of fourteen at the time. Too young to really know what it meant to believe in anything.

Nowadays, Jack Neely believed in all kinds of things he never had as a youngster; things he couldn't have imagined then and wished he still couldn't. It's easy to believe in evil spirits when your mom drinks herself into the grave at the age of thirty-seven, and your dad shoots himself in the head the day after she's buried. Even easier when when you get hooked on the hard shit by the time you turn eighteen, and you spend a couple of years in the hole after getting busted, and you find the only guy in Catawba who treated you decent busted up so he'll never walk again, just for refusing to give a smoke to a temperamental rapist/murderer.

But Ronnie had been taken away by the same kind of people who Jack had come to realize lived so close that you could smell them, even if you couldn't see them. Yeah, that was the scary thing. You could never see them, not until it was too late. But they were there. Always there.

Every seventeen years it came–just like locusts, so the stories said–but to eat souls, not foliage. On the autumn equinox. If you saw it, you were dead. It would take you, simple as that. Ronnie had seen it.

Ronnie had believed in it.

The poor, deluded kid . . . he'd gone out in the middle of the night and seen the wrong thing–or the wrong people. Neely wondered if Ronnie had smelled them before it was over for him.

Well, that's what he had believed had happened to his little brother for all these years.

Now. . . .

He made movies.

It had always been his dream, long before his parents went dead, even before Ronnie went missing (dead). But no one from a little rural town in southwestern Virginia could ever really hope to go break it big in Hollywood, especially one who didn't usually have enough money to get across town, much less across country. Dreams is dreams, they'd say, all those people standing with him on the line at Booker Furniture, not a one of whom possessed enough gumption to put a pen to paper and come up with so much as a witty line or a vivid scene or a pretty musical note or anything that might draw upon their latent right-brain-energy. The most right-braining anyone here had ever done was conjure the Fugue Devil, way back when.

But while going to Hollywood was out of the question, an enterprising and determined soul could still take a dream and make it real if he cared enough to really try. And Neely was quick to realize that the booming film industry down in North Carolina could mean that his neck of the woods wasn't as close to nowhere as it once seemed.

He picked up Carolina and Virginia Film Industry directories and started writing letters. Although not much of a reader, Neely had checked out just about everything ever written on the subject of making movies. He could converse with reasonable intelligence about cameras, lighting, sound, even a little about screenwriting. He figured if he could get a position even as lowly as a grip with some studio, he would have a ticket in. He received a few callbacks, but nothing that held any promise–until he hooked up with a man who went by the name of Running Bear.

Bear had been owner and producer of an independent studio in Wilmington that had gone bust since its listing in the Carolina directory. Green Abbey, as the studio was called, had once contracted with Ted Turner on a TV project, but long-term success had eluded it. Running Bear was in the process of finding investors to get the company back on its feet, and he seemed happy enough to send letters back and forth with Neely, if for nothing more than to talk shop with an interested party. And Neely reckoned that it never hurt to get in good with somebody in the business, especially if the break Running Bear needed actually did come his way.

But what had sewn up their relationship was the Fugue Devil, which Neely mentioned while explaining briefly how his brother had disappeared when he was a kid. Running Bear bit down on that like a grizzly on raw meat. Something about the story appeared to inflame certain Native American nerves.

Green Abbey found some money very shortly thereafter. And word arrived that Running Bear was coming to Beckham with the intent to film the very thing that had supposedly killed the younger Neely on the night of the autumn equinox seventeen years earlier.

For every seventeen years it came. Like locusts.

Green Abbey Studios, Beckham, was a pair of old passenger train cars parked side by side on the tracks where the old train station had been before it was torn down in the late 60s. The town rented the cars out to whatever business might want to use them; short or long term, didn't matter, as long as $400 a month came in on time. The cars' facing doors were connected by sheet metal and planking so you could get from one to the other without getting wet when it rained. Plus, they were hooked up for running water, electricity, hot and cold air, and there was garbage pickup once a week, but you had to pay for these extras yourself.

Prior to Green Abbey, the cars had temporarily housed a lawyer's office while a permanent building was erected on Beckham's main street. Before that, the local RE/MAX agency had used them to show off its creative use of real estate.

Running Bear didn't look like an Indian, except for a slightly dark complexion and high cheekbones. His hair was sandy brown, his eyes blue. Native American ancestry, definitely, but mixed with plenty of Anglo. He also had a regular English name, but preferred the Indian moniker for professional and social purposes.

The first thing Running Bear did was provide Neely with the appropriate government forms, a contract, and a pair of safety shoes. So it was official: Jack Neely's working hours belonged to Green Abbey Studios, a real live movie company, and within an hour of signing on, he signed off at Booker Furniture, Inc. Permanently.

His title was Executive Producer, though it didn't entail putting up any dollars. What it did mean was that he would receive a percentage of the profits and a point on the gross of whatever product evolved from the footage of the Fugue Devil that Running Bear intended to capture.

The fact that the whole thing belonged to an ancient rural legend daunted neither of them.

Neely received his orientation two days before the equinox, during which they talked of death.

"Tell me more about your brother," Running Bear said, seated at his desk–a pair of card tables in one of the plywood-partitioned "rooms" of the train car, now outfitted with computer, fax, darkroom facilities, sound mixing boards, editing equipment, a couple of couches and a refrigerator.

"Ronnie was fourteen," he said, picturing his brother's face, his straw-colored hair, his lanky physique. "He heard the stories. I heard them when I was in school too. But nowadays it's all pretty much forgotten. Times change, people aren't so afraid of what's in the dark anymore unless it's your neighbor."

"You've never heard the scream of the Wampus Cat or seen the black Big Head rolling through the forest beneath a full moon. You've never seen the Birds of Fire light up the sky like fireflies, trailing smoke and crying out like angry children. You don't believe in these things, I know. But you lost your brother to one of their kin."

"My brother Ronnie got on the bad side of one of the local rednecks. Maybe came upon moonshiners when he was out looking for his monster. They'll kill your ass for sniffing the breeze if you're anywhere around their still. They don't care that you're just a kid."

"If that was true, I would never have wasted the time and money to come here. And I know there is something inside you that grasps the truth, though you yourself do not realize it."

"How do you know?"

"It is in your letters, beneath your words. You know, many more worlds exist than those you can see or touch. And there are places in this world where the boundary that separates us from them is very thin. This is one of those places. I knew it the first time I heard from you. And I felt it the moment I arrived here."

"So you just believe unquestioningly that what I told you really happened?"

"Unquestioningly? No. Your disbelief, actually, is the hardest evidence supporting the existence of some great power here." He waved away Neely's look of indignance. "Don't get me wrong. People whose beings have been shaped solely by their physical senses seldom see or hear those things that cross the threshold, simply because their spirits are not prepared. Many, like yourself, are brushed by them, and even then close them out, perhaps for fear of what their existence actually means."

Neely almost cringed under the intensity of Running Bear's bright blue eyes. "I've known people who believed whole-heartedly in it," he said softly. "There was a man, a blind man. He claimed to have lost his eyes from seeing the thing. And there were quite a few deaths attributed to it, most before my lifetime. But the on same night that Ronnie disappeared, there were others. . . ."

"And despite your prevailing sense of reason, that is why deep in your heart the Fugue Devil is real to you. I will want to hear all the stories you know. To prepare."

"And you actually mean to film it."

Running Bear's eyes focused on something far away. "Remember how primitives used to believe that if you photographed someone you stole a part of his soul? Well, imagine actually capturing the image of this ancient spirit. No, the emulsion of film or the magnetic particles of a tape do not literally capture the spirit itself. But think of the power I will steal simply by imprinting its image on physical media as it crosses from its territory into ours. The opportunity is unimaginable."

"Let's say you're able to do this. Don't you think there's terrible danger?"

Running Bear did not immediately answer. A moment later, he said, "Tell me–do you know how the Fugue Devil got its name?"

"Well, as the story goes, there was a man from Barren Creek, a long time ago, who learned how to summon spirits by playing music. One night he stood on the summit of Copper Peak and played his violin. And called down the Fugue Devil, which took him away."

"Tell me again the rules that govern its existence."

"The Fugue Devil appears every seventeen years on the night of the autumn equinox. If you know about it, it knows about you. And if you see it, it will come for you."

"Well, you and I already know of it. And in order to photograph it, one would reasonably expect to have to see it, right? To survive that, my friend, is the challenge before us."

Green Abbey Studios employed a total staff of about a dozen, but Running Bear had brought only a single assistant with him. This gentleman, name of Hugo Eckert, acted as cameraman, sound engineer, editor; whatever the needs of the moment, he was the man. In the past, he and Running Bear had put together a couple of biker-from-hell flicks for direct-to-video release, and Eckert looked like he could have played the biker himself. Mountainous body with little excess fat, crinkly black hair in a ponytail, earrings, leather, tattoos on both arms and probably elsewhere.

And a more soft-spoken man Neely had never heard. Not an effeminate voice, but a quiet and unassuming tenor with a gentle, erudite quality that one would more likely associate with a timid, bookwormish man of letters. But he'd been in the Navy, seen the world, heard lots of stories. Neely's Fugue Devil didn't seem much of a stretch for him. In fact, Neely suspected that Eckert shared some of Running Bear's apparent reverence for the mystical.

The morning before the equinox, the company went scouting for locations in the official Green Abbey van, with Eckert as chauffeur and Neely as tour guide. Beckham nestled in a hollow between Copper Peak and Mt. Signal, home to about a thousand souls, except during school months when the college added another thousand to the population. The one main street included a few shops, a gas station, a bank, and a couple of restaurants; nearer to the college, a tavern and a bookstore overlooked the road from a tall, tree-girdled mound, and beyond this, the local post-office huddled beneath a stand of tall, ancient white pines. Just beyond, the road curved to the left, leading around the base of Copper Peak until it reached Aiken Mill, a somewhat larger town in the next valley over. To the right, overhanging tree limbs formed a dark canopy above a narrow, crudely patched blacktop road.

"I used to live out this way," Neely said, pointing down the little road. "My mom and dad and Ronnie and me."

"Where was the last place anyone saw your brother alive?" Running Bear asked.

"He was at some friend's house, on this road. He left there that night and never got home."

Neely found his nerves jangling as Eckert turned the van onto the rougher pavement. About the only reason he ever came back this way was to pick up moonshine now and again from Bill Miller when he didn't feel like drinking legal spirits. And he had to admit the memories of his old home life were still vivid . . . and painful.

"Is your brother's friend still alive?"

"No idea. I know he was alive after that night. But I don't know what ever came of him."

A couple of miles further on, to the left of the road, they saw a wide field of tall, dried grass that belonged to old man Miller.

"Slow down," Running Bear said. "It started around here." Then softly, mostly to himself: "I knew this was the right place."

"How did you know that?"

"As I told you, the boundary between the worlds is thin here. Your brother saw it around this place."

Eckert parked the van beside the road and the three of them stepped out to hear a thunderous chorus of screeching and squawking birds, which had congregated in the trees in advance of heading south. In the background, a low wind droned through the forest, but none of the nearby trees so much as rustled. An unaccustomed sense of strangeness seemed to prevail in the late morning sun that each of them felt, Neely not the least of them.

"There," Running Bear said, pointing to the turtleshell hump of Copper Peak. "Up there. That is where it first appeared to the boys. We will place cameras here."

Eckert held up a Canon High 8 video camera and looked through the viewfinder at the mountain. "I can set up a digital betacam with night lenses in the field. But there may be some diffused light from that farmhouse," he said, pointing to the Miller place, which peeked surreptitiously through the tall grasses at the far end of the field. "The 35 millimeter will give us twelve minutes. Video will give us two hours."

"Save the 35 for close up," Running Bear said.

Neely couldn't help shuddering. To think his brother might have stood in this very place the night he was killed, peering up at the mountaintop for the first sign of–something. What had he *really* seen?

"Jack," Running Bear said. "I have a lot of work to do this afternoon. Much to prepare for. Hugo will go over the operation of the equipment with you at the train cars. I'm particularly keen on having you learn how to edit. Sound okay?"

"Sure, sounds good," Neely said, relieved to be focusing on the more comfortable subject of moviemaking.

As they returned to the van, Running Bear took a long last look at the mountaintop, and Neely noticed that he bowed his head as if in reverence. Odd man, this half-breed; almost as if he were trying to make himself out to be more Indian than he really was. What if all this turned out to be some misguided venture, born of one individual's peculiar fixation? Surely, it would be the last nail in the coffin for Green Abbey Studios, and the death-knell for Jack Neely's only shot at a career in the movies.

No, he couldn't afford to think that way. In fact, it was better not to think at all of what they were doing. If they were successful in securing the footage they sought, it could mean that Neely would end up meeting his brother again very soon indeed.

Neely spent that afternoon with Eckert learning firsthand what he'd seen many times in his books–how to thread film through the editing machine, how to make cuts and splices using the digital film counter, how to match the soundtrack to the visual images. A crash course, superficial at that, but enough for Neely to get an idea of what it was like to physically put together a work print. As practice, he spent some time cutting and splicing footage from an as yet unreleased soft-core porn flick that Eckert and Running Bear had made before Green Abbey's first incarnation turned completely red. Eckert happily told him that, when completed, "Cherokee Cherry" would be the first movie to boast Jack Neely's name in the credits.

"How come you guys make these kinds of movies?" Neely asked. "You're obviously capable of much better."

Eckert chuckled. "We were hoping to make some quick dollars to finance our more ambitious projects. It had just begun to work, too. You know, we had half a dozen features go straight to video, and we got the contract with Turner to work the second unit on a made-for-TNT movie.

But our stuff ran into lots of distribution problems. Companies wouldn't pay on time, or wouldn't pay at all. Lots of assholes in this business, let me tell you. And once you start getting in with the big studios, your problems multiply by a factor of ten. We learned a lot of lessons the hard way, some of them too late. But if we can get this project off, I think we'll be back in the money."

"I hope so." He paused. "Hugo–do you really believe in this thing? That the Fugue Devil is real?"

"Don't you?"

"I don't know. I don't want to."

"Listen, my friend. I've been with Running Bear for a long time. He's got his quirks, make no mistake. But he is a man of conviction. You saw him out there today. He knows things. He feels things. I trust his instincts. I know I feel something very strange in this place. I believe in it."

Neely nodded, gazing past Eckert to a day seventeen years ago, to a young Ronnie Neely bursting with excitement at the idea of something wondrous and spectacular so close to home. If only he'd had the slightest idea of what he would actually find.

"You're thinking about your brother, eh?"

"It shows? Yeah. He was a good kid. I still miss him an awful lot. If he'd grown up, he'd have been a lot less fucked up than me."

Eckert clapped Neely on the shoulder. "You're going to be all right. Yeah."

Neely smiled, until he saw something way back in Eckert's eyes.

Fear.

Running Bear returned to the train cars at twilight.

"I spent the afternoon at the college," he said. "Interesting place. I was surprised to find no one who could tell me more about the Fugue Devil. It's the sort of legend to intoxicate your average college student. Most places they would turn out in droves to watch for it when the time is right. Like when there's an eclipse. But not in Beckham."

"The night my brother disappeared, so did some kids from the college. Some of them probably know. But it has never been widespread."

"All the more reason to understand that there is a special power here," Running Bear said. "Imagine, if the existence of something such as the Fugue Devil was common knowledge–a novelty–it would become impotent. Suppose hundreds saw it. Would it destroy each and every one of them? Does it have that kind of power? Its *real* power lies in its ability to freeze tongues. To hold dominion by fear over the select few who do know of it."

"Then, you believe that it has a weakness?"

"That is what tonight will prove."

Eckert nodded. "Since it's getting dark, I'm going to go set up the betacams. I don't think we'll have to worry about anyone messing with them."

"No," said Running Bear. "Nothing to worry about there." He then turned to Neely. "Let's you and I have a good dinner and talk business. We need to come to an agreement about your position once we go back to Wilmington. You'll need a place to live. I know of some good apartments near the studio that aren't too expensive. I want to hear your ideas. I want to know what interests you most."

"This is a lot to think about," Neely said, not sure the whole situation had yet sunk in. "It's happening so fast."

Running Bear chuckled. "I know it is. But I could tell from your letters that you are a serious man. You have a deep desire to achieve your goals. You're creative–I can see this by the steps you have taken to understand all you can about the business. You learn fast. Your ability and enthusiasm are more important to me than your experience, or lack thereof. You're exactly the kind of man I want to work with me."

"Well, thanks."

"Now. Your first and most important task is to guide us to some palatable food. Can it be found in this town?"

They ate pizza and drank beer at "The House" restaurant, considered by most to offer Beckham's finest cuisine. It was an old southern mansion that had been turned into an eating establishment back in the 60s; since then, it had been owned by about every businessman to pass through town. Neely was more than satisfied, and even Running Bear seemed pleased.

As the hour grew late, Neely realized that anxiety had stealthily crept up on him, and by eleven, his heart was racing. Not so much from a sense of danger to himself, but because of the memories of his little brother that relentlessly flooded his mind. Eckert had closed himself in the editing room to finish up some work on "Cherokee Cherry" and Running Bear was in his office doing paperwork. Neely had been trying to keep his mind on the spec book for the 35-mm camera, unsuccessfully, and jumped up, startled, when a firm knock sounded at the train car door.

Running Bear emerged from his office, waving Neely down, saying he'd get it. With a cheerful greeting, he admitted two young couples, obviously of college age, all quite attractive and neatly dressed. Neely stood up, and Running Bear introduced him as "Executive Producer Jack Neely."

They each shook his hand, imparting considerably more respect than he was accustomed to receiving. "Now let's see if I can get this right,"

Running Bear said. "This is Rob Armstrong and his girlfriend Jenny Barrow. And you are—" he paused, holding up a finger as if searching his memory, "—Jay Strand and Heather Wiedeman."

"You got it," said the first one, the one named Armstrong, obviously pleased that the director had remembered all their names.

"They're members of the college drama club. They have kindly agreed to help us out as extras on the set tonight," Running Bear said.

"What?" Neely blurted, finding himself at a loss for words. He looked warily at each of the young people, who seemed a bit puzzled and obviously afraid that they might have gotten into the middle of some creative dispute among the filmmakers.

Giving Neely a reassuring look, Running Bear said, "We'll be setting things up shortly and will start shooting right about midnight. The location is not far from here, just out from town. It's on an isolated road, but there will be studio lights, so don't worry being in an unsafe place."

"No worries," Jenny Barrow laughed. "This is Beckham."

"Good. Now, let's step into my office, we'll take care of some very quick paperwork. That way I can issue you checks as soon as we're wrapped tonight. Is that okay by you?"

"Sure," they agreed, and Running Bear led them through the car back to his partitioned office. Neely heard him begin to explain: "The scenario concerns an old legend, in which an ancient spirit is summoned from the sky by a mad musician. It is called the Fugue Devil and it appears only at certain times every few years."

A chill shot up Neely's spine. "Wait!" he called after them, his lower lip quivering. "But it's real. It's real!"

The youths smiled, figuring the producer was trying to get them into the proper frame of mind for tonight's shooting.

Running Bear waved them inside, remaining behind to give Neely a broad smile.

"You see," he said softly. "You believe. You *do* believe."

Neely rode with Eckert in their rented car, while Running Bear and the four students went in the van. As they turned onto the dark road where he and his family used to live, Neely found himself shaking uncontrollably.

"I don't like it, Hugo. This is wrong."

"Jack, settle down. Let's just get our jobs done and go. You said before it was all just a legend. Is that what you think or isn't it?"

"I don't know. I don't *know.*"

"Look. All you have to do is help me set up the lighting. That's all. We'll be out in no time. Even if it's real, it can't harm you, man."

"But those people! You mean to sacrifice them? They're just kids!"

"Now look. If you're not up for this, just say so, and you can stay in the car. But consider our priorities. We came here with a job to do. And that's exactly what we're going to do."

"They'll die."

"Okay, Jack. Let's suppose you go up and tell them they have to leave because at midnight the Fugue Devil will come down from the sky to kill them. They're city kids. They're going to think you're a lunatic. Or worse–they'll think you're making fun of them."

Eckert was right. There was no way he'd be able to stop what was about to happen. No way.

"You were chosen for this, Jack. Running Bear chose you. Don't let him down."

"Before I wrote to him he didn't even know about the Fugue Devil."

"He knew, Jack. Not in any way your or I understand. But he knew."

Ahead, Running Bear stopped the van on a stretch of road short of Miller's field, where no lights polluted the darkness. A chill wind had begun to blow down from Copper Peak.

"Keep it cool and let's just do our jobs, Jack. We're going to put the lights up just like I say, right off the road over here. You all right, man?"

Jack nodded reluctantly. "I'm okay."

"Be sure."

They got out of the car to an excited flurry of voices from the students. Jack tried to swallow his apprehension, told himself they couldn't really be in any danger. The worst that could happen was that they wouldn't get the footage Running Bear wanted so badly. And Neely would have to call off going to Wilmington. He'd be stuck here–without even his job at Booker to go back to.

What had he done?

"Okay," Running Bear said, taking the students off the road into a reasonably clear area among the brush. "This is where we're going to set up the action. All you have to do is stand around chatting, waiting. You know that at midnight, something's going to happen. I'm not going to tell you what, because I want your reactions to be completely authentic. And afterward, just stay put. The camera's going to keep rolling because I want to get as much natural footage as possible. I can edit the parts I need afterward. So don't worry if nothing happens for several minutes. Okay?"

"Sounds fine," one of them said. The kids gabbed excitedly among themselves, out of Neely's earshot.

"Jack, you know how to set these lights up," Eckert was telling him. "Get yours set up there at forty-five degree angle to the marks. Focus them slightly downwards, so there's no direct lighting above their heads. I'm going to put some tints on the field. Got that?"

"Got it." Neely set to work as Eckert had shown him, concentrating only on the job. Only on the job. No way the thing that had killed Ronnie could so much as touch any of them. They were working. This was their job.

It was just after 11:30.

A bunch of rednecks had killed Ronnie.

Running Bear himself mounted the 35-mm camera on its dolly about twenty feet from the clearing, focused it on the gathered students. Neely could hear snippets of their conversation.

"Wonder if we'll get free copies on tape?"

"Hundred dollars each is pretty good money for standing around, huh?"

"This can lead to more pictures, Jenny, no shit. We've got *credits* now!"

"I want my mom and dad to see this. They'll be really proud."

He'd come across a still in the woods. There were so many in these mountains.

Eckert came to check his work. Clapped him in the back and nodded his approval. "Good job."

They'll kill your ass dead. They don't care that you're just a kid.

Running Bear came up to him and looked him squarely in the eyes. "You'll be all right, Jack. Everything's going to be fine. Trust me. Don't you trust me?"

"I guess so," he said quietly.

"Good. Come here. Get a look through the camera. Let's see what you think of the lighting. Okay?"

He knew Running Bear was talking down to him, but he couldn't bring himself to object. "Okay."

He looked through the viewfinder at the tableau before him. It was an expert job: long shadows behind the students, atmospheric, half-seen scrub behind them disappearing into green shadows tinged with red. In the distance, an onyx mountain cutting into a midnight blue sky. He could even see the glittering stars.

"That's a hell of a good camera."

"We got this from Jim Cameron's studio. No shit. Used it in 'The Abyss.' After one movie, they often sell the cameras cheap. You know how much this thing is new?"

"About five or six hundred grand, I'd say."

"Closer to a million. I paid just over a hundred thousand."

"Wow."

Eckert was setting up the mike booms just above the camera's visual field. This was the movies. Neely had always dreamed of this.

"Almost done," Running Bear said to his cast. "Now, what we're going to do is drive a short distance down the road. The camera's going to run automatically. I don't want any presence on this set other than yours, and that includes crew. During the shooting, you just act natural. That's all. I want every reaction to what you see to be completely pure. At ten minutes past midnight, we'll be right back to break down. You get paid and you go back to your dorms. Couldn't be simpler."

"So, you got a special effects crew working or something?" asked the young man named Strand.

Running Bear laughed. "I hope you'll be impressed by what we've devised."

The group laughed as well. To Neely's surprise, Running Bear then went to the van and pulled a small cooler from the back. He opened it and took it to the kids, passing it around so each could grab a beer.

"Hey, thanks!"

"No regulations against it, and you might as well enjoy yourself while you're working." He handed one to Jack. "Drink up, my friend. You deserve it."

Jack took one, comforted by the familiar, cold metal of the can. He popped the top and guzzled hard.

It was almost midnight.

"Okay, ladies and gentlemen," Running Bear said. "I'm very shortly going to start the camera rolling. There's twelve minutes of film in here, and I mean to use every second of it. Jack, let's be sure we've got everything squared away"

A couple of minutes later, all was ready. Running Bear told Eckert and Jack to go on and he'd join them back at the train cars. Neely nodded and turned toward the dark path up to the road after giving the college kids a long last look. One of them waved to him.

He got into the back seat as Eckert slid behind the wheel. A minute later, Running Bear leaned inside. "Hugo, keep your eyes only on the road. Do not look at the sky. Do not look at the mountain. You look only at the road. Got it?"

"Got it."

Eckert shoved the car into gear and Neely glanced back at the little island of light amid the great sea of dark brush.

"You too, Jack," Eckert said. "Keep your eyes down. If you don't look out there, you've got nothing to worry about."

"I know."

"We'll be back to pick up the equipment tomorrow at sun up. Not one minute before."

They drove back down the dark road at high speed, Eckert keeping his eyes unwaveringly on the road directly ahead. Jack tried to hold his gaze on his feet, despite the constant temptation to look out at the sky. He couldn't do that. *He couldn't.*

"It's midnight," Eckert said. "It's time. I hope the betacam at Miller's field picks it up."

A heavy lump in Neely's throat threatened to choke him. Finally, he just closed his eyes to shut out everything until they arrived back at the cars. When the rumble of the engine died and the front door opened, he remained in his seat, and only moved when he heard Eckert unlock the train car door and call his name.

"Better hurry, Jack, I don't think you want to be out here all by yourself."

With that, Neely scrambled from his seat and practically leaped up the short stairs into the cozy warmth of the car's anteroom. He tried to compose himself, to keep from looking like a fool, though he figured it was all too late for that. Eckert went through both cars making sure all the windows were covered.

Running Bear arrived moments later in the van. He brought Jack another beer. "You're scared out of your skin, my friend. You don't need to feel bad. I understand completely."

"I'm sorry, man. This is just too crazy. All these memories, these feelings that this is the wrong thing to do."

"I know. But it's all going to work out. Tomorrow, we're going to be looking at serious opportunity. Lots of money. No worries."

"It's those kids. Why didn't you tell me?"

"I didn't know for sure how I was going to work things until the opportunity arose. And this was the only thing to do."

"Cheer up," said Eckert as he came back through the door to the connecting car. "There's always the chance nothing's going to show up tonight."

"There is that chance," Running Bear said with a grim nod.

Jack swigged his beer, shrugging. "Let's say it does, and you get its picture. You don't suppose seeing it on film will draw it to you, just like if you saw it for real?"

"Well, assuming that the rule that 'if one sees the Fugue Devil it will come' is true, I believe it's because the eyes themselves are the link. Eye contact builds a bridge between the individual and the demon. On film, the connection cannot be made, for awareness only passes one way–us to it. It's missing half of the equation. That is what will save us. But at the same time, our ability to duplicate the medium will actually serve to diminish the long-term power of the Fugue Devil. This is because, should knowledge of its existence become widespread, it would be forced to act against a prohibitive number of individuals. I say prohibitive because, once it crosses over, it appears to be bound by the physical laws of this universe."

"This is all in theory, right? You could be wrong."

Running Bear bit his lip and nodded. "I could be wrong."

"What if you are?"

"Then we may die. But I am certain my hypothesis is correct. Do not fear. And do not look out the window. The greatest danger to ourselves is that we do know of it, and very likely it will come near us with intent to show itself. Hugo, what time is it?"

"Ten after."

"Well. In all likelihood, our footage has been captured. And I would be very surprised if there is a living human being left at our set."

Neely's stomach lurched into his throat. Running Bear was so calm, so calculating. You didn't want to cross this man. That he could so carelessly throw away human lives. . . .

With Jack Neely as an accomplice.

"What do we do now?"

"We wait."

And so they did, for better than an hour without hearing so much as a sound from the out of doors. No nightbirds. No crickets. No distant traffic or trains. No whisper of wind. Neely drank beer while Hugo again fiddled in the editing room and Running Bear disappeared into his office.

At 1:30 a.m., Neely heard a scuffling sound outside the car, and sat up quickly, all his senses alert. A couple of low voices. There were people out there!

"Running Bear," he called. "Company!"

"What?"

A sudden furious knocking on the door nearly startled Neely half out of his wits. And an angry young voice cried, "Hey, in there! What the hell's going on?"

"Jesus, it's them!" Neely whispered hoarsely. "It didn't come!"

Running Bear hesitated, then opened the door, and Rob Armstrong stalked inside, puffing heavily. "What the hell did you leave us out there for? Is this some kind of scam or something?"

"I am so sorry," Running Bear said earnestly. "I was beeped and had to come back for a critical phone call. We've been tied up in a conference with one of our producers in Wilmington and we only just got done. This is terrible, just terrible. Come in, and I'll get checks cut for each of you. I am really sorry. Shit like this is always happening in this business."

"After midnight?"

"My friend, it comes at all hours. You have no idea how many times I've been called out of bed in the middle of the night for some piddling technical problem."

"Did you walk all the way back here?" Neely asked, barely keeping his voice from shaking.

"You're damn right we walked."

"I—I should have gotten away and come to pick you up. This was wrong, really wrong. I'm sorry."

Armstrong's expression softened a bit, but his girlfriend Jenny Barrow gave Neely an icy stare that didn't warm even when Running Bear said he'd give them each an extra twenty dollars for their trouble.

The other young man, the one named Strand lifted his eyes to meet Neely's, as if to gauge his sincerity. No doubt they smelled something fishy in all this, and Neely didn't know if he could play along with Running Bear convincingly.

"Did–did anything happen out there?" he stammered.

"You mean the fireworks that came off the mountain? That was it? There was a light that shot out across the sky, and it was gone. That what you're talking about?"

"You saw what?"

"Is that what we were supposed to see?"

"I–I think that was it." Neely felt the blood draining from his face and for the first time he saw Running Bear look as if he might lose his composure.

"I will write these for you and then you can be on your way. Won't take a second. Just a quick second," he said, rushing back toward his office.

"Hey," Strand said. "These checks are going to be good, right?"

"Of course," Neely said, voice coarse and dry. "I promise they're just fine."

"You're not looking too good, man."

"It was–it was not good news from Wilmington. Personnel problems."

Another scuffling sound came from outside. A soft, short intake of breath. Strand turned to the door, apparently surprised to find Heather Wiedeman no longer behind him.

"Hey, where'd you go?" He stepped outside to look for his girlfriend.

Running Bear appeared a moment later carrying four signed checks. "Okay, we're all set. There's still some problems to attend to here, though. We'll have to get out to pick up the equipment later."

"You're going to give us a ride back to the campus, right?"

Eckert appeared in the office door. "It's not far to the college. You guys walked over here earlier, right?"

Armstrong gave Eckert a piercing stare. "Not after walking three miles from your 'location,' freezing our asses off. It's getting fucking cold out there!"

Running Bear noticed the open door. "Where are your friends?"

Jenny Barrow turned around–just in time to hear a shrill, masculine scream erupt from just beyond the door. She cried out in surprise, leaping to Armstrong's side, nearly pushing him off balance. A writhing shadow briefly appeared in the doorway, and a second later, a wet, ripping sound silenced the screaming.

A spray of blood suddenly covered the train car door, and Neely himself let out a high-pitched shriek.

"Oh God, Running Bear! It's here! You said we were safe!"

The four slips of paper dropped from Running Bear's hand. And he slowly turned away, bringing his hands up to cover his eyes, at the same time humming a deep note in his throat.

"Christ!" exclaimed Eckert, face now as pale as Neely's own. "Okay, out," he said to Armstrong. "Get out. You can't stay here."

"What? What the fuck are you talking about, man? What the hell is that?"

A low buzzing sound drifted in from the darkness beyond the door; a heavy, rhythmic sound–almost like deep breathing.

Neely heard Running Bear softly say, "Whatever you do, Jack, do not look at it."

Eckert rushed forward then, near to panicking. He pushed at Armstrong's back. "Come on, move. Out of here. Get out of here, right now!"

"No, don't," Neely said, knowing it was futile. But Eckert *had* to get them out. The kids had seen the thing, and if they stayed inside, it would come in after them.

Running Bear's voice then rose above the others, and the two students paused when they heard him call their names. "You may leave now," he said. "After all–it's just movie magic!"

And with almost hypnotized obedience, Armstrong and his girlfriend turned toward the exit, but stopped in their tracks when they again faced the blood that streamed down the door.

"No way–that can't be real," Jenny Barrow whimpered. "It's not real, it's not!"

Eckert took the opportunity to grab both of them by the arms, his overbearing bulk pushing them along. "I'm sorry," he said. "You cannot stay here." He shoved Armstrong straight toward the exit.

Then he stopped, peering in slack-jawed wonder into the darkness. "Oh, Christ," he whispered. "Oh fucking Christ."

Armstrong, balanced precariously at the top step of the car, tipped forward, his momentum carrying him out, still gripping his girlfriend with one hand. A second later, both of them were gone. Eckert slammed the door behind them and bolted it.

He turned away from the door, and his expression nearly caused Neely to scream again. Eckert's face had drained of blood. Bone white it was, flesh drawn tight over his skull, eyes hiding in deep, dark hollows. His hands shook uncontrollably–and great tremors wracked his entire body.

"You saw it," Neely croaked. "Oh, Jesus, he saw it, now it's going to come in!"

"Hugo," Running Bear said softly. "I'm afraid I'm going to have to ask you to leave."

"God–no! I can't go out there! I can't!"

"You can't stay in here. Don't you understand that, my friend? You don't wish to endanger both of us, do you? You know what you have to do."

From outside, Neely heard the sounds of a struggle: a low, frantic moaning, a heavy thumping against the side of the train car. A scream, quickly stifled. Then the window nearest Neely shattered, and something burst through the drawn shades, showering him with red, liquid warmth before it bounced off the far wall and rolled to a stop just shy of his feet.

Jay Strand's head, torn from his shoulders, muscle and tissue hanging from the ruined neck. A pool of blood spread slowly over the floor where it lay. And Neely's voice no longer worked. All that came out was a muted hiss, and that, too, died when the remaining glass in the window clattered to the floor and something began beating rhythmically against the train car wall.

"Hugo, it's coming for you," Running Bear said, voice tremulous. "Please do us the favor of departing with all haste. The keys to the van are on my desk. Take them. Take the van and fly. You may yet have a chance if you can avoid it until daybreak."

Eckert gaped at his partner, face still bloodless, eyes as bright as train lanterns. "I–I can't move. I can't move!"

Neely summoned what little nerve he had remaining and sprang toward Running Bear's office door. He saw the keys on the desk, grabbed them and rushed them back to Eckert. "Take them, man. For God's sake, don't bring this thing in on us."

He dropped the keys into Eckert's palm. The big man nearly dropped them, but managed to snag them before they fell. At last, as if an inner struggle had been resolved, his jaw firmed, and a tinge of color rushed to his cheeks. "You're right. I can't let it come in." He gave Neely a wild, frightened glance. "But how can I go out there?"

Running Bear said, "It's between the train cars right now. It won't see you if you go through to the other car and out its rear door. Then head for the van. That will give you a head start–maybe enough to get away. Go, Hugo. You have to go now."

The car shook again and the wall beneath the shattered window began to bulge inward.

"If it comes in, you'll have blown all our chances, including yours. Go, Hugo. Go."

Taking a deep, quavering breath, Eckert nodded, and after a brief hesitation, leaped with surprising speed for the door that led to the passage. Simultaneously, Neely heaved a deep sigh of relief.

"It'll go now, won't it? I mean, it won't come back for us, right?"

"I don't know," Running Bear whispered.

Suddenly, the sound of tearing metal screeched in Neely's ears. More glass shattered, and then the lights went out.

But he could still see Running Bear, bathed in the beam of a streetlight. *The thing had ripped out a portion of the train car wall.* Without thinking, Neely leaped after Eckert, dashing through the passage to the companion car. Somehow he managed to avoid looking back and barreled his way toward the rear door, which he could see hanging open. Eckert had gotten out, all right.

Neely feared now that the sounds of the assault on the car would abate as the demon turned its attention to him or Eckert, but it did not. It seemed that its focus was not Hugo at all, but Running Bear.

He saw Eckert's bulky figure behind the wheel of the van, heard the engine cranking to life. With a desperate lunge, he grabbed for the passenger door handle, found it, and pulled so hard that he nearly ripped the whole door off. The van was moving as he clambered inside, and Eckert cast him a shocked glance.

"What the fuck are you doing here?"

"It's after him–*him!*"

"You sure?"

"I think so!"

The van's tires kicked up gravel as Eckert spun out of the little unpaved turnaround in front of the train cars. But before they'd even hit the paved road, the van slammed to stop, tires squealing. "Jesus Christ!" Eckert shouted.

He'd barely missed running over Jenny Barrow, who appeared frozen in the headlights like a mesmerized deer, eyes blazing with horror, black hair so wild and tossed she might have been an inmate escaped from Catawba Sanitarium. Neely reached to open the rear passenger door, but with a curse, Eckert hit the accelerator and spun the wheel to go around her.

"What the hell? Aren't you going to–"

"No way. It's behind us!"

Before Neely could grasp his meaning, he looked back, saw Jenny break into a sprint after the van, her hands scrabbling at the back door. But then, as if snagged by a rope that had run out of slack, she was jerked backwards–and up into the air–by something unseen that grabbed her flying hair. Neely heard her panicked screams and saw her hair and scalp brutally ripped from her skull; then the scene was swallowed by the darkness–which was all that prevented him from fully glimpsing the thing that had apparently resumed its rightful quest: the elimination of those unfortunate enough to have laid eyes upon it.

Which meant that Neely had foolishly placed himself in exactly the wrong place if he hoped to survive the rest of the night.

Helpless to do otherwise, he bowed his head and covered his eyes, praying Eckert could make the van move faster than the thing that pursued it.

"Where is it, Hugo? Is it coming?" he moaned.

"I don't know. I can't see it!"

"We've got to get away from here. Where can we go?"

"I'm heading for the main highway. At least there will be other cars. Other people."

But as the van rounded a curve, Eckert swore loudly, and the centrifugal force almost tore Neely from his seat. The vehicle skidded, thumped roughly over gravel, then tilted wildly as it slid down the shallow embankment off the edge of the road. With a crash, it was halted abruptly by a huge tree that materialized in the headlights.

Neely's head slammed into the dashboard and bounced back against the seat's headrest. He saw stars, and his thudding heartbeat drowned out the fading echoes of the collision. Shaking his head, trying to regain equilibrium, he saw Eckert already fumbling at his seatbelt, eyes bulging grotesquely from a chalky mask. In an instant, Neely was doing the same, caring not a whit if he'd sustained any injuries; if he lived through the night, whiplash or a concussion would be a blessing.

Eckert opened his door, started to climb out—and screamed a shrill scream as something yanked him out as effortlessly as one might pluck an apple from a branch. Neely locked his eyes on the ground, slid out of the van and began to run, gripped by the thrilling knowledge that he had somehow again miraculously avoided seeing the demon, even at such proximity.

Tree limbs whipped at his face, and thick brush grabbed at his legs, but he blazed through the dark woods guided by instinct, all rational thought evaporating in the sizzling rush of pure terror. Behind him, on the road, he could hear keening, high-pitched screams as Eckert was pulled apart a bit at a time, the sound goading him to run faster and faster. The only independent thought remaining was that he knew exactly what his brother had experienced on that night seventeen years ago, and he now shared a more intimate kinship with Ronnie than ever before. Maybe he *was* Ronnie, and this was a doom he was destined to suffer over and over again for all eternity. He seemed to have been running forever.

He nearly pitched headlong as, suddenly, his legs found a path clear of obstruction. He'd come out on the railroad tracks that led from the train cars around the base of the mountain to Aiken Mill. Regaining his balance, pausing only long enough to draw a few deep breaths, he bounded down the tracks that disappeared into a tunnel of darkness formed by the towering trees. Eckert's screams had faded into distance or death, and the only sound now was a mad chorus of night creatures mocking him from the dark surroundings.

After a while, finally running out of steam, he slowed to an unsteady trot, lungs heaving, heart ready to burst. He'd been heading away from town, following an unconscious desire to get as far away from the train cars as possible. But now, he realized that he was a good ten miles from Aiken Mill, and between here and there lay only deep woods–except for where the tracks closely paralleled the main road for a mile or so. And there wasn't much on the road, at that: a couple of gas stations, a car dealer, a little grocery store. But they'd all be closed, and even if he made it to any of the homes in the vicinity, no one would let him inside.

Still, he knew he could not go back toward Beckham and his own place. The demon was back there, and no force in heaven or hell could coerce him to risk facing that horror; only by the grace of God had he so far avoided laying eyes on this evil avatar. But he took some comfort in the knowledge that he still bore no death mark; not like poor Eckert or those kids, whom he himself had helped lead to their doom.

At the memory of that horrible slaughter, tears pooled in his eyes. How could he have allowed himself to be manipulated by an evil man who sought nothing but his own gain, regardless of the cost? A cost to be paid by others, at that! No . . . Neely had been too dazzled by the prospect of his dream coming true to care.

Even now, he doubted Running Bear was dead. Somehow, that clever bastard would have found a way to avoid sight of the monster, even as it tore its way through the train car to get at him. Maybe Running Bear had even managed to get out to the location and pick up his equipment, and would end up achieving his goal of exposing the demon.

Yet somehow, deep down, Neely knew better. No matter how much the egotistical Running Bear thought he could gain, Neely knew that the Fugue Devil would eventually win out. To believe a mere camera could hold dominion over such a monumental force! It was lunacy. Pure, unmitigated–and fatal–lunacy.

Once his inner heat began to wane, he could feel the chill night air working its way through his clothes, through his flesh. His neck and head hurt from the van's collision with the tree, but he didn't think there was any serious injury. He'd been lucky. The crash itself could have killed them even if the Fugue Devil hadn't been there to dole out its own brand of death.

Out here, where he could barely see his hand in front of his face, he began to feel a strange peace, a harmony with the night, as if leaving Beckham behind in some way cleansed him of the evil he'd wrought. He knew he could never atone for the blood on his hands, but if he could just stay alive long enough to see daybreak, he could begin some kind of healing.

And he'd do what he could to set things right. Expose Running Bear as a fraud–and a murderer. Whatever it took.

When the stars above were briefly blocked out by a vast black shadow, the terror did not immediately strike him. A stray cloud drifting on the soft breeze, perhaps, or a tree bending and waving lazily over the tracks.

Even the deep buzzing noise that rose around him from an unseen source did not fill him with panic—until he recognized its rhythm—the *breathing* from massive lungs.

And a shadow rose in front of him on the tracks, a shadow whose weight splintered the wooden ties and sent a ringing tone vibrating up and down the metal rails. Neely smelled something hot and sulfurous, and realized that a pair of vast wings composed entirely of shadow seemed to be unfolding before his shocked eyes.

He looked up . . .

And up . . .

And up.

"Oh my God," he whispered.

Far above, two glittering jewels sparkled far brighter than the stars. Jewels that had depth; that exposed an inner brilliance the color of the blood in which he'd soaked his hands.

"Oh, my God," he whispered again, singing it like a dirge. "I do. I really do see you. . . ."

Spiritual Radio

"In every dream there is a conflict. Man's natural tendency is to run from a threat, rather than face it. At the end of this course, you will not only be able to analyze and understand the nature of your dream conflicts, you'll be able to kick their asses."

– Dr. James McEntee
Beckham College, VA
Lecture on Dreams, October 1979

Here I go.

I'm dreaming again, just as I have for the past several nights. It's unusual for me to experience such crystal clear images; the sights, sounds and odors, all as real as they would be to my waking senses. Just as unusual is the fact that I can lucidly state, "This is a dream," and know full well that it's true, for even though my body and mind perceive my surroundings with a sharpness beyond the norm, there is no mistaking this for the "real" world of daylight. The analytical part of my mind is a constant, assuring me that these dreams are illusions, regardless of their power to tempt my emotions and my intellect. Each night, I seem to be drawn more deeply into this strange realm. I don't understand it, but I don't fight it, for that would mean staying awake, and I'm just too tired for that now.

A large green field has materialized around me; it looks like a golf course. Natural enough, I suppose, as the game is a favorite pastime. I see lots of woods around the perimeter, a creek, a long downhill slope, then a dogleg to the left. I'm standing at the top of the hill, seemingly alone. But I can hear birds singing, and—I think—a distant train. The scene is familiar, though I can't place the exact location. My head is light and I'm somewhat dizzy, but if this dream is true to the pattern from the past few nights, these feelings will clear up in a minute. The entry into dream-sleep seems to temporarily disrupt my sense of balance. But yes . . . focus is slowly becoming sharper and my head is now as steady and clear as if I were really standing on this image's physical counterpart on a Saturday morning.

Most often, my dreams are a muddled network of sprawling visual impressions, sounds, feelings of pain or ecstasy, all more or less random, usually connected only loosely if at all. They come in a tide, and I am generally swept along with it, the few choices I make insignificant or meaningless. But there is no such ineffectuality here; I have a will, a power in this world that seems unfamiliar, if exhilarating. In college, many years ago, I took a few courses on dream control, wherein the student learned to utilize his power of choice in the sleeping world, which would theoretically be reflected in bolstered self-confidence in waking life. The control process worked well enough; it did indeed help me stand up to the conflicts generated in dream-sleep, though the side benefits—those in the world of light—were nebulous at best. I haven't practiced dream control in years, so I am again puzzled by my ability to move through this place with such aplomb. I have choices here; I can explore this new realm or I can wait here until something happens.

And the one thing I can be sure of is that something *will* happen. I cannot alter what is to come, but I can control my reaction to it.

I start walking down into the dogleg, which is filled with white flowers and lush green clover. The sweet aroma is almost overpowering, which in itself strikes me as odd, for smell is a sensation usually muted or nonexistent in dreams. But I know from experience that, soon, that famous dream conflict will manifest itself in no uncertain terms. Possessed of this peculiarly heightened confidence, I don't feel afraid, as I often do in dreams. My old professor, Dr. McEntee, would be proud of me if I could relate this to him now. I should remember to write this dream down when

I wake up, for the first step in mastering the art of dream control is to record all observations, then analyze, and finally, manipulate.

"Hey! David!"

It is a familiar voice, though not a pleasant one. It is low, almost a hiss, with just enough gravel in the throat to give it an ominous edge. I turn, finding myself staring at Raymond Barton: the bane of my youth, a hybrid punk/redneck whose every interaction in my young life resulted in trouble; not for him but for me. He's straddling a wooden fence that runs parallel to the fairway. He looks out of place here–*feels* out of place. Dream characters, events, settings, all are supposedly symbols of greater things. Is Raymond a symbol of some deep-rooted fear or regret, or is he just himself? His presence conflicts so strongly with the tranquility of the setting that the land itself begins to change. Behind him, a row of dilapidated buildings has replaced the verdant trees, and a low, rumbling wind drowns the calls of the birds.

"What the hell are you doing here, Raymond?" I *am* curious, because I haven't seen the real Raymond in over ten years.

"Hell, I don't know," he says with a hard stare from beneath shaggy brows. "Do I have to have a reason for everything?"

Ah–a familiar remark from long ago. I would like to say, *Hell yes, Raymond, if you're going to invade* my *dream,* but I find myself saying, rather lamely, "I don't suppose you do." Just like it used to be, when he intimidated me so. Yeah, that's me, the Man in Control here.

Raymond's eyes gleam contemptuously. "Where are you going?"

"Anywhere I want," I say, trying to assert a bit more control. It takes some practice to master the process, especially when confronted by an undesirable symbol (if that is indeed what he is). His expression of reproach does not soften. That look, by the way, is what I remember most about him. I flex a mental muscle, forcing away my inhibitions, reminding myself that this is *my* dream, and he's only in it as long as I allow him to be.

I begin walking again; he keeps pace two steps behind, saying nothing. The grass around my feet has grown taller, and now there are crumbling hovels to either side of us. They crouch in dark mystery like ancient carcasses, some emitting sounds of life: coughing, broken voices, rattled breathing. From the door of the nearest, a withered figure suddenly steps forth: an elderly man in ratty clothes, with disheveled white hair dangling in his face like dirty yarn. He gazes at me for a moment, his eyes dark and hollow, his mouth fixed in a grim sneer, lower jaw askew. I don't recognize him. I should feel moved to pity, I think, but I am filled only with disgust.

As if comprehending my feelings, he takes one step closer to me; his face seems to grow, out of proportion with the rest of his body. Then, from his throat, a deep, snarling *"Ghaaaahh,"* spat at me furiously.

I leap back, nervous, but still not frightened. I expect this is a materialization of my feelings toward Raymond. The old man retreats into the darkness of his hovel.

"You know," I said, "these people are parasites. They're all your fault."

"Is that how you see me?" Raymond asks defensively, giving me that cold eye. His look demands an answer.

"One day, you'll end up like this. Poor, and ugly, and angry."

"Why did you come here? You're free to pick and choose your own pathways."

"I chose this path."

"You don't know where the hell you're going. How about out there–in the outside world? Any thoughts about that?"

I shake my head. Here, the "outside" world feels like something small and insignificant; a stable place, comfortable only because of its rigid physical limitations. Some people believe that the astral plane, or the dream world, is just as real a place, and that the soul's extraordinary sojourns are as much a part of living as the jog in the park you took this morning. Your dream experiences–the sensations, the people you meet–all define a separate but just as factual reality. Whether or not this is true, I can't say. All I can do is navigate through this place and trust my senses.

To iterate these thoughts to Raymond seems pointless. I turn my attention to the dreamscape again. In the distance, I see a tall, latticed tower: a radio antenna, rising high into the deepening sky from beyond a ridge of purple trees ahead. Some would say it's a symbol with sexual significance.

"Guess what that's supposed to mean," Raymond says, pointing.

"Don't start with me."

"Where are we going?"

"*I* am going that way. You can go wherever you damn well want to."

"I'm coming with you!"

"Asshole."

"Fuckhead."

I see a path now that leads toward the antenna. We follow it, passing many areas of dense foliage, tall trees and scattered piles of trash that I reckon must have come from the hovels. I look back once and they are gone, replaced by row upon row of electrical towers and power lines. Dozens of high tension wires pass directly overhead, leading toward the antenna. As we walk, I see how tall it really is– many hundreds of feet. At its pinnacle, a cluster of orange and red lights blinks slowly off an on, illuminating the rapidly darkening sky. I feel drawn to it, as if it represents an answer to some unknown question. Raymond remains behind me, silent, making me nervous.

"What do you want, Raymond?" I finally ask.

"Oh, nothing. I'm just here for the ride. To watch."

"Watch what?"

"What you do."

"A picture of brilliance," I mutter. As ever, Raymond exhibits wisdom beyond his years. I decide to ignore him and maybe he'll go away. I wonder if I could merely wish him away. . . ?

No such luck.

I walk faster, but my destination remains at quite a distance. I now feel a strange urgency to reach it, though what I'm supposed to do when I get there is wholly unclear. I decide to try something new: I stop walking. Raymond's footsteps behind me also cease. I raise my arms at my sides, take and deep breath and–*push*–with my mind. My feet slowly rise from the ground, floating up and back until I am hovering spread-eagled six feet above the dusty path. The sensation is relaxing, and I have to wonder why I don't do this more often. It finally occurs to me that things don't work this way in waking life. I propel myself with a quick little notion, and I'm now moving slowly forward, floating on a cushion of air as if it were water. While I'm only a short distance above the ground, I feel secure and comfortable. I look around, and find Raymond, my loyal companion, drifting just behind me.

"Will you please go away?"

"Eat shit."

The sky is now very dark, but, here, close to the ground, I can see quite well. The tower seems to be attainable now, but its height has become dizzying. For a moment, I feel as if I'm going to lose all balance and topple back to earth.

So. Obviously, it's a challenge. I'm brave, I'll take it on, though the thought of what I'm about to do makes me quail. Regardless, I coil myself into a tight ball, and–hey! For the first time, I notice what I'm wearing: a black tunic, like a Chinaman's. Okay, fine, I don't really have any clothes like this, but I guess it's no big deal. Anyway, I now spring upward, arms at my sides, legs trailing. I rocket skyward at a disconcerting velocity. The world below is suddenly a vast panorama of lights, roads, trees and buildings. It appears to be a large city, though I don't recognize it as Beckham, or Aiken Mill, or anyplace familiar. I'm hurtling toward the top of the tower, which seems to grow taller even as I rise. A stiff wind is blowing up here, making me feel that I'm moving faster than I really am.

I look up. The apex of the tower seems to disappear into a hole in the sky, like a vortex opening into outer space. The earth is now so far below that my stomach flutters. What if I should suddenly lose my power of flight? Would I die in my sleep? I shove the idea out of my head, for there's no surer way to make something happen than by dwelling on it. So far, I have been able to reconcile everything in this dream in my mind. The hole, though, I can not, for it seems to represent a threshold I do not want to cross, as if it's something that exists independent of my own psyche. I maneuver close to the antenna, reach out and grab one of its metal struts. Weight gradually returns to me, and I cling to the structure for dear life, like an insect on a wall. Something rumbles in the sky, and looking into that hole, I see a dark shape roiling amid broken clouds, so indistinct that it's impossible to identify.

Raymond appears at my side, expression one of wry amusement. "Acrophobia?" he asks.

"I've been more comfortable."

"Why don't you keep going?"

"Thank you, no . . . as a matter of fact, perhaps I should go back down."

"You're telling me you made a bad decision? You? What a chicken shit. Pretty typical, if you ask me."

That's the old Raymond I've always known and loathed; an arrogant, conceited ass, who has always been just stupid enough to do all the things he dares others to do. He leaps into space, then rises slowly towards the opening above. The wind drills at my hands, and a faint vibration in the tower seems intent on loosening my fingers. I don't like this dream. It's carrying me in directions I shouldn't be going. I want to wake up.

Raymond has disappeared into the distance above, and a vast roaring sound echoes from that hazy portal. Can this indeed be something from outside my own subconscious? I've dreamed of awful things before, shocking and terrible things, but I've always accepted them as a catharsis for the various and sundry negative tenants of my mind. This thing is utterly alien, a symbol of something that surely can't have anything to do with *me.*

"David!" blares Raymond's disembodied voice, at a painful volume. *"David!"*

I want to wake up now. Raymond, the familiar, if distasteful, has become Raymond the Terrible. He used to intimidate me. Now he scares me. I want out. Sorry, Dr. McEntee, don't mean to be a wimp, but I gotta run.

Wake up.

I'm in my bedroom, lights out except for the small nightlight in the adjoining bath. It's quiet outside, with only the occasional rumble of a passing car. I feel warm beneath the blankets, but inside, a chill has seized me. It takes a minute or so to remember anything of the nightmare. God, no wonder I'm cold. I look around the bedroom. My wife Sherry is sleeping peacefully at my side, oblivious to the turmoil I've been through. The clock reads 1:30 a.m., ticking in syncopated rhythm with my pounding heart. What's this? On the nightstand is a pen and notepad. I pick it up, study it in the near-darkness. It's a scribbled account of my dream up to the point where I awoke, detailing the golf course, Raymond, the hovels, the old man, the tower.

Wait a minute.

I didn't write this dream down.

I pull myself from the bed, go to the window and lift the shade. Yes, there it is: the tower. Distant, but prominent against the midnight blue sky. Its anti-collision lights blink coldly amid the thin clouds, and I see now that what I'd thought was its apex is merely a mid-point.

What the hell?

I was just in my. . . .

I am now floating alongside the tower, rather than viewing it from my window. Raymond is hanging onto one of the crossbars, smiling at me with his customary expression of belligerence.

"Raymond, why don't you go home?"

"Not as much in control as we thought, are we? Pretty rude awakening, huh? Pardon the bad joke."

"You're such an ass."

"Getting a little too hairy for you? It happens. Things start out familiar enough, then get weird, then get downright terrifying. Happens in dreams all the time, doesn't it? *Doesn't it?*"

It's time to start thinking. I realize I'm letting myself be manipulated again—flowing with the tide, as usual. It's not so easy standing up to these things, you know. It's no easier to be creative, or witty, or decisive in dreams than when you're awake. It *is* easier to be honest. In dreams, your emotions are purer because they supersede your intellect. You don't let that happen so much in the daytime.

"So, Raymond. If you're going to hang around, at least be of some use. What the hell is this thing?"

"Oh, it's a hunk of metal and glass, hooked up to electrical circuits for broadcasting and receiving."

"Broadcasting and receiving what?"

"Oh, you know. Signals and stuff."

"God, you're a piece of ape shit. What kind of signals?"

He points to the hole in the sky. His voice lowers to sly whisper. "Signals to and from . . . *there!*"

"Where is *there?*"

"Up."

"Go to hell, Raymond."

"Eat shit."

I look down. Big mistake. I can see the vast sea of lights only through a broken cloud cover. I don't like being this far up, not at all. But as I float here, a brilliant, if morbid idea strikes me.

"Bye, Raymond."

I relax my mind completely, snap the wings of thought that suspend me. It works. Suddenly, air is rushing past me, slapping at my face, and the illuminated landscape comes racing toward me. Always–*always*– when I'm falling in a dream, I wake up before I hit bottom. And I do so want to wake up. I mean, I *really* want to wake up.

I begin tumbling, all sense of balance gone. My head reels, but I perceive that the ground is rapidly approaching. Make no mistake, I feel an almost heart-stopping terror as I plummet. What if I don't wake up? Suppose I just die as my dream body connects with the earth, the illusory fragments of my brain splashed around me like the pulp of so much watermelon? I avoid this train of thought, focusing on the moment when the jolt of impact sends my eyelids flying open, and I find myself happily awake in my bedroom.

Only seconds away now. Dark tarmac whirls toward my eyes. I hear a clanging in my ears like a fire alarm–it's my heart, which is less sure than my brain that I'm about to wake up. I clench my teeth, praying–now that it's too late–that I've made the right decision. The moment of reckoning is at hand.

The moment of reckoning is incredibly soft. Acceleration ceases, the whirling winds to a halt, and the rush of air diminishes to silence. I am filled with cold dread, because it doesn't take a fraction of a second to realize that I'm hovering six feet above the ground, spread-eagled comfortably on a cushion of air that lacks the courtesy to allow my passage through it.

Raymond is beside me again, and his face is absolutely swollen with fury. "That wasn't smart," he hisses.

"It was worth a try."

"Clever, but stupid. If this were simply your own dream, it might have worked. But not now."

"What's that supposed to mean? This *is* my dream."

"Correction. It *was* your dream. It started out as yours, then we intercepted it."

"We who?"

"We," he says, pointing to the chasm above. "Up there."

"You cretin."

"Dipshit."

"What kind of signals does that thing broadcast?"

"Our kind. Not the kind you pick up on a regular receiver." He taps his forehead. "This kind."

"Are you saying you're not just a product of my subconscious?"

"Bravo man! You're not as stupid as you look."

"Jackass."

"Shithead."

"So, I suppose you're just a symbol, rather than who you appear to be.

That would make you fairly two-dimensional."

"If you like," he says with a shrug. "It doesn't matter. We've been drawing you out. Why do you think everything's been so vivid the last few nights? Your dreams were intercepted, and we're going to keep them. You won't be waking up any more, I'm afraid."

"Go on."

"No, really! Try it."

Now I'm definitely worried. During our chat, we seem to have drifted higher and higher. The opening in the sky is huge now, dark and forbidding. I again sense a movement in it, something obscured by the thin clouds that float slowly past. "Where does that lead?" I ask. "What the hell is that?"

"That's the hole in your head where the rain comes in," he laughs. "That's where you stop and we start."

I realize as I watch him that Raymond's body seems to be losing something, as if he's beginning to vaporize from within. His limbs curl awkwardly, and his head shifts strangely to one side, so that a single, glaring eye is now focused on me.

"Raymond, just what the hell are you?"

I'm sorry I asked, because his arms and legs begin to jerk spasmodically. The head, which no longer resembles the Raymond I once knew—barely even looks human—continues to twist around, but the eye doesn't move. It keeps staring, at me, through me. The eye grows larger, while the body elongates, then dwindles, becoming insubstantial. Then, the reddish sphere is all that is left.

Strange hues of blue and violet dance around the tower, and the now-pulsating eye begins rising toward the space above, and I hear sounds, with the rhythm and flow of voices, yet with a timbre unlike anything human. The "real" Raymond Barton, wherever he might be in the "real" world, was never in this dream of mine; he was merely an image plucked from my head, an instrument used by something else to intrude on my subconscious.

Indeed, if the dream universe is as real to the spirit as the physical world is to the flesh, then it is inhabited by something that is certainly not human. . . .

The tower quivers, as if it has been struck by some huge object. I rush toward it, gripping one of the beams in my hands. I focus every erg of dream power I can muster, twist, pull, thrust. The strength flowing through my arms is superhuman, born of terror, yet my efforts are fruitless. The great antenna is simply too alien for my mind to affect. I reluctantly release my grip, and again will myself to fall, hoping only to buy time. Below, the landscape has been decimated by a thick mass of dark clouds.

I remain supported in space. I am no longer under my own control.

Above, I hear a rumble, and daring to look up, I find myself suddenly stricken with an unearthly cold. My heart nearly explodes, and the sound it makes rings in my ears so that I am painfully deafened. *Wake up,* I order myself, uselessly, for all of my wonderful dream abilities are now impotent. I'm being drawn upward, and there's nothing I can do to stop it.

Then at the fringes of my consciousness, I perceive a familiar voice. "David," it says, "David, wake up. What's wrong with you?" It is Sherry. For a brief second, the view of the nearing abyss fades to a misty gray, and a surge of hope drives me to try again to wake myself. But then the dream becomes all there is once more, and Sherry's voice trails away, taking with her my only link to my "true" life.

My God, she's gone.

Gone.

From the hole in the sky, a sound like thunder shakes the tower, and I reach for it, trying to grab hold to halt my ascent. No way. It's beyond my grasp. A movement overhead draws my attention upward.

No, this all must be a lie, a joke perpetuated by some sick part of my brain. The chasm above is widening, revealing the shadows of some new reality, shadows that are beginning to grow clearer as the walls of the sky–my sky–start to crumble. Something up there is . . . *alive,* for I can hear a low humming accompanied by bizarre, shrill piping sounds, like the playing of insane flautists. The tower, no longer a necessary tool of whatever is out there, comes apart at the seams, its silvery steel latticework floating upward and out of sight. The landscape below is gone, now merely a colorless void, without form.

This is just a nightmare; it *has* to be a nightmare. I will awaken. I know this is so because there is no way I can remain asleep as the monstrous, gaping mouth in the sky–within which I can see the twisted, burnt, ravaged bodies of those who have gone before me–widens to receive me and mine.

Here I go.

Sabbath of the Black Goat

Withers heard the sounds creeping from the woods on May Eve, as daylight lingered a little longer than it had the night before, and the biting edge of the wind was dull enough so you could go outdoors without wearing a coat. His house lay in a shallow valley surrounded by the rolling, forest-cloaked hills of Sylvan County, just far enough above the floodline of Reedy Creek to keep from being washed away when the rains came. In spring, the southwestern Virginia storms often tore down from the mountains to batter the countryside around Beckham like the hammer of God. Ink-washed clouds now gathered overhead, as the chilly breeze carried the sound of distant voices and what Withers thought might be music.

"It's the Witches' Sabbath," he said sullenly as Rebecca wandered out to the porch, bringing him a bottle of their home-made brew. "Old Kirby said he'd heard 'em out by his place a while back. Doing whatever kind of celebrating they do."

His wife nodded, looking first at the darkening sky and then toward the black-veiled pine canopy. "Don't reckon they mean any harm. But I hope they don't come on our land."

"Kirby says they mostly a law-abiding sort, Wiccans. They just do their own kinda worshipping, I guess."

Withers himself wasn't a church-going man; hadn't been in near seven, eight years. Now Rebecca, she went to her church faithfully, though she never tried to push anything on him that he didn't want to hear. He took a swallow of his beer, which went down cold and smooth. He and Rebecca loved the evenings when they could sit outdoors, their work for the day finished. Friday nights, like tonight, were best, when they knew the cornfields could keep until Monday. And watching the out of doors was always more satisfying than watching the television. Unlike most of his neighbors, Withers didn't care for those satellite dishes that cluttered up their yards.

"Who do you suppose they are?" Rebecca asked. "I mean, they have to come from somewhere around here, wouldn't you think?"

"Probably up from Aiken Mill. They say there's lots of witches in Aiken

Mill."

"Well, I hope it's not anybody we know. That is a very obnoxious noise out there."

Withers nodded. Sure enough, the banging and hollering, faint but powerful, up close would be fit to raise the dead. Must be quite a few folks, he thought, all of them banging on tree trunks with clubs or something. The rhythmic percussion, muted by distance, had an almost lulling effect, despite the raucous tenor of the voices. A few moments later, the sounds were buried beneath a low rumble of thunder.

"Water coming," Rebecca said. "Luther still out roaming?"

"Yeah. He'll be around directly," he said, looking about for any sign of the old Lab. Luther didn't take kindly to rain, and usually at the first sound of thunder he'd come hauling ass back from whatever chase he was on.

A few minutes later, raindrops came pattering down on the roof, shortly turning to a steady, heavy rattle as the downpour began in earnest. Even under the covered porch, water splashed over Withers' feet as he rocked in his cane chair, so he lifted himself to head back inside. Luther hadn't bounded home yet, and Withers cast a concerned eye into the woods, hoping the old boy hadn't gone too far out or maybe hurt himself. For a second, he thought he saw a bright spark far away in the darkness, but after the one glimpse, try as he might, he couldn't see it again. The witches probably had a good size fire going, but maybe the rain would drive them off.

Withers believed in freedom of religion same as the next man, but as far as he was concerned, the Wiccans ought to exercise their rights in another neck of the woods.

Luther pawed at the front door an hour later, after the worst of the storm had passed by. When Withers let him in, the old tar-colored dog shook himself and sprayed his master and Rebecca with foul-smelling water. But before Withers could whack him, Luther ran to the kitchen.

"Wonder where he's been," Rebecca murmured. "He hates rain."

"It's getting on that season. Better things to worry about than getting wet, I guess." Withers wandered through the dining room to the kitchen to feed the dog, expecting bright eyes and a wagging tail to welcome him. Instead, he found Luther standing on his hind legs, forepaws resting on the windowsill as he stared out with ears raised.

Withers poured a bowlful of dry meat chunks from the heavy bag, but even that familiar sound didn't draw the dog from his place. Holding the bowl up to Luther's snout produced nothing more than a disinterested sniff.

"Suit yourself. But you better eat that. Nobody else is going to."

He grabbed a final beer—never more than two in a night!—and returned to the living room, settling in his plush easy chair with the Roanoke newspaper. Having turned fifty a short time back, he'd found the old chair more and more inviting as his joints increasingly protested the strenuous task of planting and harvesting his corn. Rebecca was stretched out on the couch with a Fred Chappell book, indulging in her favorite pastime. She was ten years younger than he, still fit and trim, her features possessed of a youthful warmth, her blond hair only lightly frosted with gray.

And one sweet lady, she was.

After a time, Withers realized he'd begun to nod off. Rain still clattered softly on the roof, and the living room was warm and dim beneath soft, golden lamplight. He set the remaining half-bottle of beer on the little round table next to his chair and let the paper fall to the floor.

He wasn't aware of having fallen asleep. But he was suddenly startled awake by . . . something . . . that he identified moments later as a low, whispering sound coming from somewhere outside—down the chimney, it seemed. It was indistinct; certainly not a human voice . . . yet something that rose and fell with the cadence of speech. He sat and listened, trying to determine what he was hearing. Wind? Rain falling in the trees? No. He knew these things, for he and Rebecca had lived in this house for twenty-some years.

His wife also lay in the arms of sleep, her book resting on her chest, her hands folded across her abdomen. He looked at the mantle clock: ten-thirty-five.

Pulling himself from the chair, his joints creaking in protest, he shuffled to the window and peered outside, one hand sliding along the wall toward the porchlight switch. As he flipped it, flooding the immediate surroundings with bright yellow light, he heard a grating cough from the kitchen; it took him several moments to realize that it was Luther. Gazing out at the illuminated porch and portion of yard, Withers satisfied himself that nothing and no one was approaching his front door, then he headed back to the kitchen to see what was ailing the dog.

The first thing he saw was a pair of black, arched ears framed in the ghostlit window. The Lab was back at his place, staring out at the deep forest with an alert gleam in his eyes. Instead of turning on the kitchen light, Withers joined the dog and looked out into the hazy evening, seeing that the clouds had broken and a glittering starfield gazed down at the house through the gaps in the tangled oak branches.

Then where the hell was the rain coming from that still pattered gently upon the roof?

Withers shivered involuntarily and went to the back door, opening it a crack and sticking his head out. Still cool, but not unpleasant. Except. . .

Except for the stench that met his nostrils: a foulness like a septic tank dragged up from the earth, its contents emptied in the yard, even upon the house. Despite the awful odor, Withers pulled open the door and went out to the porch, stepping into the water-soaked grass, looking up into a cloudless sky empty of raindrops, empty of everything but stars and a bloated, silver moon barely peeking over the crests of the most distant trees. Still, he could hear a racket like water striking shingles, and the last traces of a whispery voice that receded into silence the moment he turned to look at the house.

For a few seconds, a vague luminescence seemed to sweep over the house, and he realized that it was a drifting patch of mist, ascending slowly into the star-studded dome above. An almost solid-looking mass, it seemed to be lit from within, rather than reflecting the light from the moon and stars. Quickly, the vapor rose and moments later dissipated, as if a cyclone had torn it apart and hurled its molecules into the night in utter silence. Shortly, the horrible smell faded away, leaving Withers to stare at nothing with jaw agape, mind searching for some way to account for the weird phenomenon.

He started back inside when a movement in the corner of his eye drew his attention to the pitch-black treeline. Peering into the darkness, he could see nothing directly; only when he looked away could his eyes actually detect anything.

"I'll be goddamned," he whispered, realizing that something was slipping silently through the trees, very low to the ground. Back there by the creek was only bog; even when the weather was dry that place remained soggy and dank, and he rarely, if ever, ventured into it. But there was definitely something there now–faintly luminous, almost like the cloud that had passed over his house a few moments before. As the thing drew closer to his yard, his eyes began to to register its presence without having to focus on another object. But it was too faint, too vague to be able to determine just what it was.

The shape wormed its way between the trees like a pale slug, or a huge glowworm. As it neared the edge of the yard, it came to a halt, wavering insubstantially in its shroud of darkness. Withers' heart began to speed up; for a moment, he had the idea that perhaps the shape was a naked man crawling along the ground, flesh gleaming under the moonlight. But that was a ludicrous idea!

Maybe this was what had Luther all upset. Withers knew one thing: his shotgun would be a welcome partner right about now.

He turned toward the door, only to hear a soft whistling sound rise from the edge of the woods, warbling higher and higher, until it became a shrill scream.

Shhreee-shhreee . . . SHHRREEEEE. . . .

With the devil at his heels, Withers leaped through the back door into his house, all thoughts of going back out there with his gun forgotten. He slammed the door and threw the deadbolt home, his eyes falling on Luther who remained transfixed at his window, eyes bright and glassy.

My God, he's not curious, Withers thought, suddenly realizing the truth. *He's completely petrified with fear.* The poor dog could not move!

He hurried through the dining room to the living room, where Rebecca was just sitting up on the couch, rubbing her eyes and gazing at him innocently. "What's the matter, Buck? What's going on?"

"I don't know," he said, his voice cracking, despite his attempt to control it. "There's something outside."

"What do you mean 'something?'"

"I don't *know!*" From its place behind the front door, he took his 12-gauge and made sure it was loaded.

And was nearly startled into pulling the trigger when a sharp, frantic knocking came at the front door a second later.

Rebecca looked at him anxiously. He held up a hand to keep her from rising. "Okay, who is it out there?"

"Frank Kirby. Buck, for God's sake, let me in!"

Withers tugged the door open, and his next-door neighbor nearly bowled him over in his haste to get inside. Kirby's round face was the color of watermelon rind, and tears leaked from his red-rimmed eyes. "It's Sally. She's gone. She got took away!"

Withers laid a hand on the younger man's back. "What you mean by that?"

From a pocket in his overalls, Kirby took a crumpled sheet of paper and handed it Withers. "This was tacked to my door this evening when I come home."

In sloppy black ink was written:

When the Beltane fires blaze forth on the hill, with Sol in the Second House, repeat the Rites at Roodmas, which be when the Black Goat appeareth before men. She doth command the fertility of women and the potency of men, and may render fertile whom She wilt or sterile whom She wilt. There be those who will help the lean and ravenous ones through the barriers. The Dholes will aid them to break through, these the minions of ye Black Goat. Iä! Shub-Niggurath!

"It came after they stopped chanting," Kirby groaned. "I heard the window break . . . went to the bedroom . . . and Sally was gone. I saw it, Buck . . . I saw the thing!"

"What the hell are you saying, Frank?"

"It took her! She got took by a screaming white thing!" Kirby's voice broke into pathetic sobbing, and though his blood had turned to ice, Withers put an arm around his shoulder for support, guiding him gently toward the couch.

"Did you call the sheriff?" Rebecca asked, her eyes blazing with bewilderment and growing dread.

"Couldn't . . . no phone. They must've cut the lines. I just ran. I couldn't go after her, Buck . . . I just couldn't. I ran!"

"It's all right, you hear?" Withers gave his wife a stern nod. "Becca, you go call the sheriff now. You tell him we've got trouble here."

She nodded and went to the bedroom, as Withers drew the curtain aside to look out the window. "Something's happening here, Frank. I don't know what's going on, but I saw something outside . . . heard something. Reckon it has to do with them Wiccans, maybe?"

"They're not Wiccans," Kirby whispered. "I don't know what they are. But they're not Wiccans."

"How d'you know?"

"'Cause I am one, Buck! Have been a long time . . . never told you, 'cause you know how folks get the wrong ideas. But those people out there . . . *I don't think they're people at all!*"

A moment later, Rebecca appeared at the door, face ashen. "The phone's out, Buck. What does it mean? What on earth does it mean?"

"Jesus Christ," he whispered. "Make sure the windows are all locked. Get yourself the .38 out the cabinet, okay, Becca?"

Kirby was muttering, almost out of his senses. "Didn't never tell you 'cause I figured you wouldn't like it none, Buck. We don't hurt nobody. That's not our way. But them . . . they took my Sally. Dammit, they took her!"

Withers heard the sound of window latches clicking into place in the other room. "It ain't so important what you are, or ain't, my friend. If we got somebody out to harm us, well, we just ain't gonna let that happen. Don't have another gun for you, but there's plenty of knives in the kitchen."

"I couldn't go after her. Not with that *thing* out there!"

"What is it? That white thing?"

"Dholes!" The strange word came out as little more than a squeak. "Takes them back to the Mother. So she can feed her young."

Grabbing his neighbor by the shoulder, Withers tried to shake Kirby's wits back into him. "You know something about this?"

"I heard a little . . . from some folks in our group. They say there were people that used to come out here, a long, long time ago, and work these rites to bring down something from the sky. And they finally come back. That's who's out there tonight . . . it ain't us!"

"In all my years here I never heard or seen anything out there, Kirby."

"Long before you and me ever came here. S'posed to be some fertility cult or something. But what they try to breed, it ain't anything human . . . or any animal like you ever seen."

"And where do these people come from?"

"Who knows? It's a secret church, or a cult or something. It was them that left me that note! And they took my Sally. What do suppose they're going to do to her, Buck?"

Withers shook his head sadly. "Can't say, my friend. And I don't know about any *Dholes* or what have you. But there won't be anyone coming into this house tonight uninvited."

Rebecca came back from the kitchen then, her eyes wide with fear. "Luther's cowering in the corner, Buck. I can't get him to move."

"We'll have to let him be, poor dog. You get everything bolted up?"

"All done."

He went to Rebecca's side and said softly, "I'm going to get some whiskey for Kirby. He's in shock, I reckon. Keep an eye on him. I don't like the things he's talking about."

"Do you believe him?"

Withers glanced at the window, recalling with a shudder the pale shape he'd seen, and the strange cloud that had passed over the house. "I can't say for sure. But he knows something."

He was about to go to kitchen for the bottle when a deep, thudding sound echoed from beyond the windows, vibrating powerfully through the very floorboards. He and his wife looked at each other, then at Kirby, whose eyes bulged so that Withers thought they'd pop from their sockets.

"Thunder?" Rebecca asked hesitantly.

"That's not thunder," he said. "What the hell is that?"

"It's coming," Kirby whispered. "They've brought it down, and it's coming. It's come for to feed its young! Oh, God . . . Sally."

A strong booming sound shook the foundations, and Kirby fell to his knees beside the couch, murmuring softly to himself, "Iä, iä, Shub-Niggurath . . . iä, iä. . . ."

"I don't know what good it'll do, honey," Withers said, "but you use that gun if you see something. You use it."

He started for the door, brandishing his shotgun, doing the only thing he knew how to do; he couldn't sit and just wait for whatever was coming.

"Buck, I. . . ."

He turned to her, saw tears in her eyes. "It's okay, honey. I love you so much. You know that, don't you? I love you."

"I know."

He embraced her tenderly, holding her head against his chest. "Just don't be afraid. Don't be afraid."

"I'm not," she said weakly. "*I'm* not afraid."

He pulled back, looking into her sorrowful eyes. The way she'd said that. . . .

"What do you mean, honey?"

"I'm sorry, Buck. I'm so sorry."

Her eyes had risen to look past him, toward the window. At that moment, Kirby began screaming, a shrill, keening shriek like a terrified child, and he fell backwards onto the floor, one hand pointing to the window.

Withers' heart nearly burst then, for just beyond the glass, something took shape–something large and round, a color he couldn't quite identify.

An eye, as big around as the lid of a barrel.

"Jesus, *God!*"

He barely heard Kirby's cries recede to the far end of the house, and the door slamming shortly after. But it was then that the real screams began, rising into the heavens in peals of agonized despair that echoed down the chimney–accompanied by the same foul stench he'd smelled earlier in the evening.

He turned to face Rebecca. She was gazing at the window, her face dimly lit by the unearthly color from without. Something like regret brimmed in her eyes; regret and an expression of *reverence,* as if the horror at the window were. . . .

Her savior.

Jesus . . . the church she went to . . . that he never attended. . . .

It occurred to him then that his wife had not gone to bolt all the windows, but to *unlock* them.

Her sorrowful voice crept through to his brain above the pounding of his heart, before it stopped forever. "I'm sorry, Buck. But they're ravenous when they break through."

To Be As They

"Don't draw it on, *paint* it on."

Paula's slender fingers held the tiny brush the way she'd hold a pencil, each stroke a meticulous, painful sliver of sienna across an ebony background, like whiskers standing out against the face of black cat.

The painting was not of a cat, but of the fatigued-looking naked man who'd been holding his pose beneath blazing studio lamps for almost an hour. Paula obviously intended to capture every hair on the model's body at the expense of the overall composition. A typical flaw found in the work of most novices.

Paula, though, was no novice. Another four months and she'd be leaving Beckham with a Master of Fine Arts degree.

"Why this?" Fontaine asked, allowing his fingertips to delicately brush the back of Paula's hand. "You haven't painted like this before."

She glanced up at him with a slight grin. "I used to paint like this all the time. Before you met me. I wanted to see if I could still do it. This department has perverted my work, I want you to know."

"Yeah, it's perverted you into graduating with honors."

"That's beside the point."

"A photorealist you're not. And you won't be, not in your lifetime. Be true to your own style, at least while you're in my class."

"Javohl, mein herr."

Fontaine touched her hand again, tenderly, with just enough deliberate detachment to remain within the boundaries of professional decorum. In response, Paula curled her forefinger into a little wave, accompanied by a surreptitious crinkling of her nose.

Perhaps some of the students knew Paula's extracurricular sessions with Fontaine went beyond the academic. But it only mattered if someone raised an objection to the powers that be, though Marty Johansen, the department head, could hardly level any judgments; Mrs. Department Head had been a student in Johansen's undergraduate class just a few years earlier, and she'd barely reached the legal age of consent at the time. Paula was no naive freshman, but the holder of a BFA degree, with honors at that, and had seen more of the world beyond this little Virginia town than Fontaine himself had. She was 24, he was 36; at least he was nowhere near old enough to be her father.

Fontaine moved on toward a large canvas sitting by itself in a far corner of the room, above which a thicket of close-cropped dark hair bobbed up and down erratically. Ivan Luserke, the artist, did not look up or acknowledge Fontaine's arrival in any way, merely leaned closer to his painting and dabbed on a thick layer of crimson paint with a wide brush.

"Ivan, we pay the models good money to pose for us. You wouldn't mind actually painting him instead, would you?"

The subject on Luserke's canvas was a seated figure in front of a canvas of her own. Crude yet, but obviously Paula.

"Already done," Ivan said in his slow, soft monotone. "It's there, on the floor."

A much smaller canvas stood propped against the wall near Ivan's feet and Fontaine leaned forward to pick it up, careful not to smear the wet paint. The image struck him with power–the way all of Ivan's paintings did. The young man might be considered an artistic genius, Fontaine sometimes thought, admittedly most often when reflecting in the company of a cold lager. This piece bristled with energy, every muscle in the young black man's limbs prominent in shades of ochre, blue and emerald;

features exaggerated, pose stylized, but so obviously the man on the stool standing out against the red velvet backdrop that Fontaine expected to see movement in the paint.

The kid was better than he was, Fontaine thought wistfully. He didn't like Ivan, but in a strange way felt sorry for him. No, it was more than that; somehow, he identified with Ivan, even though they could not possibly be anything alike. Ivan had one of the homeliest faces Fontaine had ever seen, but something in his features reminded him of his own father. Yes, that was it. Ivan's face looked like his dad's if it were turned inside out. He had no jaw to speak of, just a straight line from chin to neck, and a small mouth that always hung slightly open. In combination with his narrow, dark brown eyes that never remained focused on anything for longer than an instant, Ivan's face wore an eternal expression of something between dismay and contempt. That, and his omnipresent checkered button-down shirts, indeed lent him a superficial resemblance to Fontaine's father.

The rest of Ivan looked like something that had been whittled from a pine sapling. Long and thin, almost ludicrously so, Ivan looked like he'd be blown off his feet by the slightest gust of wind. Jointed toothpick arms took after those of a walking stick insect, weirdly prehensile with the brush in his hand, as if it were an only slightly narrower extension of his arm.

Fontaine leaned closer to study Ivan's portrait of Paula. He had himself encouraged the students to proceed with a work of their own choosing if they finished the regular assignment before the period was over, but instinctively his defenses sprang up, as if this painting in some way violated her. He irritably brushed this highly unprofessional notion out of his brain with a swipe of his hand to his temple.

"Now, here is your light source," he said, pointing to the brilliant lights above the model. "You've captured their aura very nicely, without actually painting the lights themselves. A good decision. Here is her shadow. But here also is a pronounced secondary shadow. So." He indicated an even more brilliant violet area to the left edge of the canvas. "What is this light?"

Ivan glanced up at him, and Fontaine made himself believe that the sneer was involuntary. "That's not light. That's my music."

Fontaine nodded and stepped away, aware that asking Ivan to explain would be a waste of time for both of them. Perhaps the answer was all too obvious anyway.

These two-hour classes had become very taxing, for he had to force himself to divide his attention equally among all his students. The last thing either he or Paula needed was for him to dote upon her, thus making them both look bad in the eyes of their respective peers; on the other hand, he had no wish to deprive her of the instruction she paid so handsomely to receive by intentionally avoiding her.

Wandering on from student to student—he had twelve in this class—he periodically made eye contact with Paula, exchanging signals that, however insignificant, they both found uplifting, reassuring. Each time her wide blue eyes met his, he saw himself reflected there and was pleased. As she worked, at regular intervals she would toss her head back to keep her burnt gold bangs out of her eyes, or lift her paintbrush and place its blunt wooden tip delicately between her teeth. Her narrow, smoothly angled face, with its small nose and thin, almost masculine lips had initially struck him as being the perfect face for an artist's model. Indeed, as their relationship progressed, she had become his own "private model," if such a term could be applied without connotations of possessiveness.

He loved her. Real love, no schoolboy crush. And not unrequited.

Oddly, more than to Paula herself, he now found himself drawn back to Ivan's portrait of her. Like his painting of the class model, this one depicted her impressionistically, yet with such an air of life that Fontaine felt he gazed at a real moment frozen in time, or a single frame culled from some vivid dream realized in oil. And rendered so perfectly, so quickly. It would have taken him days to achieve this level of completion.

At the end of class, the students placed their mostly unfinished works on drying racks at the back of the room. Fontaine reminded the model he needed to turn in his time sheet so he could be paid for the week's work; then he assumed an inconspicuous stance in a corner near the lockers where Paula stored her smock and equipment. He knew she could not linger, for she had an art history class to teach next period—one of the requirements for earning her MFA.

"You're being immortalized, you know," he said softly as she opened her locker and deposited her case of paints. "Ivan seems to have a shining for you."

"That's flattering. But I prefer your shining."

"Your painting. It's stiff today. How come?"

She shrugged. "Guess my heart isn't in it. I'll get a fresh start on Monday."

"Dinner tonight, right?"

"Absolutely. Your treat."

"My treat." As she removed her smock and hung it inside the locker, Fontaine felt his usual compulsion to kiss her on the neck, but, with his customary discipline, he forbore.

"One day you're going to slip," she said without looking at him. "Better not."

He chuckled. She knew him too well. "Just be glad it's not Ivan sneaking up behind you."

She slammed her locker shut with unnecessary force. "Don't even joke about that." Then, with a half-sincere grin, she turned and disappeared.

Eubanks' Tavern saw fair crowds on Friday nights, the majority being students who elected to remain in Beckham rather than seek the excitement of, well, just about anywhere else away from town. Of course, these crowds were nothing like the ones that conquered the local drinking establishments when Fontaine had been a student here, before imbibing was limited to the twenty-one-and-over set. The food had the reputation of being among Beckham's best (hardly a world-class distinction, given the very limited choices of cuisine in town), and the pop music wasn't played quite so loudly as in the old days, so even art professors could sit in a booth and enjoy private conversation with their partners.

In public, Fontaine and Paula still sat across from each other, though the way they leaned close and occasionally touched would leave no doubt in the casual observer's mind exactly what kind of relationship they had. In a few months, it would hardly matter, since Paula would no longer be one of his students. Then, in fact, would come the moment of reckoning—for she would have to choose between her heart's desire to remain with him and her professional need to seek new frontiers.

"There just aren't any openings here," she said somewhat morosely as she sipped her frosted mug of Asberry Ale, the house special brew. "You know VCU's interested in me. And they pay pretty well."

"I know," Fontaine nodded. "Of course, you will have to do what is right for you. And that must be your decision."

"I don't want to go."

"I know."

They both fell silent, taking long sips of their beers. Paula's eyes shone at him, and in that moment he could see how young she really was, how much she would miss in this life if she remained in the little college town. But with that intuitive wisdom she so often showed, she reached across the table and took his hand in hers. "Remember, I love you, Ben," she whispered. Then her eyes went past him and the glow in her face dimmed. "I'll be damned. Look around there."

Fontaine turned and beheld the stick figure of Ivan Luserke sitting down at a table by himself, his eyes downcast, his face wearing its obligatory sour mask. A waitress scribbled something on a pad and left, and Ivan looked up long enough to catch the two of them regarding him. Fontaine gave him a polite wave, which was answered by a curt nod and an averting of the eyes.

"He seems so sad," Paula said, sounding considerably more sympathetic than her prior remarks of disgust would have suggested. "Poor Ivan."

"You're right," Fontaine said, feeling a strange pang of sorrow at the sight of the ugly young man taking a sip of his water. "He must be incredibly lonely. Look at him."

"Let's not stare," she said. "The last thing he needs is for us to make him self-conscious."

"I'm not sure that's possible," he said softly, turning back to her and waving for the waitress to bring him another beer. "There's something about him, some conviction in him. His art is quite extraordinary. You didn't see his portrait of you. Look at it on Monday. It seems warped, somehow–almost grotesque. But it's you. Really you."

"Why, thank you so much, O munificent one."

He chuckled. "You know that's not what I meant. I tell you, that young man could put us all to shame if he makes the right connections."

"Making connections is somewhat reliant upon personality. You have to have one."

"Yeah. Talent alone won't cut it. That much we know too well, don't we?"

She laughed. "And how." Her laugh was abruptly cut short. "Oh, Ben."

He saw a shadow darken the table and, looking up, found himself staring at Ivan Luserke's sullen visage. "Oh, Ivan. Hello."

"Dr. Fontaine. Ms. Decker." He stood there for several moments, invoking an awkward silence.

"Would you like to sit with us, Ivan?" Fontaine asked, unable to refrain from showing his student that much courtesy. "We'll make room here." Out of the corner of his eye he noted that Paula did not so much as frown or flinch.

"Oh, no. I wanted to say something. You know this afternoon I painted your portrait, Ms. Decker."

"Please, call me Paula. Yes, Dr. Fontaine told me about it."

He lowered his non-existent chin in something like a nod. "It did not occur to me at the time that you might not appreciate me doing so without asking your permission first. I hope I did not offend you."

Her eyes widened in genuine surprise. "Well, of course not, Ivan. I mean, we've all done paintings of other students before. Kind of goes with the territory, you know?"

"Well then. In that case, I would like to make a request of you."

Another long silence. "Yes?" she said at last.

"I would like for you to have my painting. It would mean something to me for you to accept it."

Paula looked at Fontaine with surprise, and he shrugged, not quite knowing if or how to enter into the exchange. "Well, Ivan, I don't know if I should. I mean, it's your work, and it was done in class. It means a grade to you."

"I have already given him the grade," Fontaine said with a little smile. "It is outstanding."

"If you would, please."

"Well–" Paula looked to the ceiling, just in case God had scribbled an answer there. He had not. "If it's what you want, then I'd be honored to have it, Ivan."

"Good. I will deliver it to your apartment tomorrow."

"You could just wait until Monday, and I can take it with me."

"No, no. It is best I present it to you properly. Please."

She laughed with genuine humor. "Okay, as you wish. I'll be home tomorrow afternoon if you want to bring it by." Her hand touched Fontaine's, which he understood to mean that he would also be there tomorrow afternoon.

"Are you sure you won't sit with us?"

A flicker of something like gratitude briefly crossed the homely face. "No, I have my food coming. Thank you anyway. Thank you." He turned without further word and returned to his table, seating himself just as the waitress arrived with a hot sandwich.

"Gracious," Fontaine said, then swilled half his mug. "I say again, what a character."

"Where does he come from, anyway?"

"Providence, Rhode Island, if I remember right."

"His name is European. Figured maybe he'd come straight from the boat. What the hell is he doing in this little place? They have colleges up north."

"Don't know. Maybe those schools have rules against terminal homeliness."

"That's mean."

"Sorry."

Their waitress appeared a few seconds later with their own dinners: a tuna club for Paula, and an 8-ounce sirloin on an onion roll for Fontaine. He smothered his ample supply of fries with catsup and was about to attack them when Paula stopped him with a little clearing of her throat. Looking up, he saw her face shadowed with sadness.

"Oh, Ben, look at him."

He turned slowly, and saw Ivan lifting his sandwich to his mouth, taking a tiny bite and chewing slowly, deliberately. The young man's chest heaved ever so slightly, and something glistened on his cheek beneath the warm overhead lamps.

Ivan was crying.

Fontaine turned away before Ivan could realize they'd seen him. The steak sandwich beckoned him, and he picked it up and tore out a succulent chunk with his teeth. But it seemed dry and tasteless, and even the beer couldn't wash it down. And from the red in her eyes, he wasn't sure Paula wouldn't begin to cry as well.

True to his word, Ivan Luserke brought the painting to Paula's door the next afternoon shortly after she'd finished lunch. Fontaine had arrived at her little one-bedroom flat a few minutes before, and she'd treated him to the day's third cup of coffee, as well as a kiss that gave him hope for an exhilarating afternoon alone with her. Paula let Ivan inside, and had him place the canvas on one of her easels in the tiny living room. She appraised the portrait with a critical eye, seemed rather enthralled. The broad, multi-hued strokes described her figure with remarkable precision, with little flecks of gold highlighting her perfectly arrayed hair.

"It's quite wonderful, Ivan. I appreciate it. Very much."

"The paint is still wet of course, it will take many days to dry. So it must be kept safe."

"Of course."

He gave the portrait a long look himself. "I enjoyed painting this. I am glad you approve of it."

Paula seemed to draw up something inside herself and she laid a tender hand on Ivan's shoulder. "Thank you. It's lovely."

He nodded, without so much as a softening of his severe countenance. "I will go now. See you in class." And without another word, he spun on one heel, stepped out through the front door and in an instant was gone.

Paula continued studying the painting. "Odd. I wonder what this is supposed to be." She pointed to the brilliant ghost in the lower left corner of the canvas, which bathed her painted counterpart in a soft, shimmery light born of fantasy.

"He called that his 'music,' whatever that means. But I think it actually represents Ivan himself," Fontaine said. "I think it's his way of speaking to you."

"It's . . . beautiful," she said, mesmerized. "You were right. He's got incredible power."

"I believe he's been captivated by the subject matter."

She looked coyly at him. "Can you blame him?"

"Personally, no," Fontaine said with a little laugh. At last she turned away from the painting and stepped into his waiting embrace, lifting her head to kiss him. He brushed her soft lips with his tongue, felt her body melt into his. Her hair smelled of wildflowers.

"I love you, Ben."

"I love you, Paula. I adore you. Please don't leave me. I want you to stay."

"I will."

He had not made love to her, as badly as he'd wanted to—as she'd wanted him to. He wasn't sure now why they held back. Maybe it represented too great a risk, both of them knowing that perhaps, despite what they so ardently desired, she would be leaving Beckham sometime this year. The very idea devastated him. He'd gone home last night and wept, all for himself, knowing in his heart he was selfish, but caring little or not at all.

A few inches of snow had accumulated overnight—not unusual for late February. From his aging but sturdy Southern Colonial on the high end of Starling Avenue, he could look out over the College and see the almost surreal blend of ancient architecture—the administration building, the library, the many class buildings—with the modern metal and glass monstrosities, like the new student center and the mirror-walled nightmare of the new science building. He sipped his morning coffee and gazed down at the little building where he'd first studied and then taught art. And where he'd met Paula.

He could not see her apartment complex from here, but just the knowledge that she was still nearby—easily within walking distance—tugged at his heart, as if he were no more than a junior high school boy under his first love's spell. He could not part with her. "If you love her, set her free," he repeated like a litany. But the line rang false.

He picked up the phone and dialed her number. No answer, not even her machine. Perhaps she'd gone out walking in the snow, as she was fond of doing. She might even be headed in his direction, for she was known to drop in on him once in a while. He decided to walk down the hill toward her place, and if she were out and about, perhaps they would meet.

He put on some warm clothes, swallowed the last of his coffee, and set off down the sidewalk, watching his breath crystallize with every exhalation. Woodsmoke saturated the fresh morning air, and he saw plumes of smoke billowing from countless chimneys. Many young men and women marched up and down the sidewalks, and in the distance he could hear the happy shouts of children sledding. In contrast, somewhere, a snowplow's engine muttered despondently, receding slowly in the distance.

After ten minutes, he'd seen no sign of Paula, so if she'd gone walking, it was obviously not to see him. The completely irrational notion that she might have met Ivan Luserke tapped at his temples several times, and this he batted away with a substantial measure of self-contempt. What a stupid, ridiculous idea! Even if the bizarre young artist had a flame burning for Paula, in no way could she ever return the sentiment.

At last, he saw her building looming ahead above the ice-webbed branches of the surrounding trees. Well, perhaps she'd be home by now. Or maybe she'd just slept late and hadn't turned on her answering machine the night before. No harm in surprising her with a little visit this morning. He could certainly use a cup of her famous coffee to break the chill.

He clumped up the stairs to her covered veranda, kicking the snow from his boots on the little welcome mat. Knocking, he listened for a sign of movement from within, heard nothing. He looked around toward the back of the building, saw her blue Toyota Tercel parked in its assigned spot. He had a key to her place, but he hadn't brought it with him. On a whim, he tried the door, and to his surprise, it opened easily—and a little alarm bell went off in his head, for whether she was home or away, she always kept her door locked. Even in Beckham, a relatively safe locale by any standards, no one left their doors open any more. Shrugging away his trepidation, he crossed the threshold, smelled her familiar smell, saw the tiny kitchen was in its usual perfect order, the living room, everything in place—wait.

The painting that Ivan had brought yesterday. It was gone.

No, not gone. The easel where it stood was charred black, and what little canvas remained was shriveled and blackened as if it had been set on fire. The image of Paula had been ruined; not so much as a square inch of pigment remained unmarred. But there was no other damage in the room; no sign of smoke stains on the ceiling or walls.

What the hell had happened here?

Heart clogging his throat, he barely managed to croak, "Paula?" Of course, there was no answer. He hurried to her closed bedroom door, paused momentarily to listen. "Paula? Are you here?"

He opened the door and relief washed over him when he saw the bedroom appeared empty and in good order. But no . . . a pile of clothes lay on the floor next to the bed, and that was a capital crime in Paula's eyes. He stepped forward to pick them up, when something amid the pile caught his eye—something that he couldn't understand nor quite believe. He realized then that the air in here smelled bad, a cloying, fecal stench that Paula would never have tolerated for even an instant.

A whitish, sticky fluid saturated the garments on the floor, and when he carefully lifted the bundled-up sweater, a great glob of the viscous gel splattered over his hands and plopped to the floor, trailing thin, slimy strings, some of which adhered to his fingers.

"Oh, my God."

Underneath the sweater lay a pile of glistening, half-intact organs, vaguely recognizable as a heart, intestines, perhaps a liver. As if they'd been partially digested and regurgitated.

Numerous strands of golden hair clung to the clothes, which he realized was a complete, single outfit: sweater, jeans, bra, panties, socks, all coated with the foul, organic sludge.

Something glittered amid a horrible, suggestively-shaped pool of the fluid. A gold earring, one he recognized: a hollow heart with a little diamond in the middle.

"No," he whispered. "This isn't real."

He staggered backwards, feeling his stomach lurch violently. The rank odor seemed to intensify, swirl about him, coating his clothes and skin with an oily film. He ran out of the room, out to the veranda where he leaned over the rail and let his stomach void its contents. Somebody walking down the sidewalk saw him, shook his head and wandered on, probably thinking the poor professor had partied too hard the night before. Fontaine ignored the other, saw only the wet streamers splashing to the snow-coated walkway below through a lens of sparkling tears.

Whatever was in there, it *could not* be what it appeared to be. Impossible. Patently impossible. Paula would appear any moment now, healthy and happy to see him, concerned to find him in such distress. What was wrong with him? Had he, in fact, had too much to drink last night?

When everything that could come up had, and then some, he leaned over the rail gasping for breath, unsure whether the odor that assailed his nostrils arose from his own vomit or had followed him from the apartment. Gathering up a painful lungful of air, he loosed a raw, agonized scream that shook icicles from the gutter above him, a scream that brought everyone in the neighborhood to their windows and doors, stopping the young man on the sidewalk in his tracks, turning his face whiter than the snow that blanketed the town.

And Fontaine remained there, clutching the railing in numbing hands, his screams rending the still morning air until, several minutes later, a pair of police officers arrived to silence him. They must have expected an unstable student, or someone in the clutches of the DT's, or a victim of bad drugs. They did not expect to find one of the college's most respected faculty members welded to the veranda rail, showing every sign of having gone instantly stark raving mad.

No, he was not mad. Well, maybe he had been for a short time, but after the paroxysm had passed, he found himself again. Unsteady, confused, but assuredly sane. Paula, on the other hand, had not been found, and no one could say with any certainty exactly what he'd discovered in her apartment. Some of the remains were indeed human, but as yet, no one could confirm that they belonged to Paula, nor could they hazard a guess as to the nature of the other substance that coated her clothes.

The police had questioned him thoroughly, never for a moment appearing to doubt the veracity of his statements. Plenty of witnesses had seen him walking to her apartment that morning, and the knowledge that he and Paula had been intimate was apparently more widespread than he would have preferred. The fact that the authorities did not suspect him of any foul play consoled him not a whit; all he wanted was for Paula to turn up alive.

Yet, based on what he'd seen, regardless of how utterly unthinkable it seemed, he knew Paula had been taken away from him.

They'd sent him home in a squad car, and the officers were kind enough to inquire if he'd like them to call someone to come keep him company. He declined, wanting only to be alone, to maybe lapse into the madness of the morning, where nothing and no one could touch him—where he could be with her again, see her as vividly as in life if he so wished it.

Two o'clock was too early for beer, but he twisted open a Killian's and guzzled the whole thing, then opened another, never minding the burn of alcohol in his half-ruined throat. The afternoon sun had come out to begin melting the snow, but it barely penetrated his windows or his spirits, and despite the fact he wanted to stay near the telephone, he felt he could no longer remain in his house, imprisoned by its rationality.

He set out for the art building with an open beer, a couple of more shoved into the pockets of his coat. He would go where they had met, where they had spent so much time in each other's company, he learning of her and she learning from him. How long ago had it been anyway, when they'd first noticed each other? Almost two years? Yes, when she'd begun her graduate studies, when she'd caught his attention not only with her exquisite talent, but also with her beautiful spirit. How she'd come to care for him, he'd never know; he only knew that it had happened, and since then, he'd had everything his heart desired for all of his 36 years.

The last thing he'd heard one of the officers say was that the substance on her clothes was being sent, not to Richmond, or Duke, or some other credible pathology lab, but to Beckham's own medical center. As if *they* might know something no one else knew.

He brooded on that until he reached the studio, where he was surprised to find the overhead fluorescents burning and to hear the clank of something moving within. Opening the door, he saw Ivan Luserke seated at his easel, slapping paint fast and furiously on a large canvas, his head cocked in an attitude of *listening.* Only when Fontaine stepped up to see what he was painting did Ivan glance up and give a sullen nod of acknowledgement.

Students were always welcome to use the facilities, so Fontaine had given them all keys; Ivan's presence here was no mystery. But it was indeed unusual to find anyone here on a Sunday afternoon.

"Something's happened to Paula," Fontaine said softly. "She's disappeared."

"I've heard," Ivan said. "Everyone has heard. Lots of people are talking about it."

Ivan's painting as yet appeared formless. Some kind of purplish light against an umber background. For a change, the young man's face seemed to register emotions other than bitterness and dejection. This was a frown of melancholy, reminiscent of that sad face when he'd wept in the tavern.

Fontaine felt his heart again stirred with pity, overcoming even his own pain.

"You cared for her, didn't you, Ivan?"

The narrow eyes widened and gazed at him, and they were rimmed with red. "Yes, sir, I did. Very much."

He wondered if Ivan knew that his portrait of her had been ruined. For the moment, he thought it best not to mention it.

"She was beautiful," Ivan said softly. "I hope she will be found."

"Hey," Fontaine said, reaching into his pocket for a still-cold bottle. "Would you like to have a beer with me?"

"Thank you. But I don't drink."

"You sure?"

"Yes, sir."

"Then I am going to drink this beer, if you don't mind." He twisted off the top and glanced over to the lockers in the far corner. Taking a long swallow, he said, "If you'd excuse me, Ivan, I think I'm going to go sit over there for a little while. Okay?"

"Of course."

He wandered toward the lockers, eyes fixed on the one where Paula kept her things. As a rule, they weren't locked, for the students seldom kept any real valuables here, art supplies, mostly; not exactly inexpensive, but then they'd never had any problems with notorious rings of paint thieves. He opened the door, upon which Paul's name was emblazoned in intricate, flowing strokes, finding her paint-spattered smock, her case of paints, a well-used palette, and some brushes. The most personal item was a hairbrush, its bristles threaded with strands of her fine golden hair. He picked it up and immediately her scent dispelled the sharp tang of oil and turpentine.

He finished his beer without thinking, for before he knew it, he was opening the last one and sucking it down greedily. He realized he was weeping when he looked up and saw that the lights were refracted into dozens of brilliant beams.

"I'm leaving," Ivan said, rising from his stool. "You have . . . my sympathies."

"Thank you, Ivan."

The stick man strode toward the door and, before leaving through it, said, "For what I do the muses have promised to make me as they. Good bye."

And then he was gone. The echo of the door slamming shut seemed to go on forever, reverberating painfully in Fontaine's ears, so much louder in a building devoid of students' voices, of the shuffle of feet, of the very aura of life that ordinarily permeated the building during the week.

Shrugging off Ivan's incomprehensible remark as just another in a long series, Fontaine stood up and went to regard the new painting. He started when he immediately recognized the figure as himself, seated on the stool in front of the lockers, holding a beer bottle, head bowed in sorrow. Crimson tears stained his cheeks. To his bewilderment, a ghostly light occupied the lower left corner of the canvas, washing over his stooped figure; the same light as in Paula's portrait, which he'd assumed represented Ivan himself, his particular feelings for her.

How odd. It was as if Ivan had come here knowing Fontaine would be present to model.

He turned away from the portrait, almost embarrassed to have been captured this way. His legs wobbled a bit, for the beers had gone down fast and hard. Better be careful on the way home or he could slip and fall, or worse, stumble into the path of an oncoming vehicle. But he really ought to be going now. Maybe there'd be a message waiting for him. Seeing her again was too much to hope for. But he hoped it anyway. Made himself believe that he hadn't seen what he'd seen or that it meant what it meant.

Heading for the door, he paused to switch off the overhead lights. Even the snap of the switches going down seemed deafening in the empty space, and he felt a moment of vertigo.

But the lights didn't go off. His shadow stood out stark upon the metal door–and then it shifted, as if cast by the headlights of a moving car.

Something behind him rustled. Rather like the sound of flames, disturbingly so. And looking around, he saw that the overhead lights had indeed gone off. The light that illuminated his body came from the fresh painting, from the brilliant portion of the portrait that Ivan had once called his "music." Flaring brighter, it expanded to consume the entire canvas, burning into Fontaine's retinas so painfully he had to shield his eyes.

"I want to go back," he whispered, remembering that place into which he'd retreated for a short time this morning. "I have to go back."

He turned, reached for the door handle, but afterimages of the blaze ravaged his vision, and he flailed blindly, his hands grasping only air. What the hell was happening? Why could he not get out?

A thundering noise came from the inferno behind him, and against his will, he was drawn back toward it. The flare had diminished somewhat, revealing a hot red rectangle that seemed to be a portal to some distant, hellish realm, some place where the sky was crimson and the sun burned through a haze of blood.

Then a darkness stained the glowing backdrop, growing larger, moving rapidly toward him with the sound of a rushing locomotive. He hurled his beer bottle in a futile gesture, thought briefly of the Smith & Wesson .38 he kept in his house, wishing he had it now–if for nothing more than to put it to his own temple and pull the trigger.

No bullet, no prayer, no barrier of man's devising could ever stop the thing now coming for him out of the light.

The Fire Dogs of Balustrade

"What I capture, I capture wholly and completely. The essence is absorbed and transmuted by my hands, and, should I desire it, I could transform the world."

–Ivan Luserke

"They know nothing of time or place but are in all time and in all places together without appearing to be. They walk serene and primal, not in the spaces we know, but between them."

–Abd Al-Hazred
Kitab Al Azif, John Dee, trans.

Up on Balustrade, a gathering wind roared through the natural granite columns that gave the mountain its name. The sun had set an hour earlier and, under the waxing moonlight, those rows of bleached white rock looked like a phosphorescent crown atop the blunted peak. Frank and I struggled determinedly through the dense, tangled vines that tenaciously endured the bitter winter, and several times, one or the other of us lost our footing and made backwards progress. A treacherous endeavor, this, but not one to dwell much upon; we were running for our lives.

Far behind us, a long, mournful howl rose from the woods.

"You think they're gaining on us?" I panted.

"I don't think they'll climb the mountain. Not tonight. Looks like a storm coming."

Frank pointed skyward, and I saw through the branches that a mass of hazy gray cumulus was creeping steadily toward the gibbous moon. Far in the distance, the rush of wind through the skeletal trees became a siren's shrill scream.

"Well, that's just great for us, isn't it?"

"Don't start again," Frank growled. He paused to catch his breath, and took a quick survey of our dark surroundings. "There's a light up near the top. No ranger stations on Balustrade, are there?"

"None that I know of."

Mind you, I would not have been much averse to meeting a lawman tonight if Frank were less prone to firing his pistol. I figured he'd even put a bullet in me if he felt it would help him get his way. His patience was already wearing thin since my outraged reaction to his shooting of the gentleman we'd robbed that afternoon. Frank always had his reasons to do what he did, and questioning them, especially with a display of temper, simply wasn't politic; in fact, it could be downright dangerous. Still, I respected Frank. He wasn't usually quick to anger, but given sufficient provocation he could take to violence without restraint or remorse.

Our car had broken down on the rural highway just before sunset; or rather, it had just died. Stopped moving. The alternator, I guessed. We'd pushed the old Ford sedan off the side of the road, down an embankment and into the trees where no one was likely to see it unless they were specifically looking for it. Unfortunately, the Virginia State Patrol was specifically looking for a car and pair of individuals that all too closely resembled us. Under the circumstances, we decided that an honorable retreat into the forest offered us the best chance of seeing the next morning as free men.

Frank still clutched the leather satchel that contained his victim's property. He refused to elaborate much on its contents, which had served to fuel my indignation at the needless killing. I'd seen unbecoming exhibitions of greed from Frank any number of times, but this was different. His every move seemed driven by desperation; a trait that to him seemed totally alien. He was smart, and thought on his feet a lot quicker than I ever could. When times had gotten tough, he'd helped me win a decent, if not entirely aboveboard living. I still felt I owed him some measure of loyalty. We'd been partners in swindles, burglaries, scams, and blackmail for several years now, mostly in cities like Richmond, DC, Norfolk, or Roanoke; but occasionally we'd hit some little out-of-the-way place, like the one today. But until now, I'd never been party to murder.

"You see that light?" he asked.

"No . . . oh, up there it is. To our left."

"Somebody's house, I reckon. Get your gun out."

"No more killing, Frank. I mean it."

The moon disappeared behind the rolling clouds then, but I could still see the rage seething in my partner's face. "Here we go again. Christ, George, if only you knew what I'd saved *you* from."

"Yeah–if *only* I knew."

"You will. But later. Much later. Come on, we gotta keep moving."

We struggled on up the mountainside, the cold biting us more and more fiercely the higher we went. We'd come prepared for freezing weather, but I didn't care for the idea of spending the entire night exposed to the elements. Frostbite could finish us just as surely as a lawman's gun. I took a fresh chili pepper from my coat pocket and bit one end, *crunch-pop,* welcoming the fiery burst as juice and seeds washed over my tongue.

Frank had plotted for weeks before making this hit. I knew only that the victim had been a wealthy artist who lived in Beckham, a little college town not nearly enough miles behind us. If gaining riches was Frank's goal, I didn't understand his roundabout method of obtaining them. So far, I hadn't even been able to determine why I'd been included in the bargain, other than to drive the proverbial getaway car.

"It's starting to snow," he grumbled, as a few flakes began to waft around our ears. "Let's pick up the pace, slowpoke."

I expected to come upon the source of the light we'd seen at any moment, but as we pressed on, our adrenaline-induced energy rapidly diminishing, I caught no further glimpse of our goal. Snow began to accumulate rapidly, clinging to the tree branches and our own bodies with equal disregard. I heard a dog's howl, so far away now as to be barely audible. I doubted that even the Virginia cops would be fool enough to follow us any farther tonight.

I realized after we'd gone another few stumbling steps that the ground was leveling out–yet we could not possibly have reached the summit of Balustrade, and, if anything, the incline should be growing steeper.

"This is fucked," Frank grumbled. "Where the hell are we?"

I sucked down pepper juice and swallowed the last seeds, spitting the shell onto the ground. Ahead of us, I could see the huge trees growing denser, black pillars silhouetted by pale snowlight. "We should've gotten to that light by now," I offered weakly.

Frank then surprised me by holding up his parcel and giving it a thoughtful, lingering squint. At last, he shook his head and muttered, "No way."

"Well, where to? Keep going or head back down?"

"Can't head back down," he said softly.

"Maybe a fire," I said. "We're far enough up nobody's likely to see it, and even if they do, who'd come after us?"

He thought for a bit. "Can't say as I like the idea much. But I think we're gonna freeze if we don't."

So we started scrounging for some wood; fortunately, I'd thought to bring the flashlight from the car's glove compartment. Dead brush lay around us in abundance, so it wasn't difficult to find twigs still dry enough to burn. Soon, we had a small fire blazing next to a fallen tree that could serve as a marginally comfortable seat. I then ventured out in search of some bigger wood. The density of the forest here surprised me; the undergrowth still seemed luxuriant beneath the coating of snow, and the gnarled trees pressed closer together than on the lower slope of the mountain. I couldn't even see a white backdrop beyond a radius of a dozen yards or so. Behind me, the fire crackled in the center of an island of golden warmth.

Something crunched in the darkness before me. I aimed my light toward the sound, its beam shaken by a tremor of nervousness. Nothing moved within my range of vision, just the light snow wafting steadily down through the wooded canopy. I shrugged it off, since the chances of other human encroachment up here were slimmer than slim, and none of the indigenous critters were likely to be dangerous. Still, I couldn't shake the impression that the darkness had assumed some indefinable air of hostility. I gathered what wood I could find quickly and returned to the fire, laying my collection in a heap close to the flames to help keep it dry. Frank returned shortly with a pile of his own and added it to the cache.

In the firelight, I saw that his face looked as chalky as the snow; even the glow from the fire couldn't warm that expression.

"What's wrong?"

He shook his head. "Just a bad feeling."

"I hate it when you know more than you tell. It's a nasty habit."

He glanced around at the woods, at the falling snow. I again sensed a creeping animosity from *out there,* but as before, there was nothing to do but shrug it off; I patted my gun in its holster, gaining small comfort from the knowledge that it could speak in very loud voice. I took out another chili pepper and bit one end, while Frank fidgeted nervously. At last he knelt and lifted the satchel from its place by the fire.

"Sit down," he said, opening the case and removing what appeared to be a roll of canvas. He didn't unroll it at first, just sat there looking from it to me and back again with uncustomary indecision. Finally: "The man I killed . . . his name was Ivan Luserke. He was a painter, a sculptor. A rich man. A rare thing, that, being an artist and a rich man, you know? It was his money that first got my interest, of course. But once I learned about his art, I was hooked, in a different way. I even got acquainted with him, saw his studio . . . I almost called off the job. Then I thought about just not bringing you in on it. You know, usually, I case 'em, we pull the heist, you get us out. This time, I didn't know what to do. I'd never gotten so close to one of our marks before."

"Why didn't you tell me what was happening?"

"Couldn't."

Frank slowly began to unfurl the canvas he was holding. There were apparently several in the roll, and I could see their edges were frayed where Frank had cut them from their stretchers. But when he held the first one up to the firelight, I couldn't suppress a little gasp, and hot pepper juice went down my windpipe. A slight choking fit later, I leaned close to inspect the painting.

It was an abstract—at least partially. Great gobs of color had been splashed over the surface of the canvas, forming strangely intricate geometric shapes, outwardly haphazard but with an underlying sense of deliberation. And in their midst swam a bizarrely proportioned character, with a huge head, stubby arms and legs, wide round eyes, and a gaping black hole for a mouth; the distorted body erupted from a midnight-hued mass as if being regurgitated by an ichor sea.

But what struck me so profoundly was the certainty that the twisted figure represented the man holding the piece of canvas. It was Frank.

"I think Luserke knew I was going to kill him, long before the idea even hit me," Frank said softly. "He could see things. Read people. At first, it was a challenge . . . to keep him from reading me. A game. But then it started falling apart. I saw this, and the others. I had to kill him."

Frank then held out another of the canvases. This one showed a trio of figures, but I couldn't tell if they were meant to be human or not. One of them stood on all fours, its limbs shaped more or less like a man's, only uniformly long; a featureless globe rested atop a long, bony-looking neck that protruded from an equine trunk. The other pair stood upright, appearing to gaze into the spaces to either side of the canvas itself, though, if they had eyes, they were lost among swirls of color that described features more canine than human.

"Fire Dogs," Frank said. "He called them Fire Dogs."

I instinctively disliked the painting, even though the style and subject matter were captivating. Had I seen it displayed in some brightly-lit studio, I might have thought it comic-bookish or juvenile, but out here it seemed to exude a sinister air—one that either potentiated, or was potentiated by, the feeling of unease that had already seized me.

Finally, Frank put that one away and showed me the last of the paintings he'd taken. This one was unfinished, merely a sketch with a few select areas washed in with murky-looking pigment; but it was to me the most disturbing of all, for the image that filled the space was recognizably human, though distorted much in the same way as the first.

But I was looking at a dreadful caricature of myself. The thing in that painting was *me.*

"God almighty, Frank. How the hell—?"

"I never mentioned you. I never showed him a picture of you. He never saw us together. By all rights he shouldn't have known you exist."

Peering at the crude strokes, I could not find a single contour that realistically resembled my face, my body, yet, unquestionably, the image captured something from *inside* me, something that suffered no argument as to its true identity.

"You killed him for this?"

"I killed him for all of it. Whatever he was, he wasn't just an artist. He was weaving . . . something . . . into life." Frank's eyes glistened like melting ice cubes. "He thought I was looking to agent his work . . . at least, that was the scam. I didn't realize it then, but I'm sure he saw through it from the beginning, even without checking my credentials. He talked like a preacher sometimes, quoting lines that sounded like they came from the Bible, though I couldn't say for sure. He'd talk about how art was transcendent, how it could elevate consciousness. He said *sound* could define other worlds the same way light does for us. He said those are the worlds he captured in his paintings. He could be very compelling."

"That's supposed to be your job," I said, managing a wry smile.

Frank almost chuckled. "I was at my best."

"Yet you never told me during all of this. Not until the end. That was never like you."

"Nothing was ever like this before."

I noticed now that Frank's gaze had gone past me, into the depths of the darkness that huddled close around us. Suddenly I felt an even deeper unease at having my back to those woods, with my eyes accustomed to the light of the fire.

And then, from somewhere far away, came a deep, throbbing noise, a rhythmic hum that might have come from human vocal chords were it not so heavy—so *big*.

"And that?" I asked, turning to peer into the blackness outside the circle of light.

Frank shook his head and stood up, looking quickly in all directions, eyes wide, jaw slack. He reached for the gun at his side, prompting me to do the same. For the moment, all was quiet, yet the snow-saturated air seemed to be waiting for a repetition of the throbbing hum. And a few seconds later, it came; deep, heavy, *big*, obviously still distant, vague in origin. I couldn't tell if it came from above us or below us, if either direction could apply to the inexplicably level ground on which we found ourselves. My imagination's most extreme reach could not attribute the noise to an airplane, or to an unseasonable rumble of thunder, or some aberration of wind through the mountains. No; to me, the most unshakable perception of the noise was that it was uttered by something *alive*.

"George," came Frank's sudden whisper. "Over here."

I turned and saw him staring into the darkness to my left. Following his gaze, I saw a pinpoint of light somewhere out in the forest, at an altitude roughly equal to our own. Again, I marveled at the discrepancy between what was and what should have been; how we could be standing on what seemed to be a sizable plateau when by all rights we should be confronting an increasingly steep slope. And where there had been a single small light amid the trees, a pair now burned. Then a third and a fourth, and soon, an incalculable number of flickering candle flames poked holes in the solid wall of black beyond our little fire.

"Search party?" I said, more or less facetiously.

"Not the law," Frank replied. "Not *our* law." He turned then and kicked snow and earth into the fire, finally stamping it into a sizzling, soupy mire. Thick smoke mingled with the feathery flakes that still floated down through the tree limbs, sending up a sweet aroma that had a revitalizing effect on my numbed senses. Without the fire, I could see much more clearly into the depths of the woods, and I realized that, out where those firefly lights danced slowly and rhythmically, the tree trunks achieved a girth considerably greater than any that should have grown in a southwestern Virginia forest. I wouldn't have been surprised if a small car could pass under some of the *roots* that curled out from those prodigious trunks.

"Where the hell are we?" I whispered, drawing my gun, and biting hard on my pepper. "And how did we get here?"

"He called it Cathuria," Frank said, more to himself than to me. "Come on, we've got to get moving."

"You know what those things are?"

He shook his head, and picking up his satchel of canvases, he started into the woods in the opposite direction of the lights. Helpless to do otherwise, I followed him, cursing myself for having done so ever since I'd met him all those years ago. Always two steps behind him, usually knowing better but going along anyway because up to now Frank had never stumbled. But this time, I was afraid that the edge he'd slipped over led only to a destiny that neither of us could understand or defy.

Now, my most fervent desire was to rejoin the world we'd somehow left, where an ordered natural law—or even a disordered human law—might prevail, regardless of whatever consequences awaited us. But as we made our way through the dogmatic snowfall, I soon realized that the alteration of our familiar world had not been a localized phenomenon merely to block our ascent of Balustrade, but a universal transmogrification of space, entrapping us in some province of nightmare that I could only wish were solely mine.

The trees ahead had assumed the same gargantuan proportions of those we'd left behind, and again, that deep, suggestive hum reverberated through the forest, closer this time than the last, I thought. Frank and I simultaneously broke into a run, hoping the bright, pristine stratum of snow concealed no obstacles to hamper our flight. We had no destination; instinct simply compelled us to flee, and out of necessity our minds shut down to all but the immediate stimulus of the cold snow and biting air, because these they could comprehend.

For a time, I felt as if I were running in a dream, racing like the wind with my feet never touching the ground. Eventually I chanced a look behind us, and felt a momentary relief that we had apparently left the mysterious lights in the forest behind. But then, a hulking, illuminated shape suddenly materialized amid the trees before us, and I nearly slammed headlong into Frank, who screeched to halt directly in front of me.

"God damn," he whispered. "George!"

It was a log cabin, its windows lit from within by flickering lamps or candles. Three rickety looking stairs led to a covered front porch, its edges sprouting icicles like glittering fangs. I could see a snow-coated path leading from the stairs into the woods, and here the land finally began to slope toward unseen depths, kindling a little fire of hope that at last we might be nearing the boundary that separated our world from this mad, mysterious place.

A little wooden sign over the porch identified the establishment as BLAND MASON's, and I gathered from the soft voices and clinking of glasses I could barely make out from within that it was a tavern of sorts. Frank and I looked first at each other, then back toward the abyss from which we'd emerged. From the inscrutable darkness, we could hear a distinct sound of rustling and shuffling—something heavy, moving nearer.

"Yes, let's," I said to Frank's questioning glance.

We stepped up to the front porch of Bland Mason's, and before even considering proper etiquette, opened the front door and stepped inside, finding ourselves facing a half dozen cloaked figures, all seated at tables warmly lit by little oil lamps, the light from which stopped short of illuminating their hooded faces. At the far end of the room, a gray-bearded man standing behind a long bar gazed at us impassively, holding out a pair of tall steins filled with a dark, heavy-looking brew.

"Figure ye need a stout on a night like this," said the old man, setting the steins on the bar. "Come drink'em, and for ye first, there's no charge, if ye'll put those irons away."

I looked around the room, taking in the ancient-looking furnishings, the patrons who lifted mugs to their hidden mouths and slurped at their lagers and ales. Strange paintings adorned all the walls except for the one behind the bar, which was occupied only by a tall shelf of glasses—and a few of the framed canvases obviously had been contributed by the artist Frank had so recently, permanently censored. Each of them were portraits, in the same, primitive style that marked those I had already seen, though in these—thank God—I recognized none of the subjects. But some of the other paintings appeared even more disturbing; these were lurid, life-like depictions of death and dismemberment, full of screaming mouths and agony-filled eyes, all suffering at the hands of dark, shadowy things that seemed to have been purposely painted to be seen only vaguely. I didn't examine these too closely, for fear that this time I might recognize the faces of the victims.

"Well, take ye drinks," said the barman.

Replacing my gun in my holster, I obediently stepped up to the counter and sat down, Frank now following my lead. The mysterious, cloaked patrons merely quaffed their beers, apparently satisfied to pay us little mind. The atmosphere among the drinkers, while bizarre, seemed completely relaxed, and I could hear no further noises from outside; I had the feeling that whatever we'd left outside would remain there, not that the idea was in any way reassuring.

"Where are we?" Frank asked. "What is this place?"

"Can't ye read?"

"I mean, these woods, this place. It isn't Balustrade."

The old man shrugged, apparently not inclined to answer the question.

"I take it you're Bland Mason?" I said.

"I am. You, at least, have eyes." The bartender gave Frank a sour look.

"It's a violent night out there," I said cautiously.

"Only to those what bring it with them." He looked at me knowingly. "The Dogs are out tonight."

Now, a couple of the hooded heads turned our way; I didn't care to search for their eyes. "What we saw and heard wasn't dogs."

Mason chuckled. "Ye just don't recognize them. Maybe your friend here, he should recognize them."

I glanced at Frank, noticed he was sweating hard. He pulled his heavy coat off and tossed it into the stool next to him, not caring that his gun was now exposed to the world.

"This is all crazy," Frank said softly. "Every bit of this. It's crazy shit."

"I don't suppose you have trouble with, uh, undesirables coming through your door," I said, figuring that if whoever or whatever had made those lights were of a mind to follow us, they'd be here by now.

"Not usually. The Dogs have our best interests in mind here."

"Tell me about the dogs."

"What's to tell?" Mason leaned down close to me. "Ye ran down here in a panic, ye heard them. Ye know the Dogs."

I sensed Frank's hackles rising, and he dropped a hand to his gun. I touched his shoulder, shaking my head.

"See, that's how ye get in trouble," Mason said. "Just drink ye brew, friend, and let time tell what it's going to tell."

I didn't like the glint in the old man's eyes, and for a moment, I shared Frank's urge to do violence here. But something like common sense or fear won out, and I lifted my stein to my lips with a trembling hand. It was a strong, salty stout, and actually quite satisfying after the hard run we'd just made. I took a pepper from my pocket, broke it, and dropped it into the beer.

Even better, I thought, taking a hot sip. "You brew this yourself?"

Bland Mason cackled harshly. "All my life I've made ale, and I never thought of dropping heat into it. I'll remember that, yes I will!"

When the old man stopped laughing, a dark silence filled the room. I saw his eyes flicker toward a door at one end of the bar, and he stepped away from me, as if obeying an unspoken command. This time I didn't stop Frank when he reached for his gun and unholstered it. Something was moving on the other side of the door, and now, all of the drinkers turned toward us, and I caught a few bright flickers of eyes in the shadows beneath the hoods. Suddenly I felt a sense of danger even greater than when we'd been outside.

The door behind the bar opened, and I couldn't help but utter a little hiss of surprise, bordering on relief. The man that stepped out looked so thin and weak and harmless that I couldn't imagine him having an ounce of power over anyone, even the old man behind the bar wiping out a beer mug. He had close-cropped, salt-and-pepper hair, droopy jowls that looked almost comical on his otherwise thin face, and dull, unfocused eyes that hid behind large-rimmed tortoiseshell glasses. His arms protruded stick-like from the sleeves of a ratty looking, button-down shirt, and his trousers stayed up only because of a thin leather belt loosely fastened around his waist.

But when I saw Frank's face go completely white, his mouth gaping wide enough to admit a sparrow, a spark of recognition flared in my mind.

"You can't be here," Frank spat. "You're dead. You're dead!"

Ivan Luserke shook his head, motioning for the bartender to leave. The old man disappeared through the same door from which the other had just entered. When I looked back at Frank, his pistol was leveled at the dead man's face. But even with the perceived advantage of our firearms, it was obvious who had the commanding presence here. I took a calming swallow of my beer, and Luserke glanced my way. "I know you," he said in a low, thick voice.

"I know you do," I whispered back.

"Welcome to that which Balustrade dreams," he said. "The Dogs run interesting quarry."

"The Fire Dogs," Frank muttered. "I remember."

A heavy sound rumbled outside Bland Mason's, sending a shiver through the wood beneath my elbows; the same sound we'd heard before, now so close its source could only be right outside.

"What is that?" Frank asked, pushing the gun closer into Luserke's face. "Tell me what it is."

The thin face split into a toothy grin. "Frank. I painted them. In fact, I believe you took the original piece shortly after you ruined my body. Why do you ask the obvious? You know *where* you are, don't you, Frank?"

My partner slowly nodded, as if in defeat. "You called it Cathuria."

"So I did. And here is where they reside—at least, this could be considered a portion of their dominion. They may run as they please, wherever, whenever, they please. From Kadath in the Cold Waste to Celephais to the Plateau of Leng . . . from Yaddith to Oriab to the Vale of Pnath. The walls of worlds such as yours have no meaning to them."

"You're responsible for us being here," I said. "Or it's a dream. One hell of a bad dream."

"A relative term." He looked coldly at Frank. "I had a bad dream earlier today, when your man put that piece of steel to my head. A man only commits such an act because of fear. Do you know fear, Frank?"

"Damn you, Ivan," Frank said. "I knew there was power in your work. Something I couldn't understand. Then, there's all of this. And you. *You!*"

Luserke nodded curtly. "I am. Indeed I am."

Frank's gun thrust forward and pressed against Luserke's cheek. "Can you do it twice?"

"Can you?"

"I can pull the trigger." He looked around, saw the faceless hoods scrutinizing him. Then, slowly, he lowered the gun. "But not here. Not now. You tricked me, somehow. All of this . . . a trick."

Luserke shook his head. "The only trick is knowledge, Frank. For you, everything in your life has been a trick. All your schemes, your robberies, all your material quests, nothing but cheap tricks. You use them as a means to exalt your own ego, something to color that empty space that your body occupies. But let me tell you something." He leaned close to Frank. "You are transparent. You are a vacancy. The most solidity you have ever achieved was on a piece of canvas, stroked by my brush."

Now Frank was shaking, beyond words. The sound came again from outside, a beckoning, impatient rumble. "Tell me, Ivan. *What the hell is that noise?*"

Luserke merely gazed at Frank long and thoughtfully. Finally, he said softly, "Now . . . the game shall end."

I felt a wave of cold wash over the bar and hit me solidly, like an icy tsunami that nearly toppled me from my seat. A horrid reek filled my nostrils, like sulfur and blood, and above, the rafters of the cabin groaned as if the walls were being squeezed by some monstrous grip. With a cry, Frank leaped from his barstool and grabbed a cloaked figure from the nearest table, thrusting the gun barrel against the hooded temple.

"Maybe you can take a bullet and walk away from it," Frank growled. "But how about these others? It's very tempting to find out."

Luserke shrugged unconcernedly. "Your desperation is as colorless as your greed."

Frank suddenly let out a cry, the shrill sound of panic—something I never thought I would hear from him. And seeing what now held him, I felt close to loosing a scream of my own. But some deep-rooted instinct warned me against attracting any attention to myself, lest I hurry whatever fate awaited me in this place.

The character Frank had grabbed was no longer a captive, but had deftly taken the upper hand; throwing back his hood, he now revealed himself as a hairless, mottled-gray beast with dull yellow eyes and a lipless mouth sprouting a row of jagged, protruding teeth. Frank's gun clattered to the floor as pale, spidery fingers encircled his wrists and yanked his arms up like a puppet. Worst of all, the drinkers at the tables had now disclosed their own faces, and several of those ghastly pairs of eyes fell hungrily on me.

A low, guttural voice rose from the thing that held Frank. "Shall I?"

Luserke shook his head thoughtfully. "Let's not, Richard. What say we escort him out of doors."

Frank cried, "Ivan, stop him."

The rumbling sound from outside rose in volume, and then, most horribly, played harmony to another that swelled even louder. The whole building seemed to rock on its foundations. Luserke did not speak, merely nodded to the ghoul that gripped my partner. The creature began pulling him toward the door, and Frank kicked and struggled, cursing and screaming, his efforts as feeble as he had expected his intended victim's to be.

I could only watch as one of the other creatures opened the door, and the one Luserke had called Richard disappeared through it, carrying his squirming hostage. Then I dropped to the floor, holding my ears as the hounds exulted, a sound so big, so consuming, that I felt it to the core of my brain, a pain like iron spikes being driven through my eardrums, through my skull. Frank's screams joined the chorus, and I felt hot tears welling in my eyes, knowing that, no matter how wicked a man he might have been, he couldn't possibly deserve the sentence that had been imposed upon him.

This was not justice, nor an act of revenge meted out by a dead man; it was merely the law of this unknown realm, a law beyond any conceived by human minds. I was certain now that the time had come for that law to recognize me as well. As the sounds of horror outside at last trailed away, Frank's last wails lingering pitifully inside my head, I looked up to find Ivan Luserke standing pensively before me, and I could feel the oppressive weight of all those yellow eyes boring into the back of my head. Luserke motioned for me to stand up, and weakly, I pulled myself as far as my knees. A pair of powerful, clammy hands then grabbed me and jerked me roughly to my feet.

Luserke stared at me for untold ages, so long that consciousness faded in and out several times as I stood there. Finally he spoke.

"Be glad I did not finish your portrait. Now, leave, or I will begin another."

Weakly, I stammered, "Them . . . the Dogs. . . ."

"They will not trouble you."

I gazed into the cool eyes behind those ludicrous glasses. All I could see was a blank wall. But at the very least, I found no deception.

The mass of ghouls parted as I shuffled toward the exit. I knew better than to look back as I stepped out to the rickety front porch, where the wind had driven piles of snow as deep my ankles right up to the door. As my eyes grew accustomed to the darkness, I saw that the trees had returned to their natural size, and the air carried only the sound of gently falling snow, with no trace of those *other,* living sounds that had pursued us through the night and finally taken Frank away with them. I stumbled onto the path that led down the slope, and finally, after I felt that the eyes of Bland Mason's tavern no longer gazed after me, I turned to look at the place I had left.

All I saw was a thick tangle of limbs and vines, a great deadfall that completely blocked the path. Somehow it seemed *right,* this bulwark separating me from a shadow world that only a privileged or unlucky few might ever enter—or leave again. I knew that of my late partner, no one would ever find a trace, not on Balustrade or any other corner of the world that dwelled among sensible angles and planes, the kind that reasonable men savored.

I went down the mountain, and reached the highway just as dawn's first light began to burn away the snowclouds, turning the icy white trees into sparkling, crystalline towers. Taking a pepper from my pocket, I bit into familiar fire and trudged down snow-topped asphalt toward the murder charge that waited for me at its end.

I was not prosecuted, for reasons I could not explain or dare to explore. The papers carried no stories of Ivan Luserke's murder, nor of a manhunt for two fugitives who had abandoned their car on a lonely mountain road. I expected law officers to appear at the door of my meager apartment at any time, but they never did; I even entertained thoughts of turning myself in, but could never bring myself to sacrifice whatever freedom I could call mine for an act that was by all indications forgotten. The dreamland bred strange things, and I could never truly know how far its influence crept into this world.

But since that time, my dreams have been filled with sounds that echo from unknown dimensions, and sometimes from the direction of Balustrade, the Fire Dogs bay in the night unheard by any ears but mine. There was one item brought with me that night that I have no recollection of carrying, but I obviously did, for the painting hangs in my room and watches over me, the featureless faces of the beings portrayed there patient and attentive. Of my portrait, there was no trace; I suspect that Luserke held it for safekeeping, and I can only pray that in whatever land he hides, he will never conjure with it. And the portrait of Frank—it is merely ashes, his representation as irretrievable as his own being.

I grieved for him, if only because he was a fellow man. I had respected him and hated him, but we had shared something in this life that I had never shared with another, and never would again. I think he liked me, in his own way, and I was always grateful to him for that.

Yes, the Fire Dogs watch and wait from their canvas, and oftentimes I wonder if Ivan Luserke still paints in some dark corner of Cathuria, weaving things to life in those spaces between the ones we know. There is sentience in the paint, and sometimes I speak to it, to make familiar that which is as far removed from the lives of men as the whirling nebulae at the hearts of Fomalhaut and Aldebaran.

I named the Dogs in the painting Frank, Ivan and Richard. They seem to approve.

The Horrible Legacy of Dr. Jacob Asberry

It was not the first time the painting had spoken.

Until now, Trull had never actually heard it speak, though stories of its unusual talent occasionally crept into light-toned conversations at society parties, or onto the local newspaper's back page following some generally hysterical witness's accounting of the event. Once, a group of students from nearby Beckham College broke into the old hotel in an attempt to steal the painting, but an alert Mrs. Kate Forbish, proprietor of the establishment, foiled them by phoning the police from her room upstairs. Rodney Fox, the nefarious investigative reporter from TV 6, once broadcast an exposé on the painting and its reputation for elocution, but when it failed to cooperate with an attempted interview, the celebrated gossip monger was forced to retreat in embarrassment.

Jonathan Trull had worked across the hall from the painting for over nine years, and believed nothing of these tales. The "ghostly voice" of the Broad Street Hotel surely was a gimmick conjured to draw local publicity by the late Mr. Forbish, back in the thirties. It was a novelty whose popularity had waned even before Trull had been born (he was a '56 model). Yet, when he heard that far-off-sounding, coarse rattle, not unlike an asthmatic cough, coming from the gallery across the hall from his desk, his state of mind took a distinct turn for the worse.

The spacious, antique-filled gallery was open to the public but, to Trull's knowledge, had not been visited all afternoon or evening. He left his desk and crept to the door, not wishing to startle anyone who might have somehow wandered in unseen. Poking his head around the corner, he found that, indeed, nary a soul occupied the large room, though a dying fire still crackled in the immense fireplace. Merely a log shifting, perhaps? Above the fireplace, the tall, gilt-framed portrait of Jacob Asberry dominated the room, its subject a dark, cruel-looking figure with stark, staring blue eyes, thinning white hair, and gaunt, hollow cheeks. Trull had always thought that the founder of the Broad Street Hotel would not have been a pleasant employer; no one with a face like that could have possessed an ounce of humor, nor likely any compassion. A stern, miserly man, he had gone to the great beyond the same year that the Great Depression began, leaving the hotel to his daughter. Fortunately, Mrs. Kate had not inherited his personality.

The gallery was a dim place, its walls a pale beige, the carpet deep wine, the high ceiling a rust-colored maze of intaglio tile. Even when a number of guests filled this room, the atmosphere seemed solemn, almost grim; empty, as it was now–apart from himself–it felt like a crypt. Despite this, Trull respected the fact that this gallery, and the hotel as a whole, stood as one of the last remnants of Aiken Mill's proud past. Virtually all of the other southern gothic treasures had been torn down in recent years; an unwelcome reminder of his own all-too-rapid aging.

Trull's eyes locked on those of Jacob Asberry, almost expecting to find them glaring sentiently back at him. But the painting showed no sign of having assumed any new, lifelike traits, and the thin, acerbic lips did not open to address him or even utter a supernatural soliloquy.

A cold finger tickled the nape of his neck. He *had* heard a voice! As much as he would like to have passed it off as a trick of the acoustics in the old building, he could not. Having worked here for so long, he knew exactly how sound traveled down the old corridors, through the maze of air ducts, from the spaces outside the windows.

Trull felt a moment's indecision. Should he run away, or try to unravel this mystery? After brief deliberation, he chose to stay–as long as nothing more threatening than a disembodied voice presented itself to him. He could not deny feeling a cold, nauseating fear, but at least it seemed unlikely that the voice—disturbing though it might be—could actually harm him.

"Hello?" he said softly, taking a tentative step closer to the painting. "Was that you?"

The chiseled face in the picture offered no response. Upon touching the canvas and finding only a cool, pigment-caked surface, he backed away and turned to the window, feigning an interest in the lamplit sidewalk beyond. Then—quickly—he spun around, hoping to catch the painting in some form of transition.

Nothing.

Alas, with no witnesses, he could scarcely prove his claim should he mention it to anyone. *Damn!* What a shame that such an incident, which could pretty much shatter all his convictions about reality if he let it, must remain a secret. But realizing the ridicule he would certainly face, he suppressed the urge to go running up and down the hallways, alerting all the guests to the strange, miraculous, and incomprehensible truth that had almost revealed itself to him here in the Broad Street Hotel.

In the hall, the bell on the desk jangled: a guest requiring his attention. So, Jonathan Trull returned to his work, still unnerved, but determined to perform his duties as was expected of him. Perhaps in the morning, he'd ask a few subtle questions of Mrs. Kate without actually explaining in detail what had happened to him.

But before settling back at his desk, he closed and locked the door to the gallery. If the portrait were to begin talking a blue streak, he had no desire to hear it.

"It spoke to you," said the silver-haired, rotund woman settled deeply in her plush armchair, her fat fingers folded loosely together in her lap. "That's what happened, isn't it?"

"Why, no!" Trull blurted, dismayed that Mrs. Kate had so readily guessed the truth. "No, I was just curious about it."

"No, John, it spoke, and you heard it. That's it, isn't it? No need to be ashamed."

Her voice was kind, motherly, and he could not bring himself to lie to her. He'd always liked Mrs. Kate, and knowing that she cared nothing for the rumors of the goings-on about her property, he wished to spare both of them the embarrassment of admitting what he'd heard. "Well," he mumbled, averting his eyes from her penetrating stare. "I *thought* I heard something."

"I suppose you did," she sighed, shaking her head slowly. "It happens, you know. It isn't some made-up story."

"No?" he exclaimed, taken aback. "But I thought you'd never believed in it!"

"That's what I've always told people, John. It's not good to say certain things to some people because some people shouldn't know certain things. I know some things that my father didn't know, and there are some things he knew that I shouldn't know, but that I do."

"I don't follow."

She reached out and patted his knee. "Never you mind. Would you like some tea, John?"

"Yes, please."

She poured him a cup from the pot on the table and handed it to him. The blinds in her room were drawn against the morning sun, and shadowy zebra-stripes painted her ample figure. "They're coming," she said softly. "It won't be long. I am the only one keeping them away, you know."

Trull's spirits darkened with each word Mrs. Kate spoke. He'd hoped to learn something about Jacob Asberry, not that the old woman must be getting addled. At eighty-something, her memory occasionally went on break, but she usually remained witty and level-headed.

"You know, John," she continued, "I'm not going to be here much longer. I haven't discussed this with you before, but now the time has come. When I go, the hotel is to be closed at once. Is that clear, John?"

"But Mrs. Kate. . . ."

"At once. No matter the circumstances. The guests are to be cleared out, and the doors locked. I have a good reason for telling you this, John, especially now that you've heard the portrait speak. You must promise to obey me."

Trull nodded, dumbfounded. As acting manager of this establishment, he had hoped that the care of the hotel would be left to him once Mrs. Kate passed on. But somehow, he'd always suspected that she must have other plans in mind, for she'd never so much as insinuated that the property might become his. Yet, to his knowledge, she had no living heirs. He sighed, realizing the futility of arguing with his employer. "I don't understand, Mrs. Kate. But if that's what you wish. . . ."

"It is not a wish," she said, not unkindly. "It is a necessity. My father left this hotel to me with a set of conditions that simply must be followed. Do you understand?"

"Yes, ma'am," he said. "I mean, no, ma'am, I don't. I *wish* I did."

"No, you don't. It's better this way."

"Yes, ma'am."

She stared into space for a few moments, then whispered, almost to herself: "I didn't approve of what he did. But I had to protect him. He *was* my father." Then, realizing Trull was still in the room with her, she said quickly, "Please see to the guests now, John. Do not tell anyone what you heard."

"No, ma'am." He turned to leave, giving her a long, curious look. Mrs.

Kate settled back in her chair with a deep sigh, and as someone might mutter, "Oy vey," mouthed a few odd syllables that sounded something like, "Eeya, eeya, kloogu fahtagin."

That afternoon, Trull went about his duties in a desultory daze, occasionally seized by anxiety as someone entered the gallery to relax by the fire. But nothing unusual happened before dinnertime. A few guests checked out, a few new ones in. The ancient Victorian building generally attracted retired couples who came to sample its antique atmosphere, though, once in a while, a business executive, tired of the usual Sheraton fare, stopped in overnight. Trull met them all with forced good cheer, his manners faultless as ever. But he could not forget the strangeness of his meeting with Mrs. Kate this morning, which troubled him every bit as much as the eerie voice he'd heard the night before.

As he wandered through the upstairs just before dinner, making sure that Suzie, the new young maid, had taken care of all the housekeeping, he passed Mrs. Kate's closed door and noticed a low humming mixed with mumbling coming from the other side. He paused for a moment, taking care not to make the floor creak, and placed his ear to the door. He felt a sharp pang of guilt, for it was quite wrong of him to eavesdrop. Yet, the tune he heard seemed strange, weirdly chaotic, and–he hated to admit–like something he might expect to hear from a lunatic in an asylum.

What he heard convinced him. From within came only pure, meaningless gibberish in a sing-song voice; shrill, garbled syllables that no lucid tongue would ever pronounce. He was about to enter without invitation when the voice trailed away, then called, "John, is that you?"

He slowly pushed open the door and looked inside. He sputtered, "I just came up to . . . uh . . . tell you dinner is almost ready." He felt his face starting to burn.

Mrs. Kate only nodded slowly. He noticed that the skin around her eyes was drawn, her complexion pale, and he feared that she might be ill. But she said in a normal tone, "Thank you, John, I'll be down directly." Then she dismissed him with a quick wave.

He softly closed the door and headed toward the stairs, more puzzled and concerned than ever. On the table in front of her, he had seen a large, leather-bound book, which he at first thought was her antique King James Bible. However, in the dim light, he'd seen on those pages, not verses of scripture, but strange designs and drawings scrawled in deep red ink. And on the page he'd had the opportunity to see clearly, there'd been a rather ghastly rendition of a flayed human body, muscles and organs exposed, all the more chilling because of its stark, clinical realism. In contrast, above it hovered some multi-limbed, organic-looking object, not unlike a big rhododendron bush that sprouted hundreds of eyes, rather than leaves.

He practically vaulted down the stairs on his way to the kitchen to help Chef, desperately trying to formulate a plan to rescue poor Mrs. Kate's failing mind. Unfortunately, no glimmers of brilliance were forthcoming, and, as he passed the gallery, he nearly jumped out of his skin when he heard a low, throaty voice seemingly engaged in conversation with itself. He leaped through the door, ready to confront the portrait, only to find himself staring abashedly at the long, dour face of Mrs. Penelope Prillaman, one of the regular guests, who was engaged in some monologue before a cowed-looking Mr. Prillaman: a short, squat gray-haired man with no fingers on one hand, a club foot, and several million dollars in his money belt. Both of them gave Trull an annoyed glare, and madame cleared her throat haughtily before returning to her diatribe.

Trull excused himself softly, and hurried on to the kitchen, where he found Chef bungling about with the chicken and dumplings, crying that they were out of creamed corn and short on veal, which was supposed to be the evening's special. After what he'd just seen, these mundane problems seemed a real blessing, for he was groomed for such tasks. He laid into Chef with proper indignation and commenced to setting things right, so that when Mrs. Kate came down for her dinner twenty minutes later, the chicken and dumplings were perfect, flounder had replaced veal as the evening's special, and Suzie, the new young maid, had been sent to the supermarket to purchase corn.

After dinner, Mrs. Kate had only just gone up to her rooms when the alarm came from upstairs. Mrs. Alberta Southworth, from Martinsville, had heard a dreadful thump behind Mrs. Kate's closed door, and, upon receiving no answer to her knock, had taken the liberty of going inside, only to find the hotel's proprietor lying in a heap on the floor, face deathly white, breathing shallow and labored. Trull immediately called for an ambulance, which arrived in less than fifteen minutes (for the Rescue Squad was only around the block). Mrs. Kate was trundled away on a gurney, unconscious but for a brief moment as the paramedics rolled her past Trull in the foyer. At that point, her dull, yellowed eyes gazed at him, and with great effort, she whispered, "John . . . do it now. Now!"

He stared in shock as they carried her away. The ambulance drove into the night with siren blaring and lights flashing, leaving behind a small crowd of well-wishers on the front porch. Once the excitement was over, and the guests began returning to their rooms or to the tavern next door, Trull had to seriously consider the demand his employer had made of him. In his nine years of service he had been unwaveringly loyal, having followed Mrs. Kate's every wish to the letter. But to empty the hotel and lock its doors–now, of all times, when any number of the elderly patrons might be on their ways to bed–it was unthinkable! What about some of the more active guests, who'd gone to the tavern or elsewhere to dinner? Were they to return for the night only to find themselves without lodging?

Mrs. Kate's mind, he forced himself to admit, had indeed completely snapped. Tonight, his responsibilities would keep him at the hotel, but tomorrow, he would make the time to go to the hospital–provided poor Mrs. Kate survived that long–and try to settle the matter once and for all. Somehow, he must make her understand that he simply could *not* do as she wished, at least not immediately. There were preparations to make, all kinds of legal arrangements, announcements to make. Worst of all, he would be unemployed!

If she should actually die.

He suspected that it had been her heart tonight. But she was a strong woman. Heavens, his own father had survived three heart attacks before succumbing to the big one. Yes, certainly, Mrs. Kate had a fighting chance. A woman of her spirit had *more* than a fighting chance!

With these reassuring thoughts, he managed to regain his composure and settle back at his desk in the hall. He would shortly call the hospital and inquire after her, once they'd had time to register and examine her. And if, God forbid, the worst should happen, he would have to deal with it firmly and responsibly.

The hotel was, as always at this hour, quiet and still, with dinner long over and most of the guests secured in their rooms. As usual, Trull sat down at his desk and took a few minutes to look over the evening newspaper. Down the hall, the stairway ascended into darkness, for the house lights were always lowered at night. The gallery remained solemnly quiet, and he felt no great compulsion to close its door. Within, a low, golden glow flickered on the wall from the smoldering fire.

The first sounds came from somewhere in the darkness beyond his bright little island. Initially, he paid them no mind, thinking that someone must be moving around upstairs. But after a few moments, his trained ears realized that these were not the usual noises that came from the ancient structure. Putting down his paper, he looked around, saw nothing at all out of the ordinary. He recalled the voice he'd heard the night before; but these new, rumbling groans hadn't sounded like that. For the second time in as many days, a chill shinnied up and down his back, for never in nine years had he felt that all was not right in the old, familiar gloom. And as he peered toward the stairs that vanished into shadows, he came to sense that unseen, hostile eyes had suddenly trained themselves on him. The low, rumbling sound repeated itself.

He rose from his chair and cautiously crept in the direction of the staircase, his heart now pumping wildly. Surely, no one here would stoop to playing jokes on him! He paused at the foot of the stairs and peered upward, wondering if he had actually seen a faint movement in the shadows–there, beyond the door to Mrs. Kate's room on the left.

"Anyone there?" he called softly, and received no response. He mounted the stairs, climbing slowly, carefully, so that the old boards wouldn't complain. Upon reaching the top, he looked around at the deserted hallway, at the five closed, silent doors, and at the entrance to the north wing off to the left. No movement, little sound; only the faint whisper of a television in one of the rooms.

Then, behind him, he heard it. The voice from the previous night, drifting up from the gallery. A deep, grating voice, chanting in garbled syllables that now sounded disturbingly familiar.

"A'gg ghaad kyah nog-thaah. . . ."

It was like the gibberish he'd heard from Mrs. Kate's room before dinner tonight. But that voice. . . !

At that moment, he decided to intrude upon the sanctity of Mrs. Kate's chambers and find that god-awful book he'd seen her reading. Her own wellbeing–and now, he decided, that of the guests–outweighed her right to privacy, even in her absence. He had not locked her door after the paramedics had taken her away, so he marched right inside, determined to learn the truth about that terrible book and why she might possess it.

Her apartment was, as always, immaculate, with not so much as a hairbrush out of place. The large, canopied bed was made, the dinette full of clean, neatly-stacked china and utensils, the bath freshly scrubbed, with all her toiletries laid out neatly on the shelf above the lavatory. Nowhere was the mysterious book to be seen.

Painfully discarding his sacred respect for others' property, he began a thorough search of the rooms, checking every drawer, every closet, every cabinet. Even inside the medicine chest, the jewel box, the niche where the linens were folded and stacked. No sign of the book. And yet, Mrs. Kate had not left the premises before her attack, and, surely, she could not have deposited it downstairs without his knowledge.

Confused, angry, and almost childishly afraid, Trull gnashed his teeth and swore under his breath at having been foiled. In here, he could not hear those strange noises, and he was reluctant to go back into the hall. What about the guests? What if any of them should hear the sounds and question him? What could he possibly say? Knowing of nothing else to do, he resolved to confront the apparent source of the trouble–the image of Jacob Asberry in the gallery.

He turned to leave the apartment and, suddenly, found himself facing a twisted, leering fright-mask that caused him to jump backward with a mouse-like squeak of terror. His heart almost stopped; then he realized that the features before him belonged to the dour Mrs. Penelope Prillaman, and she was glaring at him with quite inexplicable ire.

"Why, uh . . . Mrs. Prillaman," he stammered, "you startled me. I, uh. . . ." His voice trailed away as he saw the woman's face undergo a shocking change. Her eyes widened until he could see white all the way around her cloudy, gray irises, and her brow arched so that the wrinkles in her mottled forehead became deep crevasses. Her lower jaw dropped, exposing crooked, yellowed teeth, her mouth opening wider and wider–so wide that he thought the skin of her cheeks would split. And finally, a long gasp escaped her lungs with a rough, grating sound–"Gyaaggh!"–blown quite rudely into Trull's mortified face.

The odor made him gag, and he turned away with a choked sob. "Oh! Oh!" he cried, covering his mouth and nose with his hand. It was the utterly putrid stench of corrupted flesh–like a multitude of dead fish washed onto a polluted beach. Could this woman have taken seriously sick as well?

Oh, God, surely the flounder hadn't been bad!

"Mrs. Prillaman, I'm sorry," he gurgled, ashamedly turning to face her. But the woman was gazing down at him with those horribly bulging eyes, her head at an unnatural height. And then he realized that–*my God*–her feet were no longer touching the floor. Instead, they hovered almost a yard above the carpet, her thin body hanging in the air like a puppet suspended by invisible threads. Her arms suddenly began to quiver and jerk reflexively, like the appendages of a freshly-killed insect. Then, with a quick motion, the floating figure spun and drifted into the hallway, the head and eyes still fixed on Trull, who barely kept himself from dropping to the floor in a dead faint.

The airborne body whisked out of view, heading toward the stairs. For several heartbeats, Trull could only gape dumbly, but when he finally regained control of his senses, he leaped into the hall, crying out in panic, "Oh! Mrs. Prillaman! Mrs. Prillaman!"

He came out just in time to see the elderly woman pitch headlong down the stairs, to crash in a twisted heap at the foot. Her deep voice boomed up from below, "Ghyaaaggh! Ghyaaaggh!" As he reached the top of stairs and gazed down in horror, he could see her writhing convulsively on the floor, arms and legs thrashing like angry snakes stirred from winter slumber. He almost started down the stairs after her, but the glare from those brilliant eyes stopped him.

The woman's head lay at an awry angle, bent backwards from a wrecked spine. Surely, she must be dead. She *had* to be dead! But the arms and legs were still moving. And the sounds she was making!

"Ghyaaagh! Ghyaaagh!"

"Oh! Oh!" Trull cried, eyes questing frantically about the hallway, at the closed doors around him. Then, from behind, came the sound of a door creaking open, somewhere in the northern wing. For several seconds, he heard nothing more, and he feared that another floating body might appear around the corner. But when no such evil thing confronted him, and he could hear the normal groan of floorboards beneath the slow treading of feet, he breathed a small, cautious sigh of relief. Then he realized that, no matter the horrible racket they might have heard, no guests must see the wretched thing flopping about at the foot of the stairs!

He strode forward to meet the guest, to insist that, for the moment, everyone remain in his or her room. Best to call the police, and let them sort it out. Rounding the corner, he started to say, "Excuse me, could I ask you to . . . ," but then he stopped, for–to his dismay–the hall was quite empty.

"No," Trull breathed, positive his ears had not played tricks on him. "It isn't possible."

But then, of course, neither was an airborne Mrs. Prillaman.

As he stood there quivering, he began to sense that, indeed, he was not alone in the hall. *Something* hid in the corridor, something as intangible as shadow. What if it should be the thing that had turned poor Mrs. Prillaman into that monstrous mess downstairs?

"What the hell are you?" he whispered. "What do you want?"

The floorboards creaked as if someone had taken a tentative step. And from the empty air, a voice began to chant, "Eyaagh, igg shogg g'naii neb f'taghn."

Yes . . . it was the voice that had come from the painting of Jacob Asberry. But now it was free and roaming the halls of the old hotel.

He suddenly remembered what Mrs. Kate had said: that he was supposed to evacuate the place immediately in the event of her death. Did this horror, then, mean that. . . .

"No," he whispered, backing slowly away. "Go away. Leave me alone!"

The wall blocked his retreat. To his right, there was only a locked guestroom door. To his left lay the stairway and the raging, all-too-recently-human-thing at the bottom. He vaguely heard the sound of a television somewhere on the floor. Oh, God, the guests! His eyes shot back and forth frantically, while his limbs remained frozen. He felt an icy chill in the air and smelled a ghastly, fishlike stench.

Oh, no! It was coming for him–to make him like Mrs. Prillaman, to take his body and twist it. . . .

Out of the corner of his eye, he could see the old woman below; thankfully, her struggles seemed to be diminishing. The rage in her face softened, and then her mouth opened in a horrified, pitiable scream of complete awareness of her condition. Somehow, she lived long enough for her eyes to gaze upon the wreckage of her body, then her spirit rushed out of her mouth and fled, unable and unwilling to sustain its ruined envelope.

"Nooo!" he cried, as something bitterly cold brushed his face. Re-

flexively, he leaped away, moving toward the locked guestroom door. But then, his eyes fell upon the little red box on the wall, and, unable to think of anything else to do, he pulled the lever with all his strength, fragmenting the protective glass bar. A shrill, jangling bell split the silence of the corridor, so close to his ears that he was completely deafened. For the moment, the cold thing failed to grasp him, and the next thing he knew, one of the doors down the hall was flying open.

A big, muscular man, a Mr. Lawrence Tilton from Danville, stepped out and regarded him with worried eyes. He was wearing a bathrobe and black socks, his gray hair tousled. "Young man, what is going on?" he called.

Trull felt another cold brush against his cheek. All that squeaked past his lips was: "Uh . . . fire."

"What?"

"Fire. Fire! *Fire!*"

Then he was bellowing at the top of his lungs, spinning around wildly, fists flailing, as if he might beat the invisible horror to death. "Everybody out! Everybody out! Fire! Fire!"

Doors began opening, and elderly folk began to shuffle into the hallway, some plugging in hearing aids, then pulling them out again as the firebell shrieked at them. Still, the cold thing assailed him, refusing to let go in the confusion. Trull pushed his way through the tide of senior citizens, beating on doors, screaming incomprehensibly. He had to get out. He had to get *everyone* out!

"My God!" cried a short, stooped woman, a Mrs. Amelia Burke from Norfolk, who'd seen the shattered figure below. "What's happened?"

"Oh, an accident!" someone cried. "A terrible accident!"

"Fire!" Trull screamed. A cold fist had seized his skull, and, as if he were outside looking in, he saw his feet leave the floor. One of his flailing arms caught poor Mrs. Burke in the temple, knocking her down. "Sorry!" he cried but was then thrown down the stairs, his head banging painfully into the banister. He thudded gracelessly into a heap next to the broken body, and his head came to rest directly in front of Mrs. Prillaman's vacant eyes.

"Yaah!" he cried as he scrambled to his feet, arms beating at the cold that once again swirled hungrily around him. A commentary on rudeness followed him from above, but in his desperate flight, he was forced to ignore it. Thank God the guests were now filing in semi-orderly fashion down the stairs, and a thoughtful Mr. Tilton gently took hold of Mrs. Prillaman's limp arms and moved her out of the way so that the less agile among them might not trip. Then, they were heading for the front door, eyes wandering back and forth, some of them sniffing the air, no doubt trying to decide whether there really was a fire. But a distinctly foul stench assured them that all was not right in the building, and they seemed quite relieved once they had achieved the safety of the sidewalk.

Trull made to follow them out, but again, a cold, deadly hand closed over his skull, and his feet left the ground. Something frigid and wet, like a cold earthworm, tried to pry its way into his mouth, and only a supreme effort kept his jaws clenched. But it was wriggling into his nostrils, his ears . . . *it* wanted inside him, and he could not escape it. He fell into the gallery, rolling and sobbing on the floor, in full view of the painting on the wall. Jacob Asberry stared disdainfully at him, as horrible, chilling spikes of evil energy tore at his body. Trull screamed, "Get away from me! Get away from me!"

Then, the cold was all he knew.

"Get away! Get away!"

He thrashed and writhed, trying to escape the steel vises that clutched him. Then, as his vision returned, he realized that it was a gloved hand gripping his arm, and bright red lights were flashing all around him. The fire department. They had brought him outside!

Somehow, he had escaped!

He scrambled to his feet and saw a fair-sized crowd standing around the building. He expected everyone to be looking at him, for he'd surely behaved like a madman. But then he saw that his fears were unfounded, for even the fireman who'd carried him out was not looking at him, but at the old hotel that rose moodily above them.

All eyes were focused on his beloved workplace of nine years. From within the hotel pealed a deep, rumbling sound, and he saw the window panes shaking. He pulled free from the fireman's grip, and everyone began backing into the street and surrounding yards as a violent tremor caused the old structure to shake and sway precariously. Nervous murmurs swept through the crowd, and Trull heard Mrs. Burke's voice cry out, "Oh, no, it's going to fall!"

"What's happening?" he cried as, from the rear of the building came the sound of shattering glass. That foul, fishy stench suddenly washed over the crowd, causing many to gag. Trull feared that, at any moment, those cold fingers might again clutch at him in attempt to invade his body and soul.

"Look! Look there!" someone shouted, and his eyes followed several pointing fingers to a hazy, swirling shape creeping around the hotel from the rear. Then, one of the side windows blew out, spewing glass fragments into the yard next door, and a thick, smoky mist rolled over the sill. Trull saw the ring of dark, near-liquid substance increasing its speed as it rushed around the structure, forming a roaring, black funnel that rose toward the sky. The spectators began backing away in panic, and Trull scurried under a tall oak tree in the yard across the street, his pulse pounding even louder than the thundering cyclone. A jagged shard of glass whipped past his face, missing him by inches, and he dropped to the ground, covering his head with his arms. The roar began to form a weirdly modulated voice—no, a chorus of voices—rising, shrilling higher into a deafening wail, like hundreds of souls screaming in agony.

With a loud ripping sound, the old Broad Street Hotel was wrenched from its foundations and rose into the air, borne on the raging devil-wind. For several moments, it floated atop the funnel, then exploded with a deafening boom, hurling pieces of itself into the night sky like dark fireworks. The thunder echoed for what seemed like ages before finally fading, and the black funnel began to dissipate, leaving only a heavy, expectant layer of silence that slowly settled over the crowd.

Then, the pieces of the building began to rain down: huge, partially intact portions of wall, books, chairs, plates, pieces of luggage. Wreckage clattered like hail to the street, some crashing into the neighboring houses, and some—most horribly—crushing a few unlucky spectators; poor Mrs. Burke from Norfolk among them. Worst of all, from all over town, loud *thuds* and *booms* could be heard for several minutes as far-flung pieces of the building continued to fall from the heavens, and people all the way to the town limits were forced indoors for fear of being struck and killed.

Beneath his tree, coated in a foul-smelling layer of dust and grime, Jonathan Trull gazed into the empty sky, for a moment thinking that he saw a dark, swirling form blot out the stars before disappearing into the night. A kind fireman rushed to help him to his feet, only to withdraw in bewilderment as he heard the dazed young man mutter, "I'll be damned. They've checked out."

Then, looking down, Trull saw it. Right at his feet, as if placed there by magic: the thick, leather-bound book he'd seen in Mrs. Kate's room earlier that afternoon. He knelt to pick it up.

That night, Jonathan Trull was taken to a shelter at the YMCA, where he collapsed, exhausted, clutching an old, crumbling book that not even the strongest attendant could pry from his grasp.

Indeed, Mrs. Kate Forbish had died of congestive heart failure that evening—at the precise time that Trull had begun to hear the strange noises in the doomed hotel. The next day, after being sent home, he carried the book he'd finally finished reading out to his backyard and set it on fire.

The Broad Street Hotel, before it was a hotel, had been a hospital, erected by the one and only Dr. Jacob Asberry. From the entries in the book, which turned out to be Asberry's personal journal, Trull learned that the Asberry Hospital had been less a house of healing than a house of death. From its opening in 1866 until its conversion to hotel in 1930, the building had been a site of untold horror and suffering that few people, even in its day, had ever known about or even suspected.

Jacob Asberry worshipped strange gods, as his own handwriting revealed. Incredibly ancient, often going by epithets such as "The Unnameable," or "Him Who is Not to be Named," the deities Asberry revered spoke to him in dreams and demanded tribute, usually in the form of blood. Trull grew even more shocked as he learned that the hospital had been built as little more than a slaughterhouse, where "Doctor" Asberry might easily procure the sick, the injured, the dying; those whom he could remove from existence with minimal risk of discovery. Anyone was admitted, especially transient and unemployed men; those who had no families, no money. The doctor, certainly, was nothing less than charitable. As often as possible, though, Asberry daringly requested permission from wealthy patients' families to attempt "experimental treatments," or to have their bodies retained for the "furthering of medical science;" in those days, when trust played a far greater role in society than in today's world, he succeeded with alarming regularity. Hundreds of victims apparently died at Asberry's hands over the years, often in brutal, inhumane fashion. Trull grew nauseated at entries which luridly described the ghoulish feasting on the bodies of "luscious young mothers who had 'died' during childbirth." Sometimes, even the babies were "stillborn."

The authorities had never questioned the doctor for so much as the most insignificant offense. Asberry enjoyed a reputation as a severe, dedicated man of medicine, perhaps overzealous and more suited to the role of scientist than humanitarian, but without question as a man of impeccable character. Even after so many deaths, so many bodies that were never lowered into hallowed ground, no one never awoke to the atrocities being committed in the heart of the little Virginia town.

No wonder Mrs. Kate kept the book hidden. She knew about her father's work, but had never—thank God—practiced her father's unusual religion. Apparently, though, near the end of his life, Dr. Asberry had warned her that he had been "betrayed" by the ones he worshipped. He swore that, upon his death, those poor souls he had offered to his gods would return to escort him to eternal torment, rather than to the heavenly domain of those he'd served. He had taught his daughter certain banishment rituals, so that he might escape the retribution they promised. Supposedly, after his death, his spirit had found sanctuary in the gallery of the building, and Mrs. Kate wielded the power to hold the angry spirits of the dead at bay—but only as long as she lived.

So, when Mrs. Kate passed on, the only barrier preventing those poor, tortured spirits from exacting their revenge had been removed, and in they'd rushed: an insane, ghostly horde hell-bent on the total destruction of that house of pain—and, unfortunately, anything and anyone that happened to reside within its walls.

At the memory of those cold, dead clutches, Trull retreated into a comfortably warm inner sanctum, full of peaceful, orderly rooms, where he remained until that dreadful night seemed nothing more than a vague, frightening dream that he could cast away at will.

Rodney Fox from Cable 6, seeking a sensational story from the star eyewitness, tried on numerous occasions to interview him, but failed miserably each time, for Trull's mind did not come out from hiding for well over a year.

The events at the Broad Street Hotel remained wholly unexplained, and the surviving witnesses all chose to believe that some freak storm had blown in, resulting in the destruction of the building. The tragic deaths that night–nine, all totaled–were ruled accidental, and everyone figured that Jonathan Trull's temporary insanity was caused by the unusual conditions the storm had generated. Nothing similar had ever happened in Aiken Mill's history, and everyone in town, especially the families of the victims, were known to pray in church every Sunday for a holy restraining order against encore performances.

The painting of Jacob Asberry was found in the mountains of Tennessee, over 400 miles away. Somehow, after being hurled into the sky by the explosion, it was carried by the winds and deposited on earth, miraculously undamaged. It found its way back to Aiken Mill, courtesy of a farmer who discovered it on his property and learned its origin from the nameplate on the frame. It now hangs in the foyer of the mortuary that replaced the hotel.

Even after his recovery, Trull never uttered a single word about that night. He took a job as assistant manager at the local Sheraton, which was a healthy, modern fabrication of glass and metal, and the clientele were generally of the more active, business-oriented sort. Sadly, his employment was abruptly terminated a year later when he fatally assaulted a guest, who had registered under the name of J. R. Asberry. As Trull was taken away by the police, he was heard to chant something that witnesses quote as a mish-mosh of nonsensical verbiage–something to the effect of, "Eyaagh, igg shogg r'lyeh fuckin' f'taghn!" He was placed under lock and key, and later that night, he mysteriously disappeared from his jail cell.

Jonathan Trull was never seen or heard from again. No blood, no clothing, not a single personal item had been left behind. The last words that could be attributed to Trull were heard by only one inmate, who reported that Trull exclaimed, "Dammit, I never learned the words to her song!" shortly before he vanished. While no satisfactory conclusions regarding the case were ever reached, Rodney Fox, the nefarious investigative reporter from Cable 6, at long last, had his shining moment in the sun.

The Grey House

There are times when a memory is so vivid that one can fall into it and relive events exactly as they originally happened, as if the intervening months and years simply never existed. A certain smell, or particular sound, or a unique combination of sensory elements may act as a catalyst to propel the present back to the past. For as surely as the body may travel the spaces between one point and another, the spirit may at times free itself of its corporeal host and explore time by way of memory—perhaps the purest form of travel one may undertake.

It was a photograph that started such a feeling with me. That, and the nostalgic warmth of being home again after so many years of living in the far-away city. The family house had changed little since I had left as an ambitious 18-year-old—some 20 years earlier, but in these rooms lurked the unmistakable aura of a life left behind that I never realized I had missed. Now, having come to settle the estate following the passing of my mother, I found my reminiscences inevitably bittersweet. I'd achieved success in the Atlanta business community; but I'd never built what felt like a home there.

The photo I held was at least fifty years old, taken by one of my family before I was even born. The edges were crinkle-cut, the paper curled and the emulsion darkened. But the image was crisp and clear, like the day on which it must have been taken. In its black and white tones I could see the shades of autumn, feel the heatless sunlight, smell the smoke-tinged breeze. I saw the sagging, sooty roof crossing a tree-lined horizon that faded into gray mist; the broken chimney that gouged a dark, jagged outline into the soft white emptiness of the autumn sky. It was a contour to evoke feelings of age and decrepitude.

The years began to fade away.

The woods around my house had always seemed like a part of my family. From the day I was old enough to walk, I'd begun to explore them, always venturing farther and farther into their alluring depths, becoming acquainted with each towering tree, each roll and dip of the meandering countryside. With every excursion I felt more at home. Our house lay on the outskirts of Beckham, Virginia, in the shadow of Mount Signal, where the forest grew dense and unpopulated, save for the adventurers who traveled on the Appalachian Trail. A certain tranquility existed here, a serenity that I thought to be exactly what I wanted from life.

There was, however, one complicating aspect of this idyllic setting: the night. At night, especially in autumn, the wind would moan eerily through the dry, leafless trees, and the whippoorwills would begin their ghostly singing. To my youthful mind, they were disturbingly loud, even ominous. Even by the time I reached adolescence, I could not believe that such a monstrous noise could come from a small, harmless bird. To most people, I'm sure, the whippoorwill poses no more threat than a friendly, wise owl. But when I heard those shrill cries begin, I cowered under my bedclothes and cried myself to sleep, sincerely believing that, disguised as the song of a nightbird, the voices of the dead were screaming.

On the afternoon of my twelfth birthday, I began blazing a new path up the steep hillside a mile or so into the woods behind my house. My excitement was keen and adrenaline pumped in my veins as I fearlessly staked my claim on this as yet unexplored territory. It was a week after Thanksgiving, and a carpet of brittle leaves crunched sharply beneath my feet. Passing between two trees, I shredded a delicately woven web, caring nothing for the sluggish crab spider that crouched in the elbow of a limb, awaiting the freeze that would soon kill it. There were treasures in these woods, and I desired to find them all.

Suddenly, I came to a large clearing, and there it was. Beyond a ridge of green-black evergreens rose the hulking roof of the gray house, sitting silent and lonely amid the dark forest. It was really no more than a small cabin; but to find it practically in my own backyard seemed shocking, since I'd never had any inkling that such a thing existed. No smoke trickled from the broken chimney, nor did any sound hint that the cabin might be occupied. Boyish excitement rose like a little fire in me; I'd made a new discovery, and was determined to claim it as my own. I cautiously crept across the clearing and peered through the veil of evergreens to look more closely at this ancient marvel.

I couldn't begin to guess the place's true age. Its roof was crumbling, covered with black tar shingles, some of which were missing. Cobwebs and thick dust smeared the leaden windows, three of which peered from the splintered, charcoal-colored siding I faced. Beyond the windows lurked only pure darkness.

I moved to my left, where I could better view the tilted, shingled awning covering a broken stairway. An outer frame door hung open, its wire screen shredded. Three narrow panes of glass lined the wooden door, which was sealed with a black, rusted padlock.

This was surely the most classic of haunted houses.

I crept around to the tiny, weed-choked backyard and found that someone had obviously been here in the relatively recent past: a couple of tin cans lay half-buried in the matted leaves, their rims sprinkled with brown rust. Some chipped bricks had been placed in a circle, forming a crude fireplace. A few black cinders remained in their midst. Somebody detouring from the Appalachian Trail had camped here, I guessed, for I was sure no one could have lived in the house during my lifetime.

Pausing by a tree, I suddenly discovered an odd pattern in the bark next to my head. It was no natural formation, but a design cut into the wood by a blade: a cross in the center of a circle, from which radiated a series of wavy lines. I found the same sign carved into a number of trees that ringed the clearing, as if it were something sacred. I then went up to the hazardous staircase and directed my gaze into the dark recess beneath the awning. The sign was there, carved just above the doorjamb.

I breathed an excited, "Wo!" I knew about hex signs and pentagrams, and I wondered if the people who'd lived here had been witches. I began to feel a trifle nervous, as if I were trespassing on forbidden property. Looking to the sky, I saw that it was getting late; the shadows were growing long and the evening breeze had begun to pick up. It was time to be getting home.

However, I did not want to quit this place without leaving a design of my own upon it. These were *my* woods; therefore the house became part of my territory by default. So, decisively, I lifted a brick from the fireplace and went around to the side I'd first approached. Hefting the brick to my shoulder and taking careful aim at the middle window, I thrust with all my strength. I felt a swell of satisfaction as the missile struck the target with a violent crash, sending shards of glass and hunks of wood flying. The echo of that explosion rang in the air for endless seconds, receding deeper and deeper into the rapidly darkening valley. My fists clenched in unchecked glee as I surveyed my jagged handiwork.

Then there arose a sound that chilled my blood to proverbial icewater. My ecstasy instantly turned to terror as the bellowing voice of a whippoorwill erupted from within the house: a voluminous roar unlike any I'd ever heard. I had never been out in the woods when the whippoorwills started. Now, with the speed that only mortal terror could generate, I turned and fled toward my house with the horrible, wailing cry pursuing me like the devil itself.

The sound did not cease for the rest of the evening. I cried to my mother and father that something terrifying was out there; that those shrieks could not possibly come from any innocent bird. My parents' every attempt to calm me met with no success, so they shut me into my dark room to sob, alone and disconsolate. I couldn't understand why they didn't hear it: a deep, horrid bellow, more distant and far stronger than any of the other whippoorwills. It came from the old gray house.

Sometime after midnight, I must have fallen asleep. Because when my illuminated clock read 2:45 a.m., I woke up to an eerie silence so profound that it seemed worse than the howling of the birds. My curtains fluttered gently, as if to beckon me toward the window. At first, I stayed bundled beneath the covers, but after a few minutes, the lure was too strong. I slid out of bed and pattered to the window, taking hold of my drapes with a trembling hand.

Pulling back that curtain was one of the most harrowing ordeals of my life. At first, I could see only pitch blackness. Then, as my eyes adjusted, I began to make out the crystal clear stars in the cold ebony dome overhead. The trees at the edge of the yard were nothing more than tall, black ghosts, swaying slightly back and forth in the soundless breeze. I gazed into the depths of that blackness, toward the spot in the distance where I guessed the gray house lay.

Something was moving at the edge of the woods. It was impossible to see clearly, but a long, black shadow slithered silently through the trees like a huge snake. It wound purposefully among the trunks, moving along the perimeter of the yard in the direction of my window. Hypnotized, I watched it, wanting to scream for my Mom and Dad, but paralyzed from my toes to my vocal cords. As the shadow drew nearer, the sound of my beating heart thundered in my ears, and if the thing outside made any noise at all, I'd have never heard it.

A tiny light appeared amid the trees, then another, then another; like big fireflies, I thought, pale and greenish-yellow. They swayed slowly back and forth, strangely beautiful in the sea of blackness. My heart began to slow, and my rigid limbs began to relax. I might have remained mesmerized by those vivid orbs—*those eyes*—had not a sudden shrill wail burst from the shadowy mass with such volume that I thought the window would shatter.

The cry of a whippoorwill. Or so it seemed. The sound was deeper, coarser than the song of the birds.

Now I cried out, stumbling away from the window until the bedpost stopped me. I turned to run through my door, bound for my Mom and Dad's room, when the light was suddenly flicked on and I was halted by my father's strong hands.

"God damn, son!" came a growl almost as menacing as the thing outside. "What are you yelling about now?"

I couldn't speak. I could only gape at my father in pure relief, not fearing the spanking that was sure to follow this episode, not fearing it all.

But I was spared even that, for a moment later, my mother cried in a pained voice for my father to come quickly. For several horrified heartbeats, I feared that Mom must have seen the thing outside, and that it would suddenly burst inside to kill us all. But the pain my mother suffered was of a far different nature, and my dad immediately packed up and carried her to the hospital, where, exactly twelve years and one day after my own birth, my little sister entered the world, screaming.

Occasionally, I have wondered about the origins of deep-seated phobias. I have known any number of people with seemingly irrational fears of mundane objects, even such as my sister Karen, who is deathly afraid of all slithering creatures. Show her a snake, or even worse, a slug, and she will most likely fall into a dead faint. Sometimes I think there must be such a thing as ancestral memory; perhaps an individual's acute, seemingly baseless fear may be traced back to a terrible confrontation by some ancient relation with the object of that fear. This theory has never boasted much scientific credence, but it is one to which I steadfastly subscribe. One might ask what possible threat a whippoorwill could have ever presented to a distant ancestor. The whippoorwill itself? No threat whatsoever, I would say; but something imitating it, a chameleon of sorts, far more malevolent than a nocturnal songbird. . . .

So, more than 25 years later, I found the photograph that inspired these vivid recollections of my childhood, memories that have since been rationalized by the sum total of experience, education and cynicism acquired after several years of city living. Now regarding with the seasoned eyes of an adult the familiar structure in the photo, the memory of that mortal fear had something of a charming quality. Dampening the intensity of such terror from ages ago is indeed one of the blessings of time's passing. And so armed with an adult's ability to distinguish between nightmare and reality, I made the decision to return to that isolated gray house in the woods for the first time since the day I'd discovered it.

The afternoon was approaching evening when I set out, much as on the day when I'd first found the place. The same low wind rustled through the dry boughs, now sparsely adorned by the last hangers-on of the season. Farther up the first big hill, the white pines towered over the surrounding skeletal branches, still wearing their resilient, bristly coats of needles. To my right and down in the valley, I could see the angled roofs of several houses, none of which had been there when I was growing up. In a few more years, I reflected sadly, this whole area might be entirely developed, like so much of the land around Beckham. The advance of civilization was not to be halted, a fact that I sometimes greatly lamented.

From the altitude where I stood, I could see for miles in every direction. Below and behind me, the Beckham Road snaked through the valley like an asphalt ribbon, disappearing to the northeast toward Aiken Mill. My old path was dense with overgrown foliage, the result of so many years' disuse. To my left, I saw the old pine with its ladder-like array of broken limbs that I had climbed countless times as a lad. Thirty feet up in the trunk, my carved initials identified it as a part of my territory. These were still *my* woods, as friendly and inviting in daylight as they ever had been. Before me, the land fell into a steep decline, marking the frontier I had crossed only once. Beyond it, the land rose again, and at the top, my destination waited.

The thrill of youth fell upon me again. I quickened my pace to match the rhythm of my heart, plodding into the valley as rapidly as the bramble-choked trail would allow. On the other side, I could see a break in the network of spindly branches that marked the clearing. Some intuitive sense told me that the gray house would still be there.

As I neared the summit, I could see a tall row of black evergreens, hiding a barely discernible, angular shape. The evergreens had grown at least twenty feet since I'd last seen them. It was beautiful. Here again as a man, I felt no childish fear, only the renewed excitement of a twelve-year-old on the verge of a new experience. The brisk air felt wonderful in my heaving lungs.

I entered the clearing. The house stood there, virtually unchanged. A few more shingles had slipped from the roof, and the hanging doorframe in front had finally fallen into ruin. The middle window of the facing wall, shattered, gaped like a blind eye at my approach. All around the house, bare branches hung like gnarled, groping fingers. Not a creak issued from the wooden structure.

The odd markings on the trees . . . I searched them out, found them, several feet higher than they'd been those years ago. Once again I allowed my imagination to indulge in creative explanations; however, my rational mind quickly shoved all suspicions of witchcraft and sorcery behind the more likely possibility that mischievous children or even adults had once etched the designs as nothing more than exercises in primitive art. But I refused to allow maturity to spoil my enjoyment.

I decided to carry my exploration a step further. If it could be safely accomplished, I was going inside that house. I'd given the idea no conscious consideration on my journey here, though in my subconscious, it must have been a smoldering desire. I knew the prospect could be hazardous–I might fall through the floor and end up injured or stuck with no way out. But I was more than willing to take the chance as far as practicality allowed.

My first step was to try the front door. The five boards that led up to it were cracked and unusable, but the wooden struts and splayed railing provided just enough support for me to climb up and peer through the clouded windows. The darkness inside leered back at me. Trying the hollow, rusted doorknob confirmed that it was locked up, but a solid kick, I felt, would take care of both the knob and the brittle padlock.

I drew back, gripping the railing for safety, and put my weight into a swift kick. With a heavy thud and a rough clatter, the knob and lock fell into rusty debris as the wormy gray door flew open. A cloud of dust erupted from the sepulchral emptiness within. The smell of age and decay rolled out like a dense fog, nearly causing me to choke. But as I waved the dust and odor away, I began to be able to make out the features of a large, dark room, even though very little sunlight penetrated the gloom. I had to wonder how many years had passed since anyone had stepped over this rotted threshold.

I had to pick my steps very carefully. Pulling myself in through the door was easy enough, but inside, I could see yawning holes in the uneven, sagging floor. Below was only total darkness. I clung close to the wall where support would be the strongest.

The first room was the largest, taking up the full width of the house and half the length. There were no furnishings, save for a set of empty bookshelves in the far corner. Tattered, stained wallpaper hung in brown strips from the water-damaged walls. At the far end of the room to the right, a dark rectangle indicated a door leading to the next room. The air reeked of mildew, mixed with some cloying, unidentifiable, and thoroughly unpleasant odor.

Hugging the walls, I crept to the right, wary of the deep creaks that resounded with each footstep. Once, I thought, I heard a harsh sliding sound coming from below; I decided that an animal must have made its home in the cellar and had been disturbed by my entry. There was generally nothing more dangerous than an opossum or raccoon in these woods, so I paid the sound no mind. I continued into the room until I reached the shattered remains of the second window in the right-hand wall. Then, tracing what I thought would be a logical trajectory, I let my gaze wander to the center of the floor. Yes, there it was . . . lying untouched for all these years . . . the brick I'd hurled through the window.

Seeing that brick sparked a resurgence of apprehension. I stopped, listened . . . as if expecting to hear the cry of a whippoorwill. There are no whippoorwills in the city, and I hadn't heard their song for all these many years. I wondered if my phobia would resurface should one of them begin its song. I didn't think so. I was confident I had outgrown that fear.

Leaving the fragment of the past on the floor, I sidestepped a gaping rift in the planked floor and made my way to the door. In the next room I could see only formless shadows. Outside, the sun would be waning, and I would have to waste little time to get out of the woods by sundown.

Stepping into the small room, I discovered that this was the house's kitchen: a square, cramped cubicle with a single filthy window that admitted virtually no light. The squat iron woodstove in the left-hand corner looked to be a hundred years old; next to it stood a set of warped shelves, and on them rested a number of jars containing some yellowed, powdery grain. These things, so putrid with age and decay, sent a shudder of revulsion through my stomach, giving me the impression that this had once been the abode of someone slovenly and vile. The air smelled even more sickly here, and I could not keep images of disease and rot from infringing on my nostalgic state of mind.

There was only one other room, an even darker grotto beyond the door to the left. So little light penetrated here that I was reluctant to walk on the rickety floor without a flashlight to guide me. I carried a cigarette lighter in my pocket, so I decided to use it, regardless that I was in a veritable tinderbox. Lighting it and holding it before me like a torch, I gingerly stepped over the threshold and tested the integrity of the boards before placing my full weight upon them. They groaned in protest, but held up under the strain.

Suddenly, there came a violent scraping sound far beneath my feet. From a wide gap in the center of the floor billowed a cloud of dust, as if something large in the cellar had been startled and moved quickly. For the first time I considered that there might be something down there large enough to be threatening. It felt like a good time to vacate the premises before one of us discovered the other.

But what I saw in that room held me there. I could only stare in mute fascination at the state of the room, as much as I could make out in the flickering light. An unfamiliar, fetid odor crawled through the cave-like chamber that looked as if some insane decorating party had been held in years past. Black, shiny splotches of what looked like splattered tar covered the walls. Long trails of age-dried ichor snaked over the pitted floor as if a huge, pitch-covered snail had dragged itself around the room. And drawn in red on the far wall shone the ornate symbol that was carved in the trees and above the house's front door. My jaw dropped as a new, mature feeling of apprehension chilled my blood.

Braving the less-than-sturdy floor, I stepped into the room and over the puddle of dried tar. I ran my hand over the surface of the stuff. It felt cool, thick and smooth. It dripped like hardened wax into a two-foot gash in the floor, as if whatever had left the trail had slipped down into that darkened space. I leaned over and peered tentatively into the pit.

Something moved. I heard a hiss, as if a massive pair of lungs had drawn a breath. I backed away with a start.

My hand fell upon something hard and cold. Looking down, I saw that the object was a dull, tarnished gold ring. A wedding band, stuck fast in the pitch. Using all my strength, I was unable to pull it out.

Now I was puzzled and nervous, but curiosity prevented me from retreating. Standing up and moving away from the hole in the floor, I went to the only other item in the room: a dust-smothered wooden dresser.

The dresser was half-drowned in the black gel, but above its ornately-hewn trim, I could make out the word *"Shoggoth"* etched crudely in the wood. On the lowest shelf was a tiny, rusted jewel box–empty–and a decayed, moldy book bound in leather. Blowing the dust from the old tome, I discovered it was a King James Bible, and to my surprise, the cover was emblazoned with the mysterious symbol that seemed to preside over the house. Delicately turning back the cover, I found myself looking at a personalized inscription in the fragile, yellow leaf. It read:

Given this day of 1 January in the Year of Our Lord 1897 to our brethren, the honorable Gordon William Bryce. May the power of the Holy Spirit protect you from the clutches of the demon that torments you.

The name of Gordon Bryce was familiar to me.

It was my own name, minus the suffix IV.

When I was small, my parents had told me the story that my great-grandfather, the first of our family to settle in this region, had disappeared one night, never to be heard from again. Being a wholly righteous and Godly man, he'd made it his personal mission to preach the Holy Word to those who needed it. But the unenlightened mountain dwellers of his day didn't take kindly to him, and it was suspected that some of them had "done him in." That I had come to a place that had such historical significance to my family was not the outstanding fact that struck me; rather, it was my mounting suspicion that the true nature of his disappearance might be more horrifying than any old story could ever relate.

An abominable shudder shook me as another loud scraping sound rose from below. Then with loathsome deliberateness, I took the rust-encrusted jewel box from the bureau, held it over the gaping hole in the floor, and dropped the box in. It clattered sharply as it struck something in the darkness, then came to rest abruptly, as if it had been caught before it hit bottom.

Immediately, the deafening trill of the whippoorwill began. It was a blaring, urgent wail that filled the whole cabin, igniting the terror I'd known so intimately as a child . . . only now increased ten-fold, for I was in the same house with the thing I knew for certain had visited my yard in the night when I was twelve, something that mimicked the cry of a small, harmless bird.

From the hole in the floor rose another cloud of dust, then a long, black limb thrust itself out of the darkness: a whipping, barbed stalk as big around as the torso of a good-sized man. Another followed, then another, clattering against the floor with the sound of a crazed percussion orchestra. A large, rounded bulk began to rise through the opening, bending boards with painful groans as it ascended. A spray of glistening black ichor erupted from below and splattered the wall next to me. It dripped for a moment, then quickly hardened, and I knew that if it touched me, I would be trapped, to become prey for the horror in the cellar.

The last thing I saw in the house was a cluster of luminous discs atop waving stalks rising up to peer coldly at me, followed by a thick, oozing mass of dark, mottled plasma. Then, I saw only the weed-clogged path and the armies of tall trees rushing past me as I flew recklessly back toward my house under the deepening twilight sky. The harsh whippoorwill song rose in pursuit, but I did not look back. I ran with the terror of the devil upon me, blind to the branches and thorns that raked my clothes and skin.

I knew now that, almost a century ago, Gordon Bryce had been destroyed by an unearthly horror, a thing called *shoggoth* according to the carving on the old bureau. My grandfather had known that evil, and I had inherited the fear of its plagiarized voice. Had the Godless men Gordon Bryce sought to convert loosed that demon upon him, in retribution for his interfering in their affairs? Could their descendents still reside in this hidden corner of the Appalachians—*perhaps with full knowledge of the horror in the gray house?* The idea was too much for me to bear.

How I made it home without suffering cardiac arrest is almost as big a mystery. I could not bring myself to remain in my inherited house that night with that constant, bellowing cry ringing through the forest. I took what belongings I could pack in my car and drove all night until I reached the city; a haven from the thing that hid behind a voice that, in this day and age, only a select few such as myself might intuitively perceive as a falsehood.

I will never know the fate of the gray house, for I refuse to return to that valley ever again. Without consulting my sister, I sold the family house and, as compensation, sent the entire sum of payment directly to her. Not unexpectedly, she was upset with me for taking such liberties, but my simplified explanation—that I'd found the neighbors to be inexplicably hostile toward our family; perhaps a holdover from our great-grandfather's day—elicited no protest. Later, when I told her that the woods held some very ugly secrets, the actual nature of which I dared not insinuate, she gave me a deep, knowing look that chilled me to the core.

As siblings, we shared certain ancestral memories, and certain tendencies toward phobias. I think she understood.

S.

"SYLVAN COUNTY, VA—3 bedroom, 2 ½ bath Colonial home. Large porch, dining room, eat-in kitchen, unfinished basement, bonus room—could be used as rec room or library. Fireplaces in living room and master bedroom. Detached garage. Heavily wooded 5+ acre lot! Lake view! Needs some TLC. Great value for the $$$—$64,900 unfurnished, or $69,900 furnished. Lease with option to buy. Call Billie Stark for more information. MLS#765905"

TLC and then some, Galen McDonough thought sullenly as he guided his perfectly preserved 1963 Harley Duo Glide up the rock-studded driveway approaching the old house. A pair of tall stone chimneys jutted into the late afternoon sky like raised, knobby fists above a sturdy-looking but moss-encrusted roof. The columns of the broad front porch, once white, looked like sun-dried, barkless tree trunks, and the wood-paneled siding was the same color as the lumps of ice and snow in the driveway. At least the windowpanes appeared to be intact, and the door looked solid, with a brand new lock. Off to the right, he could see the lake, as advertised, through the scantily-dressed winter woods beyond a long, sloping yard.

He left his adored motorcycle at the foot of the flagstone walk and headed on shaky feet toward the front door. He'd been riding for three hours, and even with several layers of clothing and heavy gloves, the cold had cut through to his bones. But if Ms. Stark had spoken truly, the electricity and gas would already be turned on. With the key she'd given him, he unlocked the door, which swung open with a tired groan, unleashing a gratifyingly warm draft of air. Could it be that, with all that had gone wrong in the past 72 hours, he might actually be able to conclude this transaction without serious hurdle?

He flipped the lightswitch by the door, and, overhead, an electric candelabra flickered to life to illuminate the foyer. Before him, a carpeted staircase led to the second floor, and, to either side, arched portals opened to large, darkened rooms. He arbitrarily chose the room to the right, stepped inside, and groped for a switch. A moment later, the living room was revealed by the warm glow of two ornate lamps resting on squat wooden tables at either end of a long, plush-looking couch. Sure enough, apart from a healthy coating of dust on the furnishings–the Realtor had apparently not taken the trouble to cover them with plastic–the room looked smart and fairly livable.

The rest of the main floor appeared to be in reasonably good repair. Large rooms, sparsely furnished, but usable. Working refrigerator, thankfully cleaned and free of noisome bouquet. Upstairs, he found the bedrooms spacious and tidy, though covered with the ubiquitous dust he'd have to spend quite some time battling. The master bedroom, true to the ad, boasted a white brick fireplace, its rear wall scorched black from countless fires. The house was built in the 1920s, Ms. Stark had said, and had remained the property of a single family until the last member had died only a few months ago.

Ms. Stark had agreed to let him stay in the house for the weekend before making a decision, but already, he was leaning toward taking it. He didn't need three bedrooms, but he liked the idea of having a lot of space. And he didn't plan on remaining alone forever. If the interior were in as good condition as it appeared, he might even be willing to renovate the exterior. That, at least, would give him something to occupy his mind. Better than dwelling on the nightmare that had driven him here in the first place. . .

He had never intended to steal Ben Koury's wife.

What crap. You run off with a guy's wife, you do it on purpose. It doesn't happen by itself. Requires things like free will, mutual consent, malice aforethought, that sort of thing.

Galen didn't blame Ben for wanting to kill him. He might have done the same thing had positions been reversed. Galen hadn't hated the man when he began seeing Theresa, nor did he hate him now; Ben Koury was actually a fairly likeable fellow. No, it was just a matter of Ben's wife being dissatisfied with her mate–well, her whole life, actually–and discovering that Galen was the man she'd *wished* she'd met eight years ago. Galen, similarly disenchanted with his own home life, and reciprocally inclined toward Theresa, somehow found himself committing adultery one evening after she and Ben had had one of their frequent spats.

It was only an affair in the most technical sense of the word. The things they'd shared with each other . . . the enjoyment of each other's company . . . the almost predestined coupling . . . it had all seemed so very *right*—as if they weren't cheating on their spouses at all, but merely finding another partner to help fill all those little holes in their lives that simply couldn't be filled by any one individual.

None of that mattered when Ben found out. It was a wonder he hadn't killed both Galen and his wife on the spot. What he had done was much more sensible: he'd gone straight to Gina and told her exactly what her husband had been doing and with whom, and that if she were smart, she'd throw him out and urge him leave town for his own safety. Ben refused to be held responsible for whatever happened once the rein on his temper broke—an event that seemed imminently likely.

In his heart, Galen knew he could not rightfully defend himself if it came down to a confrontation. He was lucky just to have survived the resulting parley with his wife. Bitter, it was; very loud and very taxing, both physically and emotionally. Lying about the situation would have never washed. Forgiveness was out of the question. In the end, getting out seemed altogether the best solution.

But he reserved his deepest grief for Theresa. She was heartbroken, but both of them knew that they could never see each other again. She and Ben had resolved to stay together, no matter what it took, for the sake of their young daughter. But they would go through hell for a long time to come.

It was natural enough for Ben to cast blame solely upon Galen. Men fight for their territory and for their women; even unfaithful women.

So Galen had come here from Richmond, to this secluded lake in the mountains, with the idea that he could start out fresh. He needed to get away from the shitpile he'd dug himself into, and this—a place where he knew no one and no one knew him—seemed the most likely prospect. He was, in a word, rich as hell, and he could live comfortably more or less indefinitely, even if he wound up having to send money to Gina.

Who said money can't buy happiness?

Yes, it was simply best to forget Theresa, the six tolerable if not blissful years he'd spent with his wife . . . everything.

How he wished he could.

He had bought groceries and drink, enough to last him the weekend and then some, at the market in Aiken Mill on his way in. The weather didn't look promising, and a roof over his head, not to mention ample sustenance, would be imminently desirable if a winter storm broke. Fitting, wasn't it, that the sky should now take its turn to dump on him? Better to thank ye gods he'd found this place so readily, he decided, ever the optimist; he'd be a hell of a lot warmer out here in nowhereland than if he'd tried to parley any further with Gina at home.

He made the rounds through the house, inspecting the rest of the furnishings and fixtures, which generally seemed in good repair. Everywhere, though, there was dust, layer upon layer, some wadded into hefty bunnies, most of which he scooped onto the floor for vacuuming later. Once, he found himself dragging his finger through the dust on the dining room table, creating abstract designs like absurd graffiti. One of the designs spelled THERESA.

He wiped it away with his palm and heaved a disgusted sigh. He'd blown his life all to hell, and then elected simply to run away, rather than attempt to reconcile matters with his wife—not to mention the man who might well de-brain him with a blunt instrument at the first opportunity. Was it simply the easiest thing to do? The safest?

Or—was it what he had really wanted for himself all along?

Well, for now, he welcomed this isolation. This was a time for mourning, as surely as if a loved one had died. And for him, mourning was something best practiced alone.

Alone with Mr. Beam, anyway, he thought, pouring a stiff shot of whiskey into one of the cheap glasses he found in a cabinet. Mourning did have its moments. As the burn spread from his stomach through his bloodstream, he decided to have a look at the cellar—quickly, since it wasn't heated—for that was where he'd most likely find any remnants of the history had seeped into these walls. Indeed, lives had been spent here, some probably very happy, some perhaps even more miserable than his.

What good company such misery might make.

Going down and turning on the lonely lightbulb by its pull-string, he stepped into a veritable motherlode of historical paraphernalia: armoires full of old clothes, crates of books and papers, boxes loaded with cheap, gaudy-looking jewelry and knick-knacks. He began to rummage through it all, doubting he'd uncover anything of real value, as the Realtor surely would have been through here first, pursuing any free-floating bonus compensation. And apart from the books, most of which looked exceptionally old, he found little to capture his interest—until he noticed an oddly-shaped patch of darkness in the corner of his eye, revealed by the 40-watt glow of the exposed overhead bulb. Approaching it, he found a small niche in the stone wall, cut in an uneven hexagonal shape. The light gleamed off something shiny tucked within the recess; reaching in to find out what it was, he received a sudden jolt and a stabbing current of pain in his hand, as if he'd grabbed a live cattle prod. He didn't even have time to yank his hand away—his whole body lurched backward and might have collapsed altogether had he not encountered resistance from a large bureau behind him. He propped himself against it long enough to regain his balance; then, shaking off the mysterious shock, he leaned forward and peered into the dark opening, wondering what the hell could have zapped him.

The light barely defined the outlines of an irregularly-shaped metal container about the size of a small cake tin. Looking about the room, he spied a short, straw broom with a cane handle, which he picked up and poked into the opening. Gingerly, he slid the box forward, half-expecting to find it rigged with electrical wires. But as he scooped it fully into the light, he saw that it was just a plain, copper-colored box with six asymmetrical sides. A real oddity, he thought, but plainly without any electrical function.

So, what had shocked him? Static electricity?

No way.

Unable to stop himself, he put out a cautious hand and swiped at the metal with his fingertips. They touched only a cold, neutral surface. No electrical discharge. He dropped the broom and slowly, deliberately, put his hands upon the box–without ill effect–and lifted it, finding it remarkably heavy and unevenly balanced. Placing it on the bureau behind him, he lifted the hinged lid, and was startled by a sudden, ringing flute-like tone. He flipped the lid closed, and the sound ceased. When he opened the box again, the tone recommenced, warbling in his ears at an almost painful pitch, like the shriek of a bat.

Casting aside his surprise, he lifted the box into the light, and found himself staring at a strangely-shaped metal construct resting in its center. It reminded him somewhat of certain bizarre, three-dimensional modern art pieces he'd seen in his art history classes at college: a number of metal tubes and wires weaving in and out among themselves, forming an almost organic-looking figure, vaguely human-shaped when viewed from certain angles, but from others, appearing as nothing more than a tangled, metallic mass without any purposeful design. He couldn't tell what caused the sound it emitted; he guessed that the metallic strands stretching between some of the protruding armatures must vibrate much like the strings of a musical instrument. Sure enough, when he touched the thing–mindful of receiving another shock–the ringing tone muted.

With a bemused "heh," he closed the box, then turned his attention to the books stacked haphazardly on several different surfaces. Most of them appeared to be old reference books, lots of them scientific, some religious or philosophical, some without any titles or authors imprinted on the covers or spines. Opening one of them, he found only page after page of illegible, scrawled hashmarks that resembled nothing so much as certain runic symbols he'd seen on a bunch of New Age material some friends of his had once gotten into. The name "Derby" was scrawled in faded ink on several inner covers; others bore the name "Waite," seemingly in the same handwriting.

He arbitrarily grabbed a few of the books and, with his box, returned upstairs, for the clammy dimness of the basement had begun to chill him.

Closing the door behind him, he put the items on the kitchen table and poured himself another drink, feeling oddly satisfied, as if he'd discovered something intriguing, if not exactly valuable. It was probably just some novelty picked up in a junk shop for a buck, he thought, his enthusiasm momentarily dampened. Still, he couldn't get over the shock he'd gotten, which he could only attribute to static electricity, despite the stone floor and his own rubber-soled tennis shoes.

His thoughts then took another turn when he glanced out the window and saw, in the glow of the front porchlight, a swirling cyclone of snow dancing against a backdrop of complete darkness. He'd secured his motorcycle in the garage, thank God, and he was warm and set to weather an ugly weekend if that's what it came to. He left the metal box on the table and took the books upstairs with him, hoping that among them, he might find something at least mildly interesting to read before he retired for the evening.

The first one turned out to be just more hieroglyphics, and he tossed it aside. One of the others looked like a journal, which he figured might be more titillating than the other two he'd picked up: a softcover volume entitled *Ancient Iraq,* by Georges Roux, and a crumbling, leather-bound book of music, of all things, by Maurice Zann.

He found bedsheets and blankets in a linen closet next to the master bedroom, and made the king-sized bed, which must have been a true antique, with intricately carved posts at each corner that rose almost as high as his head. He briefly entertained thoughts of building a fire, for there had been a cache of firewood down by the front porch. But since that involved going out into the cold, he decided against it, even though he'd always fancied having a fireplace in his bedroom. If he took the property, he could build as many fires in the blasted thing as he wanted to. So, he changed out of his clothes and got ready to settle in for a night of solitude, determined to keep his mind on anything but the ruins of his life he'd left out on the doorstep.

He awoke with the bedside lamp still on and his book splayed open on the floor. His watch read 2:35 a.m., and his head felt like he'd stuffed it into wet cement and let it harden. No hangover–it was too soon, and he hadn't had that much to drink. He realized that *something* had drawn him from a restless sleep.

What the hell was that?

The ringing tone came from below, weaving its way up the stairs like a ghostly flute. Even from here, it seemed to charge the air, and Galen realized the hairs on his arms were standing up, as if he were about to be struck by lightning.

Just a damned minute. He'd closed that box, he knew that much. How could it be making a noise?

He rose and half-staggered out to the hall and down the stairs, briefly fancying himself a rat drawn by a tiny pied piper within an oddly-shaped metal prison. The kitchen light burned overhead–strange, for he was sure he'd turned it off!–and there, on the table, the box sat with its lid open: a gaping mouth whistling an eerie strain. He leaned down to study the wire framework within, but staying well back, for fear of receiving another shock.

The lid did not operate on a spring; there was no way the box could have just popped open. It had to have been done intentionally.

Was someone else inside the house?

He closed the lid, stifling the sound. In the sudden silence, the house seemed too large, too dark to be comfortable. Snow still whipped at the windows, and he could vaguely hear the low rumble of wind through the trees. He nervously looked around him, through the door to the darkened dining room and hall. No movement within the house; not even any old creaks and groans.

He had a short-barreled .32 revolver among his belongings upstairs. He'd had it for years, primarily for target shooting, but lately with the idea that he might have more than the usual need for self-defense. Leaving the box where it was, he hurried back up the stairs, not pausing to think that someone could already be lying in wait in the bedroom. But he made it back without encountering so much as a dust bunny in his path, and fighting back his rising panic, he scrounged his gun from his backpack and loaded it.

He could just bide his time and wait right here, he thought, finding a certain comfort in the confines of the room, for there was only one entrance to guard. Better than wandering through the house and chance getting caught by surprise.

But who could have come in, and for what purpose? Could Ben Koury have tracked him down so quickly and easily? Surely not! Perhaps someone looking for valuables, who didn't realize the house had been re-occupied? After all, Galen's bike was in the garage, and he *had* turned all the lights out. . . .

He glanced out the window, saw a wide, pale field of gray leading down to the pitch black wall of trees. And something, he didn't know what, caught and held his attention for several moments . . . something moving out there at the treeline. Branches in the wind? But no . . . something large, advancing from the cover of the woods in the direction of the house. A bulky, black shape trundling along the ground, slowly and determinedly.

A bear? Did bears live in this part of the country? Wouldn't bears be hibernating now? Whatever was down there couldn't be a man. Much too big.

The next thing to catch his attention was a sound. At first he thought it was the whistling from the box downstairs, until he realized it came from outside the window. He peered at the shape now paused in the snow, desperately trying to identify it. Impossible, though; it was way too dark and too distant. But the whistling sound seemed to be coming from the thing out in the yard, almost as if . . .

Almost as if responding to the noise the box made.

The sound rose and fell in rhythmic waves, but the silhouette didn't move any nearer to the house. He thought he detected a gentle undulating motion from the shape, like the boughs of a fir tree waving in a breeze, and he wondered if he might not actually be seeing a bush or something that got uprooted being propelled by the wind. But no, the wind was not that strong.

After a time, hypnotized, Galen finally realized that the whistling had ceased, and the shape was retreating back into the darkness.

The memory of the opened box downstairs drew his thoughts back to his own personal safety; but so far, there'd been no hint of anyone or anything moving in the dark halls, either upstairs or down. Remaining in his room still seemed the most sensible, but he had begun to feel restless, and anxious to reassure himself that no one would creep up on him tonight. So, rising from his place, he stuck his head out into the dark hall, holding the gun at the ready, and peered toward the stairwell. He saw no trace of movement in the deep shadows, nor heard the creak of a floorboard or the groaning of a door. By all indications, he was completely alone in the house.

He wasn't going back downstairs, no sir, thank you very much. Comforted by the presence of his firearm, he locked his door securely, deciding that, if a burglar broke in and stole anything, he damn well deserved to keep it. Nothing of great value in here anyway. Galen lay back on the bed, resting the gun upon his chest. He probably wouldn't actually get any sleep for the rest of the night, but fatigued as he was, his pounding heart eventually began to lull him like a hypnotic drumbeat. His mind wandered away, drifting on shadowy waves until he lost track of the time, his whereabouts, and even his fear. At last, he fell into a sound sleep, and did not wake again until dim sunlight began cutting its way through his snow-encrusted window.

When he rose, the revolver fell off his chest and thunked heavily onto the floor, jarring him to surprised wakefulness. At first he couldn't recall why he'd brought the gun to bed, but when the memory returned, so did his discomfort. Hurrying downstairs with his weapon, he found that the metal box still rested on the kitchen table, closed, just as he had left it. The lights remained off, and all the doors, which he'd bolted before bedtime, showed no sign of forced entry.

Which left him to ponder how the box had opened itself during the night, and how the kitchen light had turned itself on. Could *he* actually have been the culprit? Sleepwalking, maybe? He never had before, to his knowledge. But a more logical, and comforting, explanation eluded him. Barring further weirdness, it was best just to put the incident behind him and get on with the business of reconstructing his life. No sense in. . . .

He paused in mid-thought as he glanced out the kitchen window and realized he was facing the portion of woods where . . . *something* . . . had shambled out of the darkness to whistle eerily in the night. That, he knew, had been no hallucination, for he remembered it quite vividly now, could almost hear the sounds it made–so similar to the tones that emanated from the strange metal box. He looked down at the multi-sided contraption and slowly opened it, greeted by the powerful keening notes that more and more seemed to him, however irrationally, to be a product of some kind of vocal organ. He almost expected to hear the noises from the woods rising in response.

He bathed, dressed, and, after a quick cup of coffee, decided to explore the grounds, hoping to find–or better yet, *not* find–some sign of his nocturnal visitor. The gun would stay with him, even though it would be utterly useless should a hungry bear step out of the woods looking to have him for breakfast. Regardless, he bundled up in his riding suit and pushed his way though the nearly-frozen back door to the small porch overlooking the yard. The air slapped at his face with frigid palms, and he could hear the rush of wind over the frozen lake well beyond the treeline. The snow reached halfway up his shins, and the darkening gray sky suggested that more might begin falling within the hour. He might end up spending more than just the weekend here, for he wasn't about to risk taking his bike out on the treacherous roads.

And, besides, where would he go? Home wasn't home anymore.

Tramping through the heavy white stuff, he made his way toward the spot where he thought the dark thing must have settled during the night. Sure enough, well before he reached it, he could see a deep indentation in the snow, and what appeared to be a weaving trench leading from the woods. Even though partially filled by subsequent snowfall, the depression looked to be the scene of some kind of disturbance, for snow had been piled unevenly around it, and a few patches of grass showed through in the center. He knelt to look closely for a sign of distinguishable prints, but found none; only a number of snake-like, weaving troughs–mostly filled in by new snow–spreading out from the central hollow.

What bothered him most was the size of the depression. If a living body had made it, then it must have been the size of an elephant. The biggest bear in the forest couldn't have flattened so great an area. Unless there were at least two of them. . . .

Yeah, that must have been it. Two bears out humping in the night. That would explain the mess they'd kicked up.

But bears should be hibernating now.

Out here in the cold, he felt exposed and vulnerable, as if unseen eyes in the forest were focused on him. And he realized that he could hear no sounds of life at all. No bird calls, no distant traffic . . . nothing. Staring through the trees toward the lake, he could see the far bank of the inlet, wreathed in a misty haze; a few luxury homes stood like sentinels along the banks, but no smoke poured from any chimneys, and no one shoveled snow from any driveways. He felt like the last living man on the face of the earth, isolated, but not totally alone. *Something* was alive nearby, a presence he could feel by the slight prickling at his neck.

Then, from somewhere deep in the woods, came a faint, whistling cry, not unlike a whippoorwill: "Tekeliiii-liiiii . . . Tekeliii-liiiiii."

And that was it. Turning, Galen began trudging back toward the house, refusing to give into what was certainly an absurd fear and break into a run, but moving at as rapid a walk as the snow allowed. The foot-deep accumulation tugged at his feet, like muscular hands that had clawed up through the earth to prevent him reaching his destination. With every step nearer to the house, an increasing sense of urgency impelled to get in from the glowering outdoors.

He practically leaped up to the back porch and into the warm kitchen. Slamming the door shut, he turned to gaze back outside, at the double set of footprints leading to and from the middle of the yard. From here, he couldn't hear the strange call from the woods and hoped he wouldn't again. The most rational explanation–that it was merely some kind of bird–failed to satisfy him; not after what he'd seen and heard last night. At this point, he had to ask himself–was this really a place where he'd want to settle down? Was this terrible apprehension merely angst from a life gone down the tubes transmuting into severe paranoia?

Not sure to the former question; *almost certainly* to the latter.

For the first time since he'd left, he thought of Gina, of how *she* had been affected by what he'd done. Did she really hate him? Could she not see that, in his own sin, he'd been reacting to *her*–or rather, a partnership with her that had been subtly crumbling for longer than either of them realized? He had run straight from a situation he didn't quite understand to something he most definitely didn't understand and didn't care to try.

What if he turned around and went home? What would happen to him? To *them?*

Never too late to cancel everything with Ms. Stark. He could say he didn't like the place; after all, he was here to make that determination. He might as well swallow what pride remained and hope Ben Koury didn't take him apart with a chainsaw when he found out Galen had returned.

Trouble was, he saw, staring toward the woods, the sky had begun spitting little glistening crystals that clattered onto the roof and against the windows. *Ice, now!* And with only a motorcycle for transportation, he wouldn't be able to get away from here, not today, probably not tomorrow. Or maybe even Monday.

When he turned away from the window, he realized he was afraid.

No . . . not just afraid.

Terrified.

The journal had belonged to someone named Jacob Lamar Derby, apparently the sole tenant of the house from sometime in the early 50s until his recent death. The entries were not regular; it seemed he only occasionally wrote in the book, for there were often gaps of days or weeks, sometimes even months. And many of the entries were written in some kind of shorthand script, often punctuated by the same weird symbols Galen had seen in the other books in the cellar. The man's life, even by way of his own words, seemed cloaked in mystery—which seemed only fitting, given the nature of this property.

The final entry—which Galen read first—was penned by an obviously shaky hand:

"Can no longer be sustained by this body, and cannot move out as before. Perceptions are cloudy. Something has gone very wrong. I can no longer control the Others, even with the Zann transonifier that Thomas Asberry constructed for me. I fear they lie in wait for me. I can hear their voices."

Flipping back through page after page, he found more references to "the Others," all seemingly in terms of respect, if not outright fear, and a desperate need to "sustain this withering body." Had the old man been senile? Had he been so aware of his aging and slow slide toward death that he'd sought escape in dementia?

Much of the journal detailed the search for a compatible "receptacle"—evidently referring to a person!—and Derby's continual failing at this attempt. "I may beckon, but I can no longer swap consciousness for even a few moments. This bodes ill for me." And: "I fear that if I fail, I will be taken by the S."

Despite its ambiguity, the account made Galen distinctly uneasy. Unsettling, he thought, to be sleeping under the same roof, maybe even in the same bed, that had belonged to such a disturbed mind. Somehow, the things that had happened to him here, from the discovery of the weird box that had shocked him, to the noises outside, and the thing he'd seen in the night—all were connected with what old Derby had written in his journal. More and more, Galen perceived a strange unhealthiness about this place; and more and more, he realized that he wanted out of it. Ms. Stark, he decided, would have to run her ad again and hope for better results with her next client.

Except that, for the time being, he was nothing short of stranded here.

He drank most of the rest of his bourbon over the course of the evening, having no television, no radio, certainly no computer to occupy his time. Outside, ice rattled upon the roof and against the windows in an increasingly bothersome tirade. He could not concentrate on reading, and he didn't care to read any more of the journal anyway. The idea of going back down into the gloomy cellar to find something else appalled him, though he wasn't quite sure why.

Something from the journal seemed to be beating at his doors; some stray word he'd seen. It had something to do with that box, he believed. He'd put into a cabinet in the kitchen so he wouldn't be compelled to open it, thus allowing those sounds, which he now considered ghastly, to escape from their confining darkness.

Transonifier.

Yes . . . that was the word Derby had used. And brilliant detective that he was, Galen felt certain that the writer had been referring to the strange device inside that box. Surely, the device must serve some purpose, and from the tone of the things he'd read, he could only interpret it as malign. The fact that the sounds seemed to have drawn something out of the woods–something he couldn't explain–convinced him he wasn't suffering simple paranoia. No. Old Derby had been a bad seed, and this place remembered him all too well.

Galen had never really believed in ghosts, and still didn't, but he did believe in the persistence of bad memories, whether they be in his own mind or held by something so close to their source as an old house. Like a bad smell after something–or someone–had died, the memories remained, wafting through the darkness seeking a means to replay themselves.

A receptacle.

"Jesus Christ," Galen said aloud, staring out the window of his room into the snow-ridden darkness. How could he stand another night alone in this oppressive keep, while something whistled and shambled and watched in the darkness just beyond the treeline? Of this he now felt certain, even though he hadn't actually seen or heard anything. His increasing anxiety was rooted in primal instinct, activated by something well beyond mere imaginings.

He sat on the bed with his revolver in one hand, the near-empty bottle of Jim Beam in the other. He took a long swig, leaving just enough for another one like it. Watched. And waited.

The darkness itself startled him awake. He found himself stumbling on the stairs, not sure whether he was going up or down. In alarm, he realized he was not carrying his weapon, or even the empty bourbon bottle. And when his eyes adjusted, he saw the dim glow that he knew came from the kitchen, and heard the unmistakable, ghostly noise from the opened box—the box that he himself must have opened. He was returning to his room after performing this errand. No mere sleepwalk; he was being *driven.*

The house was cold, for he hadn't turned the heat up for the night, and a thin glaze of ice frosted the inside of the stairwell window that overlooked the woods. Peering through it, he almost expected to see that huge, black mass moving slowly from the abyss of the forest across the mantle of gray-white snow. But he saw only a few spreading shadows at the edge of the woods, which could have been anything.

And then he heard the clatter somewhere within the house, somewhere below. Something metallic, banging against a wall, or the floor. Something *falling.* He was no longer alone in the house, and the most sickening realization of all was his strange certainty that the intruder was not human.

He could understand a human threat; it was completely comprehensible to his mind, even though potentially dangerous. What he felt now bordered on the unreal, the insane. A nightmare made flesh, materializing out of Jacob Lamar Derby's demented, polluted world—which he, Galen McDonough, had somehow triggered.

He bolted up the stairs to the bedroom, retrieved his gun, its solidity his only comfort, however small. Its muzzle led the way back down, for he could not bring himself to shut himself in his room, though his every nerve railed at him to stay away from the sounds in the basement. How had it gotten inside? There was an outside door to the cellar, but nothing the size of that thing he'd seen could have ever fit through it. It would have to be *elastic.* . . .

Stupid shit! He chided himself, as reason fought down his panic. There's someone breaking into the house, probably thinking it's empty, or some poor frozen soul who's lost just trying to get warm. There are no shambling horrors in the woods who scream when a strange music box begins to play. *There simply are not.*

He went quietly into the kitchen, closed the box, then paused at the basement door, for the moment hearing nothing from behind it. Maybe the intruder had heard him coming and scrammed.

And then came the moan. A low, deep sound, like someone waking from a pain-wracked sleep. A human sound—*almost.* Something in the noise was too big, too heavy with breath to come from ordinary human lungs. But a mumbling sound followed; certainly from a human tongue, though deep and big like the moan. He placed his ear to the door and listened, hoping to discern something intelligible—some assurance that he faced nothing more or less mortal than himself, someone whose body, if it came down to it, could be decimated by a blast of his gun.

A voice, muffled, but so deep he could feel its resonance:

"Death . . . Eating. . . ."

An explosion of blood in his brain sent him reeling away from the door. The horrible, horrible sound of the thing! No human tongue could make such a sound—but what else could have articulated the seemingly meaningless but sinister words? A shuffling sound came from behind the door, something large and heavy on its way up the stairs. Not walking up—*sliding* up, he thought. Like a huge worm slowly inching its way up the wooden boards from the unseen darkness below.

"Death . . . Eating. . . ."

Then, to further kindle his terror-induced nausea, he felt a *tug* in his head; a summons, it seemed. He realized that a similar tugging must have drawn him to open the box while he was asleep. Good Christ. . . .

He was being pulled toward the door.

"God, no," he groaned, and by force of will pulled himself away. It could not have him while he was awake. He would never give in to whatever horror lay behind the door. His mind flew back to the words he'd read in Derby's journal: *I may beckon, but I can no longer swap consciousness. . . .*

Derby—or something else—was trying to get inside his head. To manipulate him; use him.

I fear that if I fail, I will be taken by the S.

"Death . . . Eating. . . ."

The sound bored deep into his brain, into realm of his spirit. Both mind and body rebelled, tried to expel the intruder like some kind of disease. But his reserves seemed no match for the raw power of the thing, and he didn't realize until his fingers closed on the knob that he'd been drawn back to open the door. He was weak, and he cursed himself. *Weak, like his giving into the temptation of Ben Koury's wife . . . weak, like his running away from the whole business, which had only brought him to this. . . .*

He pulled the door open, allowing the kitchen light to spill into the darkness, over the rough wooden planks that disappeared into the well below . . . onto a vague, grayish form that shifted and twisted subtly like some kind of monstrous serpent.

No. Not a serpent. Something vast and bulky, far too huge to have come inside through that small cellar door. For a second, the idea that it might have been down there all along—and that he'd been down there with it, unknowingly—almost sent him into a greater panic than actually standing here facing it. But he'd seen it outside, out in the snow, seen evidence of its passing. He had heard its keening voice.

"What the hell are you?" he whispered.

Something long and liquid poured *up* the stairs, with a sound like smooth flesh rubbing on rough wood. A rush of cool, fetid air washed over him, as if exhaled by the stairwell itself. And when a portion of the thing moved into the light, Galen saw chitinous hair sprouting from filmy, dead-looking tissue, like liver that had been left out to rot. The rest of the mass disappeared in the blackness below, and he could not begin to guess the true size of the thing–assuming it was all a single, unified body.

Then, the monster emitted a low buzzing sound that rose and fell erratically, as if it were attempting to manipulate the sound into recognizable syllables.

"DEATH . . . IS . . . EATING . . . ME. . . ."

There was emotion in the inhuman voice: a supreme sorrow, mixed with true, very human terror. And Galen screamed; screamed at the thing while disregarding the stabbing current in his head that warned him to run . . . *RUN.* He only stood there and watched the gray mass ooze up a step, and then another, coming more and more into the light, exposing more of the filthy, glistening pallor of its corpse-hide.

It was Derby, he knew; the *S.*, whatever that was, had indeed taken him, and was now trying to claim him as well. He had somehow summoned it here–by means of the strange device he'd found downstairs. Then the thing, in turn, had tried to summon *him!*

No, not the thing itself, but Derby. The human part that remained, that so desperately wanted to preserve itself, from within its monstrous prison had beckoned him . . . caused him to sleepwalk . . . to open the box that would bring Galen and the S. together.

The touch of something on his shoe shocked his senses awake. Looking down, he saw a quivering appendage reaching out of the darkness to spread over his foot and crawl up his leg. With a horrified cry of "NO!" Galen tore himself free and spun away from the stairwell; he pushed his way through the back door, giving no though to where he was going or paying any heed to the ice that pelted him from the leaden sky. He raced into the garage and jumped on his beloved Harley, kicking it to life with so much force he bent the metal shaft of the kickstarter. Then it was out into the downpour, past the house and the thing within, and all he could see was the long, unbroken swath of snow-covered driveway winding through the forest on its way to the main road.

In seconds, the trees were rushing past, his tires throwing up great gouts of thick white snow, ice crystals slashing at his exposed face and arms. He slid; nearly spun out . . . somehow managed to maintain his balance. The tires thudded over rocks hidden beneath the snow, jarred him so badly his teeth came down on his tongue, drawing blood. But he barely felt it; the only thing his senses could now identify was a sound, wafting down from the house with such terrible intensity that it threatened to swallow him, draw him back to some fate he didn't dare imagine.

The shrill, keening cry he'd heard this morning from the forest:

Tekelliiii-lleeeee . . . Tekelliiii-lleeeee. . . .

A sound that did not fade from his ears until he was well out on the deserted road to Aiken Mill, spinning through deep slush, half blinded by the precipitation. He realized after a time that he could no longer feel his fingers, and his arms were turning an ugly shade of blue.

But if he froze to death, it was a death he could comprehend.

Later, God knew how long, barely conscious, somehow maintaining his balance on the bike, he came upon a snowplow. He didn't have to stop and hail the driver . . . the man was out to meet him well in advance.

Three days later, Galen arrived back in Richmond, weary and ill, but with extremities intact—which the doctors had assured him made him a hell of a lucky man. A few more minutes out there and he'd have never ridden a motorcycle again. As it was, he'd had to rent an RV and hook his battered Duo Glide onto the back for the return trip. Foolish, the acerbic old doctor had told him, for anyone to have even dreamed of going on such a long haul by motorcycle this time of year. And why the hell had he come tearing down a snowbound road without so much as a coat on?

To this question, Galen offered no response, nor would he explain where he'd been or what had happened to him since he'd left Richmond, seemingly ages ago.

He had resolved to go home and face Gina. Perhaps she would have him back, perhaps not. Whatever came of it, he had to try. He could not be weak.

The house—*his* house, as he thought of it—was dark when he pulled into the driveway. Seven o'clock; she would be home from work by now. No car in the driveway. Most likely in the garage. He took a deep breath, and found his hands shaking. But he'd been shaking ever since he'd made his mad dash from the Derby house, and for all he knew, the condition might be chronic. He had forced the events of the past few days into some dark compartment of his mind, hopefully never to be released. To let them loose might mean losing whatever grip he had managed to keep on himself.

He unlocked the door, finding to his relief that Gina had not changed the locks. No light burned in the living room or hall, but a fluorescent glow came from the kitchen. No sound from in there. He started to call her name, but something from the back of the house caught his attention, and for one wild moment he thought of the sounds in the basement of the Derby place, and the eerie, high-pitched noise from the metal box.

Going down the hall to the bedroom, he heard a heavy sigh, and something crept out of the dark place in his mind until it registered that the sound he'd heard was completely human. He stepped in through the open door, and there was Gina, in the bed—their bed—with the sheets wrapped around her obviously naked body. Her mouth formed a soundless "O" as she caught sight of her husband in the door. And Ben Koury, next to her, regarded him first with an expression of fury; then, as the significance of his position settled upon him, with something like embarrassed frustration.

"Galen," Gina said softly, her voice delicate and tentative. "I—I didn't think you'd be back."

Koury, dark eyes glowering at him from beneath shaggy brows, muttered, "Feels good, doesn't it, sport?"

Gina shot him a withering glance, then looked back to her husband. Whatever she was about to say dissolved in the air when Galen turned around and started to walk away, softly mouthing something that came unbidden to his lips.

"Death . . . eating."

"What? What did you say?" Gina called, on the verge of sobbing.

He did not respond. The numbness he felt was a good thing. Now he, Gina, and Ben Koury were all on equal ground. He could simply walk away from this, holding his head high, knowing in his heart he was justified. If the last remnants of his old life were now shattered, he simply didn't care. Everything here was *fine.*

There were worse things.

The Herald at Midnight

I walk by night, for the land is my friend, no matter its type or guise, and I prefer to make its acquaintance without interference from the people of the sun. I have lived in many places, but I never stay in one of them for more than a few months, for once I have explored, discovered, and absorbed the character of a locale, I am compelled to move on; to expand my horizons, one might say. While those who infest the land largely shape its character—be it benevolent and healthy, or wasted and forbidding—the land has a life of its own, and I am certainly more a part of it than the species to which I at least temporarily belong. While I have traveled to many cities, and learned their streets, their ways, and their folk, it is the small town that most keenly draws my interest. In it, I find the land at its truest, and it is here where, unknown to most, the land craftily shapes its people.

This town was named Aiken Mill. An affluent community, its foundations stood on wealth earned many generations ago, its core population imbibed with ancient and proud southern blood. Dwellings were built into the environment with respect, and the small business district, which was curiously free of most contemporary franchises, paid tribute to the days when commerce was not worldwide but local, and transactions between men were bound by trust rather than legal documents. Here, brick and hardwood reflected the colors of the woodland in which the town nestled. Tall chimneys rose along with high white pines, birches, and cedars in natural formation; the green-clothed trunks on individual lots marched away to merge with others of their own kind rather than falter at artificial lines drawn by human developers. The house I selected for my time here was a hundred-year-old Tudor, spacious, but manageable for a single, semi-reclusive inhabitant, located in a part of town quaintly known as Druid's Hill. Plentiful oaks and maples sheltered the windows from errant sunbeams and lined both sides of the avenue to mold organic tunnels where one might stroll in insulated silence.

For my nocturnal sojourns, I always wear black. I neither carry a light nor wear silly reflective devices, for these things insult the night. I have often been amused and/or infuriated by those who carve their way through the darkness gleaming like neon-clad harlequins. Instead, I move mainly unseen, though I make no particular effort to conceal myself from my neighbors. I do not fear their vehicles, or the animals that often guard their homes. These things may be thwarted with minimal effort. My energy is devoted entirely to communing with the parasite's host.

Several years ago, I fashioned a walking stick of hickory; lightweight but strong. The handle is shaped like the head of a horned serpent, with hollow eyes and jaws spread wide. The wood always feels warm, for its life has never been fully extinguished, and it knows my touch as intimately as a lover's. My hair is long and black, and I had grown a moustache and goatee shortly before I came to Aiken Mill. I enjoy this façade, for it suits the night and serves to set me apart from others without undue exaggeration. Little is more foolish than appear among them as a cliché.

It was eleven o'clock on a Saturday evening when I left my house and strolled down the avenue, inhaling with relish the chilly, smoke-scented air. By day, from the hill upon which my house sat, I was afforded an excellent view of the surrounding land; its rounded, gold-tinged hills, the tall, blunted summit of Copper Peak rising behind them like a mammoth tortoise shell. But at night, I could see only huge, solid masses of shadow and ghostly mosaics of black and gray, speckled with pinpoints of light from the houses and roads that were cut in tiers along the wooded hillsides. At the bottom of my lane, a lake nestled in a low-lying hollow, and from there, no lights burned their way through the black veil. After sundown, little traffic marred the silence of Druid's Hill.

I had never introduced myself to my neighbors, for to do so would have been an affront to personal tradition. As I walked slowly down the hill, I saw the curtains flutter in the windows of the house next to mine, and a handsome, middle-aged woman peered out curiously, her face tinged with the pallor of unease. I am quite accustomed to such reactions; it neither annoys nor pleases me. But to acknowledge her existence would also have been an affront to tradition, so I walked past with my sights set firmly on Lake Charity.

This dark body of water was not large, but ran deep, occupying the concavity between two tall ridges. As I approached, I could hear the muted quackings of its most prolific residents, as well as the occasional, throaty belch of the huge bullfrogs that thrive along the banks. My walking stick clacked rhythmically on the pavement, and as I moved deeper into the shadows at the bottom of the avenue, the ducks began to paddle toward the center of the lake, preferring a wider buffer between them and the new arrival who offered nothing delectable. When I reached the wooden railing that ran along the bank of the lake's near end, I could see the pale, feathered shapes sailing smoothly through the black, oily-looking water. After staring appreciatively at them for a minute or two, I resumed my pace and turned onto Brynmawr Trail, a lane that snaked up Druid's Ridge toward the Beckham Road, the main artery to and from town. On this avenue, the houses loomed gigantic, their hulking silhouettes dwarfing the surrounding Bradford pear trees like ancient chateaux. The lights in their windows merely hinted at the lives concealed within; I detected no movement, no voices, no sign whatsoever of human activity, and certainly no awareness of my own wraithlike passing.

Here, immaculately trimmed lawns and expensive cars boasted to passersby the expected standard of propriety, without insinuating bigotry or pretense. I admire honesty, no matter if one is rich or poor. But whether this town truly warranted admiration, I had yet to determine; the land had obviously worked a sort of quiet magic on its inhabitants, and they, in turn, had paid homage by more than mere ornamentation. The air swelled with a rare healthiness, so unlike the oppressive atmosphere of many towns no more complex than this one. I felt a warmth in the air that came from the earth itself: a welcoming, comforting draught that meant I had been recognized.

Shortly, I heard the rumble of a car engine, and, from behind me, the beams of headlights burned my shadow onto the pavement before me. As my shadow shortened, the engine grew louder and lowered in pitch as the car slowed down. As it entered my field of vision, I took note of its driver: an elderly man with thick glasses and a bald head, peering at me with some consternation. I found myself moved to chuckle as the old man veered unnecessarily toward the middle of the road, as if to avoid running me down. His attitude suggested that he would have been only slightly more unnerved had the walker been Satan rather than me.

The car slowly disappeared from view, and silence came down like a curtain over an empty stage. But moments later, another car approached from the direction opposite the first, moving considerably faster than the posted limit. This was a small Japanese coupe, its driver a young man of high-school age. He took no notice of me whatsoever, though the beams of his headlights washed over me like hot spotlights. The wind of his passing whispered that he was on his way to a special rendezvous; perhaps to the first meaningful liaison of his young life. I wished him well.

You see, I do not hate all men, nor do I particularly care for any of them. There are those I respect, and those to whom I defer; and, certainly, there are those whose paths ought not to cross mine. The signs in Aiken Mill so far were inconclusive. My sentiments might swing either way.

I passed a sprawling mansion that must have contained thirty rooms, its brick siding webbed with clinging ivy, its multiple chimneys stained black and dribbling smoke. Only a few lights burned in its upper windows, and I perceived a great loneliness, a sense of loss from its solitary occupant. Whoever dwelled in that place shared my love of the land, yet I could tell that his or hers was incomplete, for a subtle stench of decay wafted my way across a weed-ridden lawn.

Another pair of headlights gleamed ahead, and this time, as the vehicle approached, it slowed down. The car was a huge gray sedan, its driver a young man of perhaps forty. As he pulled up beside me, he rolled down his window and called, "Excuse me, sir."

I bent down to look him in the eye. "Good evening," I said softly.

"Do you live around here?"

"Why, yes I do."

He looked a trifle uneasy. "I haven't seen you around before."

"No."

"Do you usually walk at night?"

"Yes. I enjoy it."

"You know, that might make some people in this neighborhood . . . uncomfortable, if you take my meaning."

I gazed curiously at him but said nothing.

"Where is it you live, if you don't mind me asking?"

"I live on Coventry, near the lake. Are you a police officer, perhaps?"

"No, I'm not police."

"The mayor? A town councilman?"

"No, sir, I'm just curious about you walking around at this hour."

"I understand. But I would say no one has anything to fear from me, mister. . . ?"

"Noland. Bob Noland. I run the neighborhood watch here, you know. I wouldn't want there to be any . . . misunderstandings."

"Thank you for your concern, Mr. Noland." With no further ado, I turned my back to him and continued on my way, swinging my walking stick leisurely. The car rumbled slowly away, and I could feel Mr. Bob Noland's eyes in the mirror fixed intensely on me. He was a Southern Baptist.

Once the car had disappeared and its sound faded into the distance, I began to perceive a faint humming in the air. I paused to listen. It was a low, almost mechanical-sounding drone, steady and unwavering; at first I thought it be merely the machinery from some plant out on the main highway, for sound travels oddly among these ridges. At times, the evening whistle from a factory on the far north side of town would ring out as if it came from down by the lake, here on the south end. This phenomenon has always interested me, and from studying its many variations, I have learned much about the land. On this night, I decided to walk as far as the Beckham Road, strangely drawn as if by the song of a siren.

As I neared the summit of Brynmawr Ridge, a grating, rattling engine obliterated the low humming, and a pair of headlights hit me from behind. Seconds later, I heard the squeal of brakes, and a battered, rust-encrusted Camaro of indeterminate year and color appeared beside me, pacing me. The driver, a youthful man with long sideburns and a pencil-thin moustache called out to me, "Hey, ain't you pretty!"

"Thank you," I replied.

"Those are fine boots you're wearing."

"Indeed."

"I thought you were a girl from behind, but I guess you ain't. Shave your face and I bet you'd be an all right-lookin' bitch."

"Possibly."

"Hey, how about a lift. I bet you'd like to ride with me."

"Thank you, no. I'm enjoying my walk."

"You want to snort some coke?"

"I do not." I gazed at him with unconcealed amusement. His stare faltered.

"You're a real smart-ass," the man said, then spat on the pavement at my feet. With a roar, the car sped off, his exhaust heavy with the same vulgar stench as his hot, polluted breath. He came from the west end of town and cruised these roads out of envy, I suppose. He was not a robber or rapist or murderer; he was merely a lonely, unhappy wretch of man whose life meant considerably less than that of the bullfrogs I could still hear far in the distance. I was hardly afraid of his kind. And he was simply too stupid to fear mine.

When at last I reached the Beckham Road, the moon was past its zenith, and a chill had crept into the air. From here, I had a pleasing view of Aiken Mill; through a dense stand of pines below me, I could see the lights of town, spread through the valley like a vast pile of glowing embers. The sound I had heard was louder here, but I still could not be certain from which direction it came. It was a song, I decided; melancholy and mysterious. I began to shiver in the breeze.

I now turned back in the direction I had come, picking up my pace, for the night would soon become uncomfortable. I barely glanced at the houses as I passed, focusing solely on the sound, letting it carry me toward my destination. It whispered, sang, and beckoned. Its volume did not diminish as I drew nearer to my house. Only when I arrived at my driveway did it finally fade away.

When I stepped through my front door into the sweet warm air, I had begun to have an inkling of what I had heard, and what it meant to me personally.

I continued my excursions on subsequent evenings, sometimes taking the same route, sometimes turning down Hunter's Glen Road and walking around Lake Charity. I seldom turned right on Coventry as I left my house, for that way led toward town, and the population and traffic increased accordingly. No matter where I walked, I could now hear that distant, whispering, madrigal song, always alluring, always challenging me to discover its actual source. I knew the latter was quite impossible; however, the more I listened to it, the more I realized that it was being carefully modulated by the contours of the earth. The land was transmitting a message to me.

Brynmawr Trail to the Beckham Road became my preferred route. I never tired of it, for every night there were subtle changes: variances of moonlight, broad ranges of color in the reflected light in the sky and over the lake. Each journey provided me with new sensations, new ways of experiencing the land. Sometimes, I even walked in daylight, finding the change in atmosphere refreshing. I was determined to translate the sound on the wind, and I was certain my favorite route must hold the key. But the song could only be heard after dark; never in sunlight.

Bob Noland passed me on occasion, and so became accustomed to my nocturnal ramblings. Still, I smelled distrust in his wake, and, after a time, I began to realize that a similar odor had begun to permeate the air—so subtly that at first that it was almost undetectable. The neighborhood was becoming aware of me, and the true essence of its people was seeping from behind those closed doors, the brightly lit windows. I'm certain they wondered about my motivation, my apparent independent means. I had always been invisible, and I prefer it that way; but this town was built on special land, and it struck me as being the place I wanted to remain for a time, despite the increasingly troublesome vibrations of the local infestation.

Well after midnight one evening, as I reached the sprawling thirty-room house of loneliness, my ears detected the far-away grumbling of that pathetic Camaro, which was apparently heading in my direction. I had seen it a few times since our first encounter, though if the driver had seen me at all, he never let it be known. This time, I could sense a purpose in the growl of the engine, and I knew he was not alone. He was looking for me.

I made no effort to hide or escape from him, so he found me quickly. The Camaro's brakes squealed, and the car screeched to a stop directly behind me. I did not turn around when I heard the slamming of the driver's door, then the passenger's. I knew this meeting would not end peacefully.

"Hey, fuck," called the Camaro man. "We come to see you."

I stopped and slowly turned to regard him. His eyes were glazed from alcohol, and he carried a scarred-looking nighstick. His partner, a long-haired, scrawny creature with a pockmarked face, sidled up to me with his hands behind his back. He was carrying a weapon of some kind. He grinned lewdly.

"It's a nice night," I said. "You would enjoy it more if you were walking . . . somewhere else."

"I knew you were a goddamned smart-ass. Frankly, I'm tired of seeing you prancing around at night in my town," Camaro man said.

"I'm sorry to hear that."

"You *are* gonna be sorry!"

The pockmarked longhair positioned himself behind me, and Camaro man stepped up with his face close to mine, breathing gin-tinged steam. "We don't want to see you out here no more. As far as I'm concerned, you're just a trespasser."

"Ah. How odd. I was thinking just the opposite."

Like lightning, a hand flew up and struck me across the face. I felt a shock through my jaw, and my cheek began to burn. I kept my balance, however, which obviously surprised the both of them.

"By the way," I said. "This is not your neighborhood."

I saw him raise his nightstick threateningly. "You're just aching to get hurt, aren't you? Oblige him, Kenny."

From behind, something struck me in the ribs, and a sudden jolt of pain nearly sent me reeling. My walking stick fell from my hand, and only a supreme effort of will prevented my knees from buckling. But my eyes caught a quick flash to my right, and I turned just in time to see a fist loaded with brass knuckles rocketing toward my jaw. I twisted and managed to avoid the blow, but Camaro man's foot swept forward and caught me squarely in the chest. My breath exploded through my lips, and I felt a sharp pain shooting through my entire body. Still, I refused to so much as teeter off-balance, and my lack of cooperation obviously infuriated my attackers.

"Come on, you fuck. Get mad at me," growled Camaro man.

I sensed that Kenny, still behind me, was gathering his energy to strike me again. I kept my eyes on Camaro man, who glared at me with contempt.

"Being a smart-ass gets people into trouble, wouldn't you say?"

I nodded slowly. "You are quite correct."

I heard a movement from behind and I suddenly felt a heavy blow to the back of my head. My vision went red for a second, and my knees wobbled unsteadily; but I slowly turned to see the longhaired delinquent shaking his head in disbelief, rearing back to strike again with the brass knuckles. As his arm shot forward, I felt–and heard–a *crunch* at my jaw and tasted blood. Stars flashed in front of my eyes, and now the pain was spreading through my neck and shoulders. I nearly lost consciousness.

But I did not fall. I *would not* fall.

"Damn!" Camaro man roared. "You son of a bitch!"

Both of them began to back away as my trembling legs began to stabilize. Kenny looked uncertainly at his partner, and slipped the brass knuckles back into his pocket.

"We're gonna let you alone to reflect," Camaro man said, the threat in his voice undermined by his mounting bewilderment. "I'm telling you, you better stay the hell indoors from now on."

I suddenly heard the familiar, smooth rumble of a car engine in the distance; and as it drew nearer, I saw the headlights of Bob Noland's gray sedan coming around the curve. The car slowed and hissed to a stop as the driver took in the sight of my two assailants scurrying back to their own vehicle. The Camaro groaned to life, and with a pained roar backed up, turned around, and vanished in the direction of the Beckham Road.

I did not need to look around to know that Bob Noland's eyes were studying me with rapt curiosity. He did not get out of his car, and I did not expect him to be a good Samaritan. His suspicious eyes merely blazed as I turned to face him. He said, "Looks like there was a misunderstanding here. I warned you."

"And I thanked you."

He gazed at me for several moments longer. I smelled his disgust; the scent was almost intoxicating. His arrogant righteousness swirled over and around me like a shroud, fed by the complementary vibrations from the surrounding homes. The distant song now swept across the pavement, shimmering up through my hands and feet, creeping up my spine and tickling my ears. It whispered reassurance to me. The land was my friend.

"I hope you learn from this," the Baptist said. "I don't wish you any harm, you know. But sometimes people need a firm hand in order to be set right."

"You are more correct than you realize," I told him.

He shook his head in dismissal. "You really are a fool." He put his car into gear and drove off, glancing back in his rear view mirror to make sure I understand that he loathed the sight of me.

Shortly, the agony in my gut dulled to a tight numbness, and I tested my legs by taking a few steps to make sure they would continue to support my weight. They did. I retrieved my walking stick, which, thankfully, had not been damaged. Certainly, it would have been an adequate weapon had I chosen to defend myself. Yet, to retaliate against these puny creatures would have been nothing more than a symbolic act and, in itself, no less stupid. Perhaps in another instance, I might have seen fit to dispatch my attackers, but here, in Aiken Mill, the land dictated the need for action beyond symbolism.

I limped home and soaked myself in hot water. The night was quiet and relaxing, and, after bathing, my injuries felt less severe. My head still ached but was clearing rapidly. My leg supported my weight without undue pain, and my chest loosened so that breathing no longer hurt. By tomorrow night, I would be ready to walk again.

I would take one more walk in Aiken Mill before it was time to leave. I had not anticipated bidding this land farewell so soon, but now I realized the necessity in a new and terrible way. No one had frightened or intimidated me; if I had wished to remain and confront the Camaro man or Bob Noland or any of the town's other guardians, I would have, and emerged unscathed. But I acknowledge the things that are larger than I, and I respect them, even the infestation of the land, if need be. Here, the earth was speaking to me in a way I had never known before, and it behooved me to listen.

That last night was cold and clear, the stars quite brilliant in the midnight canopy. I imagine Camaro man and his friend had been cruising since early evening, anticipating another encounter with me. I could feel the current of his movement in the air, and smell traces of the foul exhaust of his vehicle. Once, I heard Bob Noland's sedan far in the distance, but he did not travel on Brynmawr; at least not yet. I doubted that I would ever see him again. As usual, I followed my route up Brynmawr Trail, drawn by the low song on the breeze. It had begun to modulate itself into syllables, ever-so-patiently sending out its message of greeting. By the time I reached the summit of the ridge, where the lane joined the Beckham Road, the source of the sound had at last become clear to me.

It was out there, echoing from Copper Peak. The mountain, of course, was merely a conduit; the true source of the voice was distant—unimaginably so, even for me—and was meant specifically for those such as myself with the ability and the desire to listen. As it spoke, my purpose for being here—yes, even my reason for existing—began to crystallize in my mind. I knew now why I had wandered for so long, and why the land had befriended me. Such a revelation is by its nature both terrifying and exhilarating, and its overwhelming import, its irrefutability, nearly reduced me to the same scale as the microscopic organisms that swarm purposelessly in a drop of lakewater.

But then, with my role and its significance patently clear to me, I gathered my wits and my walking stick, and turned to peer at the golden, glowing embers of Aiken Mill, far down below the ridge. It was midnight, and the song from Copper Peak began to waver uncertainly until it finally died. I had heard the sound for so long that my ears could scarcely withstand the silence. But the silence, I knew, was only temporary. I felt a thrill of anticipation unlike any I had ever known, a trembling in my body that originated from an unfathomed, heretofore unknown part of myself.

Far from where I stood, I heard the growl of the Camaro's engine, and I felt the driver's ire pounding down the road ahead of him like an angry stalker. In the absence of the once-familiar, ghostly voice, the sound of the approaching car seemed flat and one-dimensional. But now, beneath the engine noise, a new voice began to rise: a low, deep rumble that became an actual quivering of the earth, setting the nearby trees to trembling and bending as if blown by a low gale. I heard the distant shriek of brakes, and then a loud, metallic crash as the Camaro smashed into a tree. Human voices flared in agony and bewilderment, and somehow I realized they were meant for me to hear, amplified by the land itself. Far away, Bob Noland's car left the road and shattered at the bottom of an embankment. Nearer at hand, the lights in that sprawling mansion of loneliness flickered and went out.

Long ago, up on Copper Peak, a door had been left ajar, and numerous times in the past it had swung fully open before closing again. But now, that door had been flung wide, and out there, in the night, I could see a pale, misty glow illuminating the mountain's edge against the black sky like a phosphorescent cloud. Above that rounded, shadowed hump, a jagged, black crease appeared in the sky; a sickle-shaped scar that gradually began to both lengthen and widen. Darker than the night itself, it opened slowly like a gaping mouth, and from it—trailing brilliant streamers like diving birds of fire—the stars began to fall.

I could feel the change as it began to come over me. This was the moment to which I had been born to bear witness; the culmination of my life's journeys. My walking stick grew hot, fusing itself to my hands, and my muscles and bones began to transform, twisting me out of the shape I had known for so long. My walking stick was also changing, growing, stretching, the mouth of its serpent-like head spreading wider and wider. When I lifted the device, I found its narrow end hollow, and perfectly shaped to accommodate my mouth. Placing its tip within, I began to blow with all the wind I could summon from my now mammoth lungs.

The deep, droning cry that emanated from the mouth of the instrument swept over the ridge, down into the valley, out toward Copper Peak, and beyond. A voice from the mountain called back, and the night began to grow bright with the golden flares that continued falling from the heavens. The ground pitched and quaked erratically, shattering buildings with the strength of a force nine earthquake. Around me, I could see tiny figures scurrying and cowering, and the disbelieving screams that rose in harmony with the song I blew brought to me the pleasure of a destiny fulfilled.

My message delivered, I would soon be leaving this town, and I would have to reluctantly bid the earth farewell. For me, there would be more wanderings, true; but on these I would no longer be a seeker but a collector. On this night, for those few, endless minutes that I played my song beneath the light of the falling stars, many who saw me believed that the seventh, final seal had been broken, and that the last trumpet had sounded, and that in the twinkling of an eye, all would be changed.

And all those who so believed were entirely correct.

MISFITS
- or -
A New Arrival at Paradise Lost

Nothing has ever chilled me more than the sound of a man screaming; the high-pitched cry of a soul being ripped from its body. I remember once hearing the flight recorder of a doomed airliner, and in the final seconds before the abrupt silence, the cockpit crew screamed in terror as they realized their lives were about to end. It made my heart quail, brought tears to my eyes. It was that kind of terrible shriek that halted me in my tracks just as I reached to open the front door of the little bar and grill I'd come upon. The sharp, raw cry drilled into my ears like a steel bore and stopped me cold, even though it was a sound that had become all too familiar during the past 12 months. Sadly, I knew exactly what it meant.

From the holster beneath my long coat, I quickly and quietly drew the H&K 9mm semiautomatic my husband had given me. It had been almost a month since I'd last had to use it. Having come into town without encountering any resistance, I had dared entertain the notion that things *might* have turned for the better.

Sometimes my own naive optimism disgusts me.

I crept along the side of the dirty brick building, picking my footing carefully to keep from betraying myself. Trash was strewn all over the alley, though, and avoiding the noisier bits, like the cans and bottles, proved to be tricky.

Yes, mortal terror gripped me, and my hands were trembling. The 9mm semiautomatic is a fine weapon, but in a confrontation like the one I expected, its effectiveness depended on a precise aim rather than the more popular spray and pray method. I could hear a low shuffling sound behind the building, 20 feet or so ahead of me. I moved forward slowly, glancing back every other step to make sure that a second assailant wouldn't surprise me from behind.

Thump. Rattle.

Damn it! My toe had struck an aluminum can and sent it rolling. Fighting panic, I lifted the gun to blast any target that appeared, for the thing behind the building would surely know I was here now—if it hadn't become aware of my presence even as I walked into town. Tension charged the air with an electric reek, and I barely fought down the instinct to flee in blind panic.

A loud scrape came from around back, then a sharp cough that ended in a pained hiss. A second later, I heard the clattering sound of a chain-link fence being shredded, followed by heavy, crunching footsteps that retreated quickly into the wooded grove behind the building. I found myself panting with relief.

But I didn't like it. A stalker generally will not run away unless he has buddy who will just as happily do you in. Still, a sense of duty compelled me to see if there was anything left of the screamer behind the building. Gathering my nerve, holding my weapon at the ready, I leaped around the corner, keeping my finger tight upon the trigger.

There was no second stalker. Nor was there any hope for the individual spread around the asphalt apron like so much strawberry jam. From the remains, I gathered it had been a young man; late twenties, thin, reasonably well-built. From the half-mashed object that stared up at me from the pavement, I deduced that at least one of his eyes had been blue. Leaning down to examine an arm discarded near the trio of metal trash barrels, I saw that the flesh bore several scars, some old, some recent, all quite extensive. Up to now, this man had been a survivor. My heart went out to him.

A section of the fence that separated the tavern lot from the adjacent grove was torn and trampled, and from the wreckage hung an unrecognizable strip of anatomy. The trees beyond the fence were impenetrably dark, and a low, chilly breeze had begun to whistle eerily through the branches. The stalker might be watching me from back there at this very moment. I turned and hurried back toward the front of the building, wanting now just to get inside before the sun went down.

Gun raised, I reached for the handle of the tinted glass door and tugged. With a hydraulic hiss, the door swung open to reveal the dimly lit interior of the tavern. It was too dark to discern much, but, by the glow of a Michelob sign, I saw a couple of silhouettes moving. Stepping inside, I hugged the wall to minimize the chance of being shot by a nervous guard. I heard several male voices, but none sounded excited, upset, or otherwise prone to overreaction. They felt, I suppose, that as long as the new arrival was human, they had little cause for concern. I wondered if they were aware of the carnage out back.

I cautiously approached the bar, where a gaunt-looking man of about 60 rested on his elbows, watching me warily. There were eight others in the room, both men and women, and I quickly noted their strategic positions. Several gunbarrels surreptitiously tracked my every step, and I sensed as many pairs of eyes appraising me carefully. I focused on the bartender, wearing as pleasant an expression as I could muster, and lowered my gun to demonstrate my benign intentions. I said softly, "Could I get a beer?"

"Yes'm," he said curtly and turned to fill a mug from a longhandled tap without saying a word. He placed it on the counter and went back to resting on his elbows, eyeballing me thoughtfully.

Before taking it, I said, "I can't pay for this, you know."

"On the house." He gave me the tiniest suggestion of a smile.

The faintly humorous light in his eyes seemed sincere, so I nodded my thanks and took a sip, grateful for at least these few moments to let my taut muscles relax. The beer was a little flat but cold.

I motioned to the bartender with one finger, and he leaned down close to me. "You know," I said, "Somebody just bought it out back."

Barkeep raised an eyebrow. "Do tell?"

"Real mess. You didn't hear the screams?"

He shook his head, putting on a thoughtful expression. A jukebox was playing an old Willie Nelson song at low volume, but I didn't think it could cover any loud sounds from outside. A long, tinted window faced the font, but the side and rear walls were solid. I supposed they might have been heavy enough to make the room reasonably soundproof.

"Must have been Davenport," a man to my right offered. "Cocky son of a bitch. He probably invited the thing right down on him. You get a look at him, lady?"

"Pieces of him. He was tall, thin, blond. Had at least one blue eye."

"Davenport," the man said with a nod, taking a sip of beer, then settling back to gaze at me curiously. He was a grizzled fellow with a thick, ragged beard, dark brown eyes, and a missing leg. Two crutches leaned against the counter next to him. Beside his beer mug lay a long-barreled Smith & Wesson .38. Propped behind him was a sawed-off twelve-gauge.

"Who was he?"

"Sentry. Always keep one outside." He jerked a thumb toward a door behind the bar. "Got a trapdoor to the roof back there. Sentry's supposed to give us notice when something–or someone–comes into the vicinity. Davenport had taken to leaving his post for an extra shot of beer."

"Which must be why he didn't warn us about you," a woman off to my left called. "I bet he tried to take on a stalker all by himself."

I gave her a curious glance. She was young, about 25, with attractive features beneath a billow of chestnut-colored hair. "Take off your coat and stay a while," she said with a note of authority. I complied, not wishing to start any kind of row with these people. I laid my coat on the bar and the barkeeper took it, hanging it on a rack next to several others at the end of the counter.

"Wow. Hey lady . . . nice ass," came a deep voice from a shadowy corner to my left. I saw a hefty black man seated at a table with two young white women. He flashed me a toothy grin; I smiled back with as much derision as I could muster.

"That's Crate," said the woman. "Don't worry, he has a big mouth but a heart of gold. I'm Anthea. That's Tripod Jack." She pointed to the one-legged man. "You have a name?"

"Yes," I said, but offered nothing more. Each pair of eyes stared at me expectantly. I drained my beer glass and handed it back to Barkeep. "Please?"

He took it, gave me a refill, and settled back to gaze at me some more.

Anthea rose and slowly approached me. She was tall, half a head above my five-foot-six. Like me, she was dressed entirely in black: black turtleneck, black dungarees, black flat-heeled boots. A leather holster hung low over her hips, housing what looked to be a .357 Magnum. She regarded me coolly, but without menace.

"What brings you into town?"

I reached into my back pocket and felt the tattered edges of the photograph. Pulling it out, I handed it to her, watching her eyes as she studied it. Her mental gears whirred for several moments, but at last she shook her head.

"I haven't seen him. Your husband?"

"Yes," I said. "This was his hometown, many years ago. He'll be coming here . . . if he's still alive. His name's Locke. Colin Locke."

Anthea handed the photo to Tripod Jack, who also shook his head. "Name of Locke ring anybody's bell?" she called out. A murmur of negatives rose from the group. She gave the picture to Crate, who passed it along. When everyone in the room had gotten a look, Anthea gave it back to me.

"Sorry . . . Mrs. Locke."

I slid the photo back in my pocket. "It's been years since he's been here. But his mother lives out on Barren Creek Road. He wanted to make sure she was safe."

"There you are!" exclaimed Barkeep. "I remember some Lockes out there. Dave and Margaret, right? The old man died several years ago. You remember them, Jack?"

Jack nodded slowly. "I think so. Me and Baker here are about the oldest locals left. I reckon we've known most everybody who's lived in Aiken Mill for the last 30 or 40 years. Yeah, I remember them. So, you're married to that little boy of theirs." He eyed me appreciatively.

"Where are you from?" Baker the Barkeep asked.

"Chicago. We got separated when all this began. We were trying to make it back here. Colin figured it would be better away from the city."

"You came all the way from Chicago? Alone?" Anthea asked, wide-eyed.

"Mostly, yes."

"Lady," Tripod Jack said, "that's some story. Just you and that popgun you're carrying?"

"I've had others. I lost my Glock somewhere in Ohio."

Flash:

The night the stars fell, we'd been hearing the sounds for hours: a strange, seemingly sourceless *hum* that surrounded us, made us feel sick, finally becoming a deep *thump . . . thump,* like the beating of some gigantic heart. Colin, our daughter Ellen, and I watched the rift forming in the sky from the backyard of our house in Evanston. The stars had shimmered, then a black spot, darker than the night itself, began to form near the southern horizon. Slowly it spread, like ripples in a pond, until it became a gaping wound, hollow, empty—finally destroying the entire sky. The tiny globes of light came next, hurtling toward the earth like monstrous fireflies, their erratic movements belying any suggestion that these might be ordinary celestial particles. Soon afterward, it became painfully obvious that there was nothing heavenly about them.

The stalkers appeared the next day. I was in the kitchen that morning—a bright Saturday—and on the television came the first reports of the mass murders. Over the course of the day, the numbers increased shockingly, as did the sightings of the things in the sky and in the streets. When martial law was declared that afternoon, Colin knew we couldn't stay in the city. From the news reports, metropolitan areas were being hit the hardest. We locked ourselves indoors that day, sometimes hearing screams from outside, but—thankfully—never seeing anything. We lost our power, our telephone, our water. The police and national guard, unable to fight or even comprehend the nature of this new threat, soon bugged out.

The next morning, at dawn, we loaded our van and made our escape.

"How did you and your family get separated?" Tripod Jack asked.

"There were stampedes," I said, remembering our flight from the city. "Crowds draw stalkers like blood draws sharks. It was insane. We saw people leaping off of buildings, throwing themselves in front of moving cars. Colin hit more than one himself. Just outside of town, we got stopped by a bunch of kids who had found some automatic weapons.

They took me and Ellen, and they were going to kill Colin . . . but a stalker appeared. Three of gang hustled Ellen and me into their truck . . . the stalker finished off the rest of them. I saw Colin. He escaped. Saved, by a goddamned stalker, can you believe it? If he's still alive, he'll be coming here. I *know* he's still alive."

"How did you get away?" Jack asked.

I shrugged. "There were only three of them."

"And your daughter?"

"She lasted a month. Died of pneumonia, back in Ohio. She just couldn't take it."

"I'm sorry," Anthea said. "How old was she?"

"Nine."

Flash:

Ellen stood in front of me, warily eyeing the 9mm I held out to her. She shuddered as if I were offering her a rattlesnake, but she took it.

"It'll kick, but it won't knock you down," I told her. "You have to deal with it. I've got to be able to trust you."

"I know," she whispered. "But what if I can't shoot it?"

"You can shoot it," I said. "Look here. First, you cock it . . . like this. Good. Now, to aim, you look down the barrel. See the point on the front sight? Line it up with the notch on the rear sight."

"I'm shaking, Mom, I can't. . . ."

"Don't worry. Look at that tree over there. See? Aim at that knot. Good. Bring your left hand up and hold your right wrist steady. Now . . . put your first finger around the trigger. Don't pull it. Squeeze it, so it won't jerk in your hand. When I say shoot, you shoot. Got it?"

"I guess so, Mom, but. . . ."

"Ellen!" I glared at her fiercely. "We're going to get through this, but you've got to help, okay? Now. Are you ready?"

She gulped and nodded.

"Shoot."

The loud *boom* jolted her, but she held the gun fairly steady. She looked at the smoking weapon, then at me.

"I shot it!" she cried, not sure whether to be terrified or ecstatic.

I approached the tree, thirty feet away, and looked up at the knothole. Just to its right, some bark had been skimmed off.

"Fine shot, especially for a first time. Now, tell me again. Where do you aim?"

"At its eyes, Mom."

"And why?"

"It can do things with its eyes. You can only kill it if you hit it in the eyes."

"Very good."

"Can I shoot again?"

"No. Remember, if you shoot twice, they can find you. Come on, now. Let's get moving."

"You miss her," Anthea said. "I'm sorry, I didn't mean to upset you."

"It's okay," I said, forcing the memory away. "I deal with it. She just got sick, you know?"

"Yeah. But maybe it was for the best . . . compared to what could have happened to her."

I shivered. "That's what I tell myself." I took a swallow of beer and looked back at the three characters in the corner opposite Crate and his two women. "Who are they?"

"That's Danny, Jill, and the Stretch—he was a basketball player. We're all regulars here, in case you haven't guessed."

I nodded with a wry grin. It was the same in every little town. The local hangouts became part-time fortresses. The cities were occupied war zones; in the sticks, assaults were guaranteed, but were far less frequent. Still, each of us knew the day would come when the cities were completely conquered, and small towns would be the next battlefields. I'd heard it had already started happening farther north. Here in southwestern Virginia, I hoped, there might still be a time of reprieve.

I let my mind drift away from the violence beyond these doors and concentrated on the people around me. They seemed relaxed, though I didn't doubt that inside they were coiled springs. I remembered how casual they'd been about my arrival, and how coolly they had accepted the news of their comrade's grisly demise. They were either incredibly naive or damned sure of themselves. I didn't think it was the former.

The song on the jukebox had ended, and the room fell expectantly silent. Crate slid his chair back with a resounding scraping noise, stood up, and went to the window. Outside, the sun had set, and only a faint glimmer of blue remained above the horizon. The streets were dark, and no other buildings nearby were lit. Now and again, a car would pass by, usually without headlights. Crate stared for a minute, then said, "I'll check the roof. We're going to have company tonight."

I glanced at Tripod Jack. He smiled.

"Crate's never been wrong. He smells 'em. Must be that damn big nose of his."

The black man pounded Jack on the arm as he passed. "I'm going to break your crutches, asshole."

When Crate had left, I said softly to Anthea, "I guess he didn't smell the one that killed Davenport."

The look that she gave me chilled me to the core. I zipped my lips, certain now that I had to watch my step around these people. It would not pay to fall into disfavor.

Baker the Barkeep took my mug, still half-full, and topped it off. "Last call," he said.

Tripod Jack hefted his shotgun and glanced at the front door. Outside, I saw a couple of shadowy figures striding quickly down the opposite side of the street, presumably searching for cover for the night. Sometimes the stalkers struck in daylight, but they usually saved their best efforts for the after hours. At night, it seemed the world had reverted to its primal state: wild, treacherous, and ambivalent. My travels through the States had taught me a whole new respect for Mother Earth. It was strange: but for the loss of the two I loved most, I had never felt more alive.

Jack pulled a pack of cigarettes from his shirt pocket and flicked one out, offering the pack to me.

"I quit," I said, "but I guess I'll take one." It was a Merit Ultra Light, and I had to laugh. "You look more like a Lucky Strike man."

He lit mine, then his, with a battered old Ronson. "I'm on a health kick."

We smoked in silence for a few minutes. I watched Anthea sipping a gin and tonic, her eyes occasionally meeting mine and seeming to frost over, as if she dared not make any attempt to get close to me. In the corner, the two young women at Crate's table, whose names were Suzanne and Collette–sisters, according to Jack–sat in silent repose, tapping their fingers on the tabletop, one of them now and then reaching down to caress a tall gray cylinder resting between them. After a minute's long-distance examination, I realized they had an RPG. *Christ.* I hoped they weren't drinking martinis.

Danny, Jill, and the Stretch sat closest to the door. Danny was a lanky, longhaired redneck, wearing a black T-shirt emblazoned "The Ungrateful Dead." Jill couldn't have been more than 17, a little pudgy, with greasy dark hair and masculine features. She twirled a heavy revolver on one finger. The Stretch's weapon, which I thought looked like a genuine Uzi, rested on the table with its muzzle aimed at the front door. Even seated, the young man appeared to be a giant. His long, powerful legs straddled his chair as if cocked to launch him like a rocket. He was probably only 18 or 19, but I figured that by the time he ever got to play basketball again, he'd probably only qualify for a senior's league.

Suddenly, I heard a shuffling sound above. Anthea's eyes turned upward, and her knuckles went white, but her expression remained passive, as if the greatest danger we faced was running out of drink. I found myself drawn to her; she had the calm reserve of a born leader, an aura of dignity that suggested harm would never find its way to her. I wanted her to like me.

I felt a cool hand touch mine. "I guess this is old hat to you, young lady," Jack said.

"I'm not bored, if that's what you mean."

"Is your gun loaded?"

"Yes."

Softly, he said, "If you be so kind, please turn slowly toward the front window. Look at the street sign over there, at eleven o'clock. Tell me what you see."

I did as he said. Something was moving over there, something indistinct, but large. My stomach fluttered. For a moment, I didn't think I'd be able to speak, but I finally managed to whisper, "Oh, yes. It's out there. Looks like it's moving to our left."

I heard the metallic rasp of guns being brought to bear. Anthea maneuvered herself behind the bar, resting her Magnum on the counter, aiming it at the entrance. Barkeep took a position next to her, facing the rear door. I heard three distinct raps on the ceiling, followed by two more.

"That's Crate," whispered Jack. "The stalker is sounding us out. It's moving around to our left, all right."

"Are there any restrooms back there? Any windows?"

"Yes, but they're too small for him, unless he's a Cancer Cloud. Not this fellow, though. I think it's Joe the Fireman."

"You name them?"

"Know thine enemy," he said with a shrug.

I heard a rattle at the rear door. A moment later, Crate appeared, his broad features taut and grim.

"It's our old pal Joe," he said softly. "And I saw something in the sky. They may be massing here soon."

"Then this is a bad place," I said. "I've seen the way they hit areas of concentration. It's ugly."

A cloud briefly darkened Anthea's face. "We've defended against three, maybe four at a time. What do you think, Crate? We going to get more than that?"

"Probably not tonight. But tomorrow. . . ."

"They must be coming out of DC and Richmond," I said. "That means the cities have fallen."

Tripod Jack and Anthea gave each other knowing looks. "Then tomorrow we're bugging out," she said.

Suddenly, something banged sharply on the ceiling, and I heard the unmistakable creak of metal being bent. Barkeep slid back a couple of steps, making sure he had a clear shot at the rear door. Anthea swung around to back him up. Jack and Crate leveled their weapons at the front door, anticipating a possible second intruder. I was just about to move into the space Anthea had vacated when the front door exploded, showering me with fragments of glass and metal. I felt a sharp jab as one of them lacerated my left palm.

I heard a deep, guttural rumble that rose quickly into a coarse howl, and I scrambled around the corner of the bar, seeking what little protection it had to offer. I quickly rolled into a crouch and aimed my gun at the ruined doorway, ignoring the blood that trickled down my wrist.

My finger tightened on the trigger as a tall silhouette materialized at the entrance. Slowly, a long, muscular arm covered with thorn-like scales reached in and scooped aside the wreckage of the door. The stalker had to stoop to gain entry, its broad shoulders scraping against the sides of the doorway with a sound like a rake being dragged over corrugated metal. Its eyes glowed hotly beneath a protruding brow; they were shaped like a viper's, reddish brown, alert, searching. Its head swung back and forth, minimizing my chances of hitting its only vulnerable spot. I saw the Stretch drop behind his table and cut loose with the Uzi. The shots rattled off the beast's hide, forcing me to duck as zipping bullets ricocheted around me. Anthea screamed, and I turned to see her head disappear beneath the counter. I prayed she hadn't been hit. I turned back just as the stalker focused its gaze on me. My gun locked onto one eye and fired. The monster recoiled from the shot and rumbled ominously, but it remained upright. I'd missed my mark.

Damn it!

Joe the Fireman rose to its full height, its head banging against the ten-foot ceiling. He was a big one, fully armored with barbed scales and segmented plates on his chest and abdomen. The legs were long and anthropodal, its feet clawed like a giant hawk's. The brute shook its wolf-like head as if to rid itself of the pain; then its eyes began to rove around the room. The five ivory horns arcing forward from the back of its skull seemed to glow faintly. Ellen had once called them devils, and there was no better name to describe them.

Ellen, maybe you were *lucky to have escaped as you did.*

I caught a glimpse of Anthea moving around behind me. Thank God, she was uninjured. Tripod Jack knelt at the other end of the bar, bringing his shotgun up to fire. I squeezed my eyes shut, expecting to hear the thunder of its discharge . . . but it never came. Instead, I heard a shrill cry, and I opened my eyes to see the stalker reaching behind a table to drag Collette from her hiding place. She tried to spin away, but the thing jerked her into an awkward embrace and raked a clawed hand down her back. Her scream gurgled into a wet hiss as the creature laced its talons into her hair and gave a quick tug. Her head separated from her body with a ripping sound, and blood sprayed into the air like crimson champagne. Her sister, Suzanne, leaped forward with an incomprehensible cry, then fell backward as the stalker dropped the decapitated corpse. Collette's body hit the floor and twitched several times. I felt my stomach heave.

"No!" Suzanne screamed, and she reached for the RPG behind her table. I stood up, offering a distraction, knowing that if the weapon went off in here, the stalker would most likely be the only survivor. The reptilian eyes rolled toward me, locking onto mine. Suddenly, I felt a warmth building deep inside me. I tried to raise my gun, but it seemed as heavy as an anvil. I had screwed up big time. You never, *never* looked a stalker in the eye.

But I'd halted the action long enough for Jack to call out, "Suzanne, no! Not in here!"

The stalker raised Collette's head and slung it at Jack with major-league force. He tried to duck but was too late; the grotesque projectile struck him squarely in the chest, knocking him backward. I heard the air rush from his lungs as he went down, followed by the clatter of his .38 spinning across the floor.

The blasts of six guns discharging simultaneously doesn't just deafen; it rapes the eardrums and shatters the mind, like a jackhammer pulverizing concrete. The flashes turned everything in my field of vision magnesium blue, then blood red. Crate, Barkeep, Anthea, Danny, Jill, and the Stretch had fired at once as the monster exposed its eyes. I couldn't hear the screech it made above the thunder in my brain, but I saw its huge hands fly toward its face as greenish-gray fluid spurted from between its clawed fingers. I think the next shots would have brought it down if the rear door hadn't blown inward, hurling Crate and Barkeep to the floor. Anthea rolled away, while the others spun to face the new attacker. Across the room, Jill and Danny opened fire; a moment later, they were cut down by some unseen force. Two sickeningly huge splashes of blood on the wall behind where they had stood assured me that they were both permanently out of commission.

This new creature was unlike any I'd yet seen. It hovered in the doorway; a long, squid-like thing with several arthropodic claws extending from a thick, conical mass. From a gray, mushroom-shaped head, ten amber-colored, globular eyes scanned the room. I smelled a cool, mildewy odor that grew stronger as it approached. As the ringing in my ears began to subside, I could hear a low, purring rumble.

The room was frozen, held in the grip of the stalker's mesmerizing power. My insides twisted in a fear more intense than any I'd ever known. The creature called Joe the Fireman was brute strength; a difficult foe, but one my mind could grasp. This new one was so *alien,* so intimate in its mental assault that I nearly dropped into a faint.

They'd called them extraterrestrials that first day. But by studying the Doppler effect as they'd come out of the sky, scientists had determined that they were *extradimensional,* appearing on Earth through some kind of gateway held open by sound. Yes, for days prior to their appearance, we'd been hearing that strange, mournful *hum* in the air, followed by a long series of deep, thunderous rumbles that seemed to come from nowhere—and everywhere. The stalkers came out of those sounds.

Mushroom-head floated forward, struck the bar, and splintered it effortlessly, passing through the wreckage like a wraith. I felt its gaze on me; a hot, murky sensation that made me want to wash myself. It drifted toward Suzanne, who'd fallen next to her sister's body. I saw her look up slowly, her face a melange of disgust, dread, and anger, but shadowed with the cold acceptance of one who knew she was staring death in the face.

But she could not have expected to be lifted by invisible hands and suspended in midair like a human marionette. Convulsing in pain, she was pulled to the center of the room, her arms and legs thrashing wildly and unnaturally. Her back arched violently, and her head twisted around until I thought her neck would snap.

Joe the Fireman, one eye ruined and leaking, glared on in approval.

From Suzanne's throat rose a choked growl: "Weelluugghyuuhh," she rumbled. "Weelluugghyuuhh."

Crate tried to move toward her but was held back by an unseen barrier.

"What the hell," muttered Tripod Jack, pulling himself into a sitting position at the end of the trashed bar. "What's she saying?"

The young woman's face contorted helplessly as a will that was not her own forced her lips to move. "We . . . come . . . we . . . invited . . . here. . . ."

"What the hell?" Anthea echoed.

"Weelluugghyuuhh . . . we . . . we . . . love . . . you. . . ."

Suzanne's lips cracked in a sickening parody of a smile. I shuddered at the perverted implications of the words. We had somehow *invited* them down upon us?

Mushroom-head purred deeply, and I felt a moment's panic as an electrical force tugged at me. It passed, but then I saw Crate shuffle forward, his terrified eyes betraying his absence of volition. Retrieving Jack's shotgun, he lumbered forward until he stood just below the floating girl, lifted the barrel, and aimed it directly at her panic-stricken face. I tried to move, to call out, but my body was beyond my control. Crate's mouth formed the words, "No, no," as a flicker of realization came to his eyes. Then he pulled the trigger.

The explosion sent shock waves through the room. I staggered and probably screamed, but I was unable to hear the sound of my own voice. Blood and body fragments showered the room, painting it deep red. Suzanne's remains crashed to the floor.

Crate was weeping, but he could only stand amid the gorestorm like a crazed huntsman. Shouldering the gun, he turned slowly, his eyes questing. His gaze met mine briefly, then he turned to Anthea. I could tell she wanted to back away, to scream, to move, but Mushroom-head would have none of that. I felt the sudden thrust of its will as surely as if it were directed toward me; but it was Anthea's eyes that abruptly went blank, and her pistol that dropped from limp fingers. She clumsily unfastened her gunbelt, letting it fall noisily to the floor; then she began to work at her pants, unzipping them and pulling them down, swinging her hips like a strip-tease dancer. When they were bunched around her ankles, she tugged down her panties, and, with an artificial flourish, bent over to touch her toes. Then, lowering the shotgun from his shoulder, Crate pushed its snout ungently into her rear end. As his finger tightened on the trigger, I heard her whimper softly.

The gun went off with a click.

Empty!

My heart leaped, as if the reprieve were more than temporary. Mushroom-head buzzed angrily, and for a split-second, I felt a weakening of its will. It was all the time any of us needed.

In a flash, Crate spun around, bringing the shotgun up in a wild arc. It struck the creature in one of its amber eyes, drawing a shrill whistle from some unseen voice organ. Immediately I had control of my limbs. I raised my gun and fired. Another eye disappeared in an explosion of viscous fluid. The Stretch's Uzi flared, its rapid *rat-tat-tat* seeming to go on and on, as if it held an endless supply of ammo. Eyes burst in huge splashes of gold-tinged gore, and more trills of anger–and what I hoped was pain–rose above the sound of the shots. When the firing stopped, I figured the magazine was spent. Instead, I saw the Stretch lifted from the floor by a huge silhouette, then pitched across the room like a discarded washrag. He screamed once, then struck the bar and collapsed into a heap.

A moment later, I came to understand why Joe the Fireman had earned his name. His good eye flashed once, and the Stretch's body burst into flame with a dull thump. Waves of heat rolled from the inferno, and, within seconds, the remains of the bar had caught fire. I thought I saw a writhing figure within the pyre, but I prayed that I was wrong. Then, there was only raging heat and rippling light.

Anthea's legs had tangled in her pants. Cursing, she grabbed her Magnum, and, with a smooth roll, turned and fired. Joe the Fireman lost his remaining eye and slammed against the wall, howling in agony. He slid to the floor, his horned head thrashing, one arm twitching violently.

Crate hustled around the burning bar, and I saw him drag the unconscious Barkeep away from the spreading flames. Tripod Jack did a backward crawl on his elbows and one leg, propping himself against the jukebox, out of harm's way. Running to Anthea, I took hold of an arm and pulled her toward the front door.

Mushroom-head floated amid the crackling fire, orange tongues lapping at its writhing, clawlike appendages. It shrieked long and loud, then flew backward through the doorway behind the bar. I heard a crash in the back room, and a receding cry as the battered creature retreated into the night.

"So much for the free beer," Crate said, watching as flames consumed the entire building. A loud, wrenching crash split the night as the roof caved in, sending a huge fountain of glittering sparks skyward. A column of black smoke rose from the ruin–a signpost to the scene of battle for any interested eyes. I doubted any that were would be human.

Anthea fastened her gunbelt around her waist and gave me a meaningful smile. "Thanks for saving me," she said in a low, weary voice.

"Rough place you've got here. It wasn't exactly what I expected."

She shrugged. "We'll have to find a new safehouse. It's going to be hot around here now."

"You lost some good people. I'm sorry."

Her eyes gazed into the past. "You don't know how many. A month ago, we had 20. The month before that, 50. I always felt like there was safety in numbers. But you've done all right by yourself."

"I don't know if I call this 'all right.'" I pointed to the fire and sighed. "What are you going to do now?"

"First things first. Find cover. If they're coming out of the cities like you said, then trouble is brewing." She stared at me until I began to feel uncomfortable. I gave her a questioning look. "Come with us," she said at last. "I have a feeling you can teach us a thing or two."

"Hey," Crate said, pointing to the sky. "Gotta go."

Tripod Jack, leaning on the one crutch he'd managed to save, nodded. "He smells 'em coming."

Baker the Barkeep chuckled softly and smiled at me. "Better stick around ma'am. Not a one of us has exactly got a place in this world anymore, if you take my meaning. Those of us that's left oughta stay together."

I shook my head. "I still have to find Colin. He could already be here. I've got to get out to Barren Creek."

Anthea touched my shoulder. "There's four other pairs of eyes here. Five pairs see better than one."

Crate looked a little worried for a moment. "If we don't disappear quickly, we're not going to have any eyes left to look for anybody. Listen."

We fell silent. Far away, I heard a low beating sound. A deep, repetitive thud, almost like a monstrous, distant heartbeat.

It was gradually growing louder.

"They're coming," I said.

"It's settled," Jack said. "Crate, give me a hand."

The black man took one of his arms, helping him keep his balance.

"They catch us here, it's over for all of us."

"Let's split up," Anthea said. "We'll hole up somewhere the rest of the night, do a little scouting tomorrow and check out our situation. Meet at sundown tomorrow at the Methodist Church on Starling Avenue. We take it from there. Everybody agreeable?"

"It's good," Barkeep said. "I'll take Crate and Jack down to the Jefferson Hotel. We should be okay in their basement."

"You come with me, then," she said. "Hey . . . just what is your name?"

"Angela."

"Nice to meet you. Now, let's the hell out of here."

We turned down the street, away from the burning building, moving at a good clip. Crate, Tripod Jack, and Baker headed in the opposite direction, Jack's one crutch clacking on the pavement. Before Anthea and I reached the first corner, they had disappeared from view.

We began to run down the dark, deserted street, past empty buildings, dead traffic signals, and abandoned automobiles as the deep booming sounds increased in volume. The air was cool and felt exhilarating as I breathed deeply and steadily. This had become my element, it seemed. Sometimes, I could barely remember anything other than running. Around me the stars were falling again and the air thudded with the sound of arriving stalkers.

"Where are we heading?" I asked.

"This is the way to Barren Creek Road."

I nodded, feeling for the first time since the death of my daughter that I was not completely, utterly, and forever alone. I ran into the night with all the speed I could manage, even then barely keeping up with the dark, chestnut-haired figured ahead of me. The idea of companionship was almost alien, but alluring. Just maybe, with the help of this new family of mine, I would be able to find Colin.

Or he would find me.

Us.